ACHE

David Rogers

Rachel,
I don't know
you, but I can only
assume you're
cool
enjoy

Published by Accent Press Ltd 2014

ISBN 9781783755349

Acknowledgements

I'd like to thank the following people for their encouragement, support, input, and/or influence during the writing of this book and the times that bookended it: Mom and Dad and the rest of my family, Emma Kennedy, Natasha Ball, Kelly Allan, Catherine Cambanakis, Bhing Tubera, Samuel Thomas Airey, Alexander Paul Wyatt, Rachel Pollock, Charlotte Pollock, Jennifer Bilham, Shilan Raza, Dominic Sullivan, Sue Devenish-Meares, Oliver Zarandi and all other Kaplanites, Sim Scammel, Ryan Knowles, Amelie Tang, Will Olivier, Poppy Bradbury, Martin Spychal, Joe O'Connell, Emma Taylor, David Percival, Andy Croft, the staff of Café Chula, Record Club, and Tower 47 (Camden) and Foyles Café (Soho) for stimulation and distraction, Greg Rees and everyone at Accent for their hard work, diligence, and support.

Enormous thanks to Rona Cran, who deserves her own paragraph on the acknowledgements page for the many ways she helped with the edit.

For inspiration: Banks, Bukowski, Burroughs, Ellis, Hemmingway, Kerouac, McCarthy, Palahniuk, Tartt, Thompson, Vonnegut.

For accompaniment: Alt-J, … And You Will Know Us By The Trail of Dead, Bass Drum of Death, Battles, The Beach Boys, The Beatles, Beirut, Big Black, The Black Keys, James Blake, The Blood Brothers, Bon Iver, Botch, Brand New, Calories, Caretaker, The Cinematic Orchestra, Circle Takes the Square, Alice Coltrane, Converge, Elvis Costello, Miles Davis, Deerhoof, Deftones, The Dillinger Escape Plan, Drive Like Jehu, Eagles of Death Metal, Eagulls, Every Time I Die, Factory Floor, Far, The Fall, Franz Ferdinand, Future of the Left, Gallows, Glassjaw, Al Green, PJ Harvey, Her Parents, Hey Sholay, Hooded Fang, Hot Snakes, Hundred Reasons,

Interpol, Kyuss, Jamie Lenman, Liars, The Locust, The Mars Volta, Curtis Mayfield, Mclusky, Minus the Bear, Mudhoney, My Vitriol, Neutral Milk Hotel, Nine Inch Nails, Nirvana, OFWGKTA, Of Montreal, Owls, Parquet Courts, Pavement, Pixies, Pulled Apart by Horses, Queens of the Stone Age, Refused, Reuben, Rival Schools, Savages, Shellac, Slayer, Elliott Smith, The Smiths, Sonic Youth, The Strokes, Earl Sweatshirt, thisGirl, Vampire Weekend, Tom Vek, The Ventures, The Walkmen, Wavves, Weezer, Will Haven, Kanye West.

None of this is real.

Part One

LONDON

1

CitySweets is tipping her head towards the digital calligraphy of her phone. I get close enough to confirm I'm her date and she smiles with the kind of overbite I like. She stares as if she doesn't want to get caught, already picturing me scratching her skin with the serrated edges of my stubble and wondering how hard my body might be.

While fingering the cigarette pack in my pocket I remember writing on my profile I was a non-smoker, so I make plumes of steam with my breath instead. It's cold tonight but that's a plus as my winter wardrobe is probably my best.

I consider the girl I'm in love with as I escort this evening's match to the Jazz Café, Camden.

We arrive at the venue and stand near the stage. Cymbals are tightened onto stands as trumpeters manipulate the valves of their instruments. I ask *CitySweets* if she likes live music and she nods with enthusiasm from behind the liquid in her glass. A little of it trickles down her chin; she swabs at it with the sack of veins she keeps in her mouth then wipes herself dry on her sleeve.

We look at each other with nothing to say.

I sigh deeply, giving her my coat, my scarf, and my drink. She holds the coat against her breasts and lets the scarf hang between her legs. I tell her I'll be back shortly before retiring to the gents to study my reflection, running fingers through my hair and adjusting my shirt. I undo a few buttons then fasten them again.

It's important to me that I make a good impression, although I'm unsure why.

I reenter the bar. I wait for her to notice me and when she

does I start walking again, confidently avoiding other people by turning my hips and twisting my shoulders. I take the wine from her first and drink it all in one go. Then I take my coat and scarf, making sure their ends are not trailing along the floor, and I say to my date over the pulse of a spinning record: 'It's your round, isn't it?'

An hour passes and it lasts two hours. I whisper something into her ear which she doesn't understand but I don't have the energy to repeat whatever it is I said. She straightens out her spine and pushes out her chest, grasping at coquettishness.

It's warm in here but I still can't quite bring myself to forgive her for the sweat patches under her arms.

I start to think I'll sleep with her tonight and the thought is overwhelming and depressing and it fills me with despair.

I sip at my drink in search of a distraction before helping out the band by tapping out a rhythm on the table. I stop when my phone starts vibrating.

I stand and walk to the bar. Alcohol has rendered me unsteady on my feet but it's barely noticeable.

I buy another glass of wine while I inspect the message I have from Jess. I brought her here a month ago and she got drunk enough to take me to her bus stop when the night was over. We kissed until the number 9 arrived and I followed her onto it, asking the driver for a ticket to the same place – a single.

No need for a return, not from where we were headed.

The message says that Marcus' trip finishes tomorrow morning and if I want to see her before he gets back to London, *it has to be tonight.*

I lock the phone, slip it into my pocket, and return to my date.

I find her resting face-down on her forearms.

I hail a taxi and throw *CitySweets* onto the back seat. As I'm turning away she drags me into the car with her, announces the name of her street, and launches herself into my mouth.

4

My tongue becomes a weapon that I try to fend her off with.

She grabs my coat in bunches and I'm anxious she'll crease it or mark it with the sweat on her hands.

She climbs onto me as the taxi swerves through London traffic and I can feel the heat of her even through our clothing.

She misjudges a kiss and clatters against my teeth.

I start to feel the same old fluid sloshing around inside my gut.

She opens my shirt and twists my nipple, hard enough to make me wince.

I start to feel the same old panic.

I reach for the side of her head and get under her hair and feel out her skull. I pick out her drunken eyes with my own. I ask her to tell me she likes me and she obliges as she rubs my body and licks my neck but deep, deep down, in the places she'll never be able to reach, I find myself not believing her.

We arrive at her house and she pays the driver and walks me to the front door. She swings it open and shoves me inside, kicks off her heels, and shrinks four inches.

She takes my wrist and leads me upstairs, banging most of the steps with her shins.

All stuffed animals are hastily removed before we fall onto her bed. I'm feeling unsettled as I can no longer make out the shape of her face and it's impossible for me to picture what she looks like. She could be anyone. I think back over the night that's passed but all I can focus on is the message from Jess.

CitySweets' silhouette removes my clothes and kicks them onto the floor. As she's taking off her own I climb from the bed, locate my trousers and shirt, fold them up as neatly as I can without being able to see properly, and place them on her chest of drawers.

I could probably make her come without even touching her.

I get under the sheets and pull her warm skin against

mine.

When it's over I ask if the number 9 bus stops anywhere near here and I can feel her inhaling and exhaling and looking at me in the dark.

2

I'm giving a lesson I neglected to plan. I never plan. I just read from the textbook in an authoritative tone.

Exercise A. Exercise B. Exercise C.

I'm not providing answers because I don't have any myself.

Exercise D. Exercise E.

The best thing about Jess, if I had to choose, is her huge blonde hair. It's so curly that it's almost rope.

Turn the page. Exercises F-K.

I often let my mind drift to her during lessons. I use this particular moment to review the time we first met.

(Exercise L-P, in pairs)

It was at a warehouse party eight months ago, two months after I returned from Paris. I watched her from across the room as she drank glasses of gin and tonic and snorted cocaine from the cover of a hardback book. Occasionally she'd nod her head in time with the song that was playing and laugh at a joke that a friend shouted into her ear.

I waited for my moment and when it came I approached her with a rum cocktail and my name and she accepted both with grace. Whenever she moved towards me to speak I thought I could detect her scent – a sweet perfume that brought to mind citrus fruits.

I mixed fresh drinks and opened screw-top bottles of beer for her so she didn't have to dent her palms.

Other men watched and their envy was apparent.

Once the party had peaked, she wrote down her number and gave it to me. I didn't call her for a week afterwards; not because I didn't want to but because I was too afraid.

I'm still afraid of her in a perplexing way. The way I feel about her is quite terrifying.

Hamood lifts his hand to ask a question. Rather than responding I finish the lesson ten minutes early because, as ever, I can't concentrate on anything other than Jess.

I walk into the staffroom and head straight for the kettle, only to be frustrated by the sight of people already surrounding it. All teachers need stimulants if they are to get through the working day. The finest educators are the ones tweaked on a double espresso, a thimbleful of speed, or a snuffle of cocaine. I once caught one of my colleagues sucking on a teaspoon heaped with instant coffee granules and he still had bitter brown crystals embedded in his gums when he left for class.

That kind of thing happens more than people think.

A man could cycle straight through *Exercises A-Z* with the right pre-show ritual.

I decide not to risk waiting for the crowd to disperse. I crack open the can of energy drink I've been carrying around in my bag. It spits at me with displeasure and I guzzle two-thirds of it down without blinking.

Alex begs me to run through how the past perfect continuous tense is formed but by now I'm past caring. He goes for the collar of my shirt and I slap him away. He turns to Matt and asks the same question and Matt struggles to contain his distress when he says, 'Shit I don't know either oh God oh *God* ...'

None of us really know how the past perfect continuous tense is formed. In fact, none of us really know anything at all. Old teachers, new teachers, we're all the same – our most intimate companions are coursebooks, textbook notations, and suggested lesson plans found on suspect websites.

Amidst the chaos I drain the last luminous dregs from my can, look up at the clock, and realise our five-minute break has passed, meaning it's time to go and teach our students all about the past perfect continuous.

In other words: *Exercises T – W*.

On the way up to the classroom, I notice I've received a text from *CitySweets* that describes how good a time she had on our date.

8

I delete the text, delete her number, and never see her again for as long as I live.

Once we've wasted enough time, the lesson ends. There should only be a brief two-minute changeover between the second and third session but as I need a new packet of cigarettes I decide to step into the street and walk to the shops. I take my time looking through all the different boxes although I know the brand I want, the brand I always go for. I'm halfway back to school before deciding I should also visit a nearby kiosk to buy a box of matches. I ask whether or not they sell condoms too but the woman working there just looks at me like I'm disturbed.

She isn't too far off the mark, I suppose.

On returning to class I find Terry sitting at my desk, seemingly tormented by having to cover me in my absence. This was supposed to be his free period. On the board behind him he has written: *Finish this morning's exercises INDIVIDUALLY.*

The students seem to be working autonomously so I make an effort not to interrupt them. Instead I reclaim my seat from Terry and cycle through the telephone numbers of girls on my contact list to see how many of them I can place. If I remember correctly, *LooseLucy1988* looked good and smelled great but was too shy to speak, even after three bottles of beer. *BlueTulip* was an emotional catastrophe who started talking about her ex-boyfriend before we'd even had a chance to sit down. *Vikki_12*, *xXxLaurenxXx*, and *HackneyKitten* are examples of girls I can't recall, regardless of how hard I try. The evenings that we spent together had no consequence other than the fossilisation of their numbers in my phone.

Sergey puts up his hand to bring my attention back to class. I ask him what he wants.

'I finish,' he whispers.

'Well then, Sergey,' I say, as if what to do in this situation must be obvious by now: 'check your answers, check them again, go on to the next unit.'

He looks down at his book with a sigh.

He scratches at it with a well-used biro.

I eat some of my sandwich. It tastes horrible but has just 374 calories. I dislodge a chunk of it from the roof of my mouth with a sip of coffee. Other teachers feed themselves with one hand and scan websites and thumb through books and cover their bloodshot eyes with the other.

'OK,' Karen the Director says. She holds papers against her chest. Perspiration pools on the bristles of her upper lip. 'OK, are we all here?'

Rob takes a head count, as furious as ever. His face is a clenched fist. His shirts tend to be immaculately ironed, which I have to admire, but they're almost always ugly; the colour of bruises and limes, pin-striped.

'That's everyone minus Carly,' he says.

'Where's Carly?' Karen the Director asks. Rob whispers something to her and she's flustered when she has to say 'Oh yes, of course she is. That means we can start. Right, Item one on the agenda is textbooks for new arrivals – basically, we don't have enough of them – so for now if you could photocopy the relevant page for the week's unit and distribute them at the start of the lesson,'

'Photocopier Two's broken again,' Trudy says. She sounds aggrieved, as if she's saying: *my husband has had another stroke*.

'OK. I'll make a note of that. Can you just use Photocopier One for now, Trudy?'

'Also knackered,' Terry says. He looks as angry as Rob. He still hasn't come to terms with losing the first ten minutes of his free period to my tardiness.

Karen the Director clears her throat and looks off to the side. This is news to her.

'How can we be expected to teach without books or photocopiers, Karen?' Trudy asks.

'I don't know. Rob?'

Rob doesn't move. He keeps his arms folded.

'Don't we have a pile of books left over from last term in the basement?' Shelley asks.

'The syllabus has changed since then,' Rob replies. 'We can't use the old books.'

'Can the students we have in class at the moment share books with new arrivals?'

'Ideally, no,' Karen the Director says. 'Every student needs his or her own copy of the material. It all should be included as part of their course.'

'Can't we get more copies in from the Clapham branch?'

'No can do,' Rob responds. 'They don't have enough books, either.'

The spiral I've been carving into an unused worksheet turns dense enough to slit a hole in the paper. Stairs above us creak beneath the feet of students already on their way to afternoon lessons.

'I think I've got it,' Alex says. 'We could print copies from the shared drive. I remember Jason from IT telling me they've been backing up all course materials onto the G drive for the past few months. Everything we need is probably on there already.'

The relief of each of the teachers is audible. Matt pats Alex on the thigh and grins.

'Great idea,' Karen the Director says. 'Does the printer work?'

'No ink,' Terry says.

'Why don't we just burn the school down? We could say the new books were lost in the fire.'

Rob looks at me and says, 'If that's supposed to be a joke, it's not at all funny.'

I want to tell them to think about what's *really* important in life but the sound of soles on the stairs above us has stopped and a bell rings to signify how late we all are.

There's never enough time for us to think.

There's never enough time for us to get things done.

'We'll have to stop there. We should have another

11

meeting about this tomorrow though so put your heads together,' Karen the Director says. 'And I'm sure we all wish Carly a speedy recovery. I'll pass a card around later. It'd be great if you could all sign it –'

Her words are lost beneath the scraping of chair-legs and the collective groaning of my miserable and deflated colleagues. Before going to class I head outside for a final smoke and as I lift its filter to my lips I have to wonder when it was that things got so complicated.

3

I go to the fridge for a beer before heading to my bedroom with the intention of clicking through the newest visitors that my *LovedUp* profile has received.

I get a lot of hits, I get a lot of messages, and with these girls I self-medicate.

I sling my jacket onto my desk chair and throw myself onto the unmade bed. My bag lands on the floor and decants itself. Shreds of paper bleed from it – pieces of homework I'll never get around to marking.

After a few precious moments spent gathering my thoughts together with a cigarette, I press into the keys of my laptop to wake it up. I click refresh and am greeted by eight *wolf-whistles* and six unopened messages with subject lines like *Hey!* and *Hi!* and *lol hi* ☺.

I delete fresh messages from *CitySweets* without even reading them.

I have a new message from a woman in her late thirties with the username *MyPudding*. I read it through two, three, four times before deciding not to bother responding. I also have a message from a girl called *Lollipop86*. I click it open and scan it. It lists all the things we have in common and complains about all the socially handicapped piranhas on *LovedUp* who routinely send her hideously authored advances.

She hopes I'm different, oblivious to the fact that this website is where hope goes to die.

I pay no attention to the details she's agonised over; descriptions of her favorite films and music and pieces of art. I read her *About Me* section just to confirm she's viable. She uses lines like, *I know how to have a good time* and *I don't take life too seriously* and *in my spare time I act and do Pilates* so I enlarge her profile picture and click through to see the rest: there's one of her pouting in a club, one of her

13

riding a horse, one of her lying on a beach in a two-piece swimsuit (good body, not great body), one of her graduating in a cap and gown (not flattering), one of her wearing a Dorothy costume onstage.

I open the .doc file I have saved onto my desktop, then copy and paste it into the digital space marked *Flirt Back*. It's a piece of writing I've honed over the last few months. It sets me up to be something more than any human man could ever be – attentive but not clingy, happy-go-lucky but highly sensitive, a rebel, a gourmet, a *great* lover with a big prick implied by my willingness to use the term *I know how to be there for a girl*. I even use the word *sincere* at one point. It works like voodoo. They skim the text and scroll through my pictures and their hearts and their minds and their souls and their vaginas all cry out in unison: *this is the one for me*.

After clicking *Send* I click *Home* and start waiting.

With nothing better to do I pick up my guitar and strum the four chords I know over and over again. I've always wanted to be able to play the guitar. It's a terrible shame someone nurturing this much angst might never get to grace a stage.

I have so much to give.

Before long I decide to abandon the instrument and replace it with my phone. I rest against my amp and cycle through messages from Jess.

To paraphrase a line from a song I wrote about her: *she remains the only one I'd love to hear from.*

4

This is stupid.

I'm looking into her bedroom window. I can see the pinkness of her through it. I can just about make out the white strap of her bra. Her hair hangs heavy, a jungle of wires. She sometimes plaits it with beads. It usually smells unclean yet delicious, often smoky.

She's not alone.

Marcus walks into the room, stripped to the waist. He says something to her then switches off the light.

The absence of stars doesn't help.

This is so *stupid* ...

I intended to walk home but didn't make it that far. I sit at the bar of The Enterprise and tear strips from a beermat as I picture him tearing strips from her; her skirt then her tights then her underwear.

I order a few bottles of wine to try to shift some the dirt that's accumulated in my head. I almost burst into tears when, having been riled from a drunken coma, my most recent glass still not emptied, I find that someone has left me their telephone number scrawled in bitty eyeliner pencil.

I somehow materialise within the bowels of another late-night establishment. Even at this distance Jess has a hold of my brain and she's turning it. The music in here is deafening but I can still hear her voice speaking over it.

I lose face by reaching for the bar and missing it completely, stomping a foot in search of balance, rattling my teeth, and lacerating my tongue. A girl in a tight black T-shirt cocks a buttock to reach for the bottle of whiskey on the top shelf. I give her four coins from which there's no change.

I hoist my waist over the bar and scream at her: *Don't you think it's a little too* loud *in here?* She shrugs. She's used to it, as much as she's used to being pestered all night by drunks like me.

I trip towards the dance floor to start getting down to the too-loud music. I'm thinking of Jess and of what I can do but my ability to think rationally is folding in on itself, getting smaller and smaller, folding in on itself until nothing but corners remain. All I really know is I'm drunk and alone. I space out to the gut-pounding bass and drums and cup an imaginary waist between my hands, one hand empty and one hand with drink, and the waist is small and the drunker I get the smaller it gets until I'm holding my glass in both hands.

The DJ plays his records and he might not realise it but he's playing me too.

I look around for further distraction but there are no girls here – only colours and shapes. On my way to back the bar I fall over my own bent feet and onto the beer-soaked sick-stained shag of the carpet surrounding the dance floor. I'm taken up from the bottom of the ocean of moving feet shoals by a rough authority that ejects me from the depths of the club. I hit the pavement hard.

I contemplate waiting outside for the barmaid but after twenty minutes or so I get bored enough to attempt passage home.

I locate my building and hug the railing up to our flat on the top floor. The keyhole is elusive; I prod at it and poke at it but can't find its jagged orifice. I'm pretty drunk. It's only after what feels like for ever that my key finally sinks into it. I push the door open and fall onto the shitty rug and unclaimed letters and junk mail of my homestead.

Jack turns on the light and I lift my head to let him know I'm cognisant. I strike the floor with my forehead, hard enough for coloured dots to make themselves known on the backs of my eyelids.

'What the fuck?' he says, but not in angry way. He's amused. I always amuse him, which is no doubt why he enjoys living with me so much. He moved here from Australia a few years ago in search of what he calls his *destiny* and contracted the kind of mental illness that has him convinced that one day and one day soon, through hard graft and perseverance and an untold amount of blowjobs and cocaine, he'll make it as a successful actor. He fails to realise that he'll be forever blowing this city. London is not his. London is not anybody's. His is a lost cause – another desolate Australian, this city collects them. It rolls them around within itself like ball-bearings.

I hear John, Jack's boyfriend, moving around in the kitchen behind him. John is his chosen English name; his Asian name is Liu Fung. If I ever referred to him as John out loud then Jack would take me to task for it. *Why should he be westernised?* he'd ask, and has done many times before now. *Why should he reject his ethnicity? It's what makes him who he is. It's what makes him the man I love as much as I do. Fuck the way our society works. Fuck the way they try to fit people into their own world view. He has no reason to change who he is just to make the lives of others easier.*

London treats Liu unfairly. He works in a café and gets paid less than minimum wage. I can see a sliver of him from here. He's making coffee, which is something he must be sick of doing by now. In this way, disrupting the evening he'd been spending with Jack by turning up steaming drunk yet again, I am mistreating him also. I attempt to say *sorry* but the word is muddled by the booze in my blood and comes out unrecognisable.

Jack grabs me under each armpit and I attempt to fight him off without knowing why. He heaves me through the hall and we pass the bedroom he shares with Liu. They'd moved into the room separately and initially had rented a single bed each for fifty pounds a week, although once they'd had a chance to bond they pulled the two beds together and sourced for themselves the cheapest rent for a couple's room in all of Camden.

I am utterly mortified when Jack lifts my quilt to dump me under it and a photograph of Jess falls like a whisper to the floor.

He peels off my T-shirt and my jeans, leaves me in the dark but returns a few minutes later with the coffee. The sudden resurgence of light when the switch is flicked on inflates me with horror.

'Drink,' is all he says. He doesn't trust me enough to let me hold it. He drifts it around my chin and I slurp it up, spilling some onto my naked chest but feeling no pain. His hair tickles my skin and I scratch the spot he's irritating.

'Where've you been?' he asks. 'Your breath is pure ethanol.'

'Out.'

'*Out,* he says!' He turns to his boyfriend for confirmation that this is hilarious but Liu's observing everything with a slight frown creasing his forehead. 'Yeah, we can see you've been *out*, genius, but *where*?'

I could use this opportunity to confess how infatuated I am with a girl I can't quite obtain and that tonight I hid in front of her house to spy on her. I open my mouth and belch into his face and he pulls away and says, 'Fucking hell, mate, you are so *disgusting.*' He waves a hand in front of his nose but can't quite disguise the smile he's wearing. He tips the cup into my mouth until most of the coffee has disappeared.

'Sleep it off,' he says as he gets off my bed, 'and all the best for tomorrow's hangover. I'm sure it's gonna be a good one.'

He throws an arm around Liu's shoulders and the two of them leave me to my suffering. This time they let the darkness envelope me fully and the burden of light does not intrude upon me again until the following morning.

5

Jess opened her jacket and let it drop to the floor and I remember the sound of her keys jangling in her pocket when it fell. The taxi outside pulled away, leaving us to each other. Her skin was white, so pale, peppered with freckles, rippling around her nipples. Her hair was a mess of curls. She stepped towards me on one foot. Her stockings, black, clutched her thighs, cupped her feet housed in tall high-heeled shoes, wet with rain, slick, blood-red leather. Above their elastic was a tease of hair, then the indentation of her stomach, two round breasts, bare, rising and falling at the mercy of her lungs, her delicate neck, up, up to her teeth, her nose. She brought her face into mine, her tongue pressing against my own. I pulled her against my belly and lowered my hands to her lower back, her soft round behind. I drew her against me. She's forever against me. Her tongue is always in my mouth; it's a wall, a fleshy barrier I hold between my teeth. Her heels clunked against the wooden floor. I took her to bed. We looked at ourselves, at each other; her naked but for her stockings and me in a shirt she unbuttoned slowly, methodically. I wondered in that moment whether all music had been written for us, and we lay against each other and closed our eyes, and we drifted around each other like smoke, and we used the time as well as we could, every minute, every second, every start and splash of spit, and I started to learn then what bodies were built for.

Our time together passed as it always does, as it always has to, because of Marcus.

I brushed her hair. I kissed the top of her head and her nose. We listened to music and drank our rum. I was swollen with love but love never came into it, not as far as she was concerned. It was not love that had brought her to my bed, after all. She tripped and fell into me, that's all, or rather, she tripped and I fell into her, three times that night and many times before and since.

Marcus. There's always Marcus. To her, he is love. To her, he is everything. I'm left behind with only thoughts of what could be and the misery each moment without her brings.

This is all I have, but it must surely be better than having nothing at all.

6

I'm holding *Lollipop86*'s purse and standing at the bar of White's in Covent Garden while she urinates. I use this time to compose questions to ask in case our pool of conversation is drained too quickly. I look around the room for inspiration. Everyone here is immaculate. Straws stretch from crushed ice in cocktail glasses, penetrating pink lips. I imagine how short a distance they'd be able to walk in such sharp shoes.

I take my wallet out of the pocket of my jeans and look through the few notes I stuffed into it from the cashpoint on the way here.

A possible question to ask if things start going terribly: *exactly how much money do you make?*

My date takes her purse and her wine and escorts me through the pack. Somehow she finds a table for the two of us, cluttered with empty glasses and plates. I take it upon myself to locate a tray and stack the crockery onto it, moving it to the bar while *Lollipop86* drapes her black suede coat and velvet gloves over the back of her chair.

She starts telling me about her job in HR and explains how much she loves doing something so *worthwhile*. She asks me about my job so I tell her I'm a teacher of English as a second language. She uses this revelation as an opportunity to tell me she went to an all-girl boarding school. She shows me a picture of the house her uncle owns in Tuscany and recites well-rehearsed anecdotes of all the summers she's holidayed there.

I can't deny she's beautiful. She has immaculate skin and subtle waves in her yellow hair. She speaks with a soft musicality played by the thoroughbred nature of her roots.

She is from good stock.

I watch her lips move and mirror her in every way possible.

She likes to sing and dance and the last show she starred in was her local am-dram company's adaptation of *Oklahoma!* in which she played one of the leads. I ask her to show me the accent she adopted for the show and she pitches to me this lazy American drawl that draws attention from surrounding tables. She shows me the picture of her as Dorothy, the same one she uses on her profile, and she looks better in it than I remember. I tell her my housemate calls himself an actor and when she asks me what the difference is between *being* an actor and *calling* yourself one I can't help but laugh, and it's a genuine laugh, and it makes me feel good in a way I haven't felt for a long time.

We're halfway through the time she fluffed her lines at a school play when my phone starts to vibrate. Jess is calling. *Lollipop86*'s lips are moving but I can no longer understand what she's saying. It's now beyond the realms of possibility for me to be able to process her words. Her stories have been demoted from amusing to meaningless.

I cut her off mid-sentence and hold a finger up to indicate a minute. I walk outside, slide open my phone and say *hello*. Jess sounds sad. I ask if she's OK. She says no and calls Marcus a *bastard*. I ask where she is and she gets angry and says: 'What, do you want to come over and stick it in me? Make everything all right again?' She says *all men are the same* then hangs up.

I try to call her back but my efforts are diverted straight to voicemail.

An idea projects itself onto the inner canvas of my skull: *girls are inherently evil.*

Lollipop86 mauls me in bed and makes everything hurt. I imagine she watched one too many tapes while at boarding school, learning what to do for a boy from a pirated copy of an old porn film – the volume set low to remain undetected by the patrolling matron or prefect, crouched in front of the screen in the dark, consumed with confusion and disgust and emitting a thick, musky odour into the air of her dorm room, hormones thumping around her teenage body as she learned and engrained the kinds of techniques that are now leaving me so cold.

She chokes herself on it when it goes into her throat. A stream of saliva slithers from the end of it when she resurfaces for air and pants and pants and wipes her tongue on her arm.

Panic comes and goes.

She asks over and over if I want to fuck her and when said in such a delicate and refined way, the words formed with such eloquent diction, it truly is heartbreaking.

I wrap the condom around my wilting cock and she climbs onto it as if I were a pony in one of her riding clubs. I enter her and she does exactly what I'd expected her to do – she bounces and rocks and writhes around on top of me in a way that's anything but pleasurable. I grab her hips and roll her onto her back so I can take control. It changes nothing – she insists on overacting, she overreaches, and I can't help feeling sorry for her and sorry for all women if this is what they think we're asking for.

She rakes hands through my hair and tells me to lick her. I don't want to but I'm too depressed to argue. I go down there, down to the depths of her, and write the names of my favorite songs with the tip of my tongue.

I can't take much more of this tedium so I straighten myself up and kneel over her. I unroll the condom and fling it across the room. I stroke myself as if being timed and feel genuine pleasure when I come because then I know it's all over.

I climb from the bed and locate my underwear, my clothes, and my coat.

I make my excuses and leave.

7

Karen the Director sits at a spare desk and pretends to write in detail about my capacity to teach. I stand in front of my students, fifteen people from across the world, all watching and waiting for something to happen. I look down at my notes, but there are no notes – just an empty piece of paper with the word *NOTES* printed on it.

I tell the students to move all chairs and tables to the side of the room. I instruct them to walk around the class and to speak with each other for five minutes each, changing partner when the time is up. I explain that the subject of today's discussion is their favourite … *thing*. I ask them to describe their favourite thing and to explain why it's their favourite thing, to pose follow-up questions about their partner's favourite thing and to make a record of what's being said about favourite things for use in an essay to be written for homework.

After a few agonising moments of inactivity, the boldest of the group (*the nineteen-year-old waiter from Brazil*) walks to the middle-aged Russian diplomat and asks: 'What you favrite theeng?' Then the French risk-assessment manager of Société Générale creeps up to the Korean engineer in his sixties and offers: 'What eeez yrr favriite tiing?'

Soon the room becomes thick with viscous accents and a palatable nervous tension. I look over at Karen the Director and she replaces the cap of her pen and closes her folder, as if she's seen enough.

Before leaving the classroom she gives me a thumbs-up, rubbing the sleep from her eyes.

On the tube home I start writing a text to Jess ready to be sent when signal has been reclaimed but can't help getting distracted by the girl sitting opposite. She has a lip piercing and an eyebrow piercing and is smeared in dark lipstick.

She's wearing ripped tights and has short dyed-orange hair. A lengthy tattoo of coiling vines and snowdrop berries is suggested by the rips in her Dead Kennedys T-shirt.

As the train starts to slow she gets out of her seat and moves closer to me. She stands and holds onto the bar above us. She shows me all of herself and I drag my eyes across every part of her body. Her scent is a heady blend of perspiration and pot smoke that makes my nostrils flare.

She alights at King's Cross. I watch her as she jumps into the arms of a man wearing a scuffed leather jacket, a mass of green spikes standing erect on the top of his head. They disappear somewhere along the platform as I start rolling home again.

I think about what colour I'd like to dye my hair when all of this is over.

I take out my mobile to tweak my message. As any author would, I worry something might be missing from its final draft. I type a few kisses, then limit them to one. I consider calling her by the pet name I once gave her (*Bunny*) but eventually decide against it, fearing I'd only embarrass myself.

I leave the train at Camden Town. I walk alongside the MTV building and send up a little broadcast of my own: *Jess, I'm here for you. I'm always here for you. Give me a call when you can x.*

Jack and Liu are in the living room watching a cookery show on TV. Liu's lying with his head in Jack's lap. His freshly painted toenails are separated by balls of cotton-wool.

I collapse into the armchair we found discarded on the street a week ago. We haven't bothered cleaning it since bringing it into the flat as Jack claims doing so would make the whole thing less *bohemian.*

'You look shitty. Had a hard day at school?' he asks.

'Fuck you,' I respond, and he lets out a laugh.

'What? What did I say?'

'It's not what you said, Jack; it's the way you said it.'

26

'God, *someone's* not in a very good mood.'

'Yeah, well, I have a lot on my plate.'

The two of them continue to watch the carrots being diced, the tomatoes being quartered.

'Care for a spliff or something?' Jack asks. He turns to his boyfriend and says, 'Think that's a good idea, Liu? He looks like he needs to chill out a bit, doesn't he?'

Liu shrugs silently, as if to say: *who the fuck cares what he needs?*

'No, I'm fine,' I tell him, quite sure that drugs would be more of a hindrance than a help. I hold my phone and squeeze it, making the plastic crackle and pop against itself. I'm willing it to vibrate. I'm breathing as shallowly as I can for fear of scaring away any potential messages from Jess.

I catch myself off-guard when I feel the pressure of tears building behind my face. I look away from the television and out of the window. I focus on the sounds of cars as they drive past. I think of Jess in a variety of ways, placing her in a few of the positions she has occupied throughout our short history. I see her lying naked on her front on her bed. I watch her as she dances to Nine Inch Nails. I stare at her breasts pressed into my chest as we share our saliva and our sex. Every memory acts as a whiplash – they each leave behind a scar that I scratch at and rub and tease and prevent from properly healing.

I turn back from the window and see that Jack's been studying me.

'All joking aside mate, are you honestly OK?' he says. 'You do seem a bit down.'

He's stroking Liu's hair, whose brown eyes I've always thought of as being only a shade away from black. Liu regards me now with these two circular voids and I chew on the soft fleshy membrane inside my cheek in a desperate attempt to get myself straight.

'Yeah, I'm fine. I'm going to my room. I've got some marking to do.'

'You're not fine though, are you? Come on, out with it,

boy – tell your Uncle Jack and your Uncle Liu all about it.'

'Don't patronise me, I'm not in the mood,' I say, to which he responds: 'Fine. Forget it. Just go and be depressing somewhere else, would you? You're bumming Liu out.'

'Whatever,' I say, and get up to leave. Before I have a chance to open my door he calls out from the sofa, 'But we'll be here for you if you want to talk about it later!'

I walk into my room and say aloud that, *it's OK, it's all right, you don't need anyone,* but feel yet more desolate and deprived when I look around and realise how alone I am.

Consider the girl on the tube. Think about the tattoo she had. Imagine it coiling around her hip bones, wrapping around her thighs, playing across the lengths of her legs ...

I should be picturing her bending over my desk and asking me to use her blood as ink, to tattoo my name upon the milky desert of her back, but instead I only see her leaping into the embrace of the punk on the platform.

I lean against the mirror and we stand I and I, eye to eye, forehead to forehead. Tears come and I let them fall. My telephone remains inanimate as I unleash my frustration onto the glass and the wetness from my nose smudges it enough so I'm distorting the reflection of myself.

8

I make my way to The Water Poet in Spitalfields to meet up with a few of the teachers I worked with in Paris. I'm casual yet smart in new jeans and suit jacket and this is for Louise more than anyone else. She's the colleague I doted on the most. I used to think of all the things I'd like to do to her as she made photocopies and snipped exercises out of old resource packs. We'd all meet in the staffroom of the school before venturing out onto the city streets, a bag of clippings and papers and board-markers thumping at our sides as we rushed from one building to the next, and I'd spend that time not preparing lessons or marking homework; I'd sit watching the hurried movements of this girl, pencil skirts sketching out an hourglass figure, shirts unbuttoned to tease the black lace outline of the bras that fought with her breasts.

The pub is full and it takes a few laps of it to find them. There's Rick and his French girlfriend Alice, Elizabeth (not my type, although I'm aware she's always been totally into me), and Gary and Phil. They each offer full-beam smiles as I approach, apart from Alice.

The first thing out of my mouth is: 'where's Louise?'

The table collects empty glasses as we all play catch-up. I talk to Rick who's the only one of us, along with his girlfriend, that still lives in Paris. We speak about art – he tells me that the newest exhibition at the Pompidou centre focuses on feminism and that a 12-foot-high woolen vagina currently hangs at the entrance. On one particular piece, he explains, the artist has painted three self-portraits hideously disfigured by phallic growths sprouting from her cheek, her chin and her nose. I ask him what he thinks it means. He says he doesn't know and turns the question back at me so I say *vagina good, dick bad*, and he laughs a lot, takes a swig of his beer, then laughs some more. Alice moves in for a translation and when Rick re-sets the mold of the words I gave him into French, it sounds infinitely more beautiful and profound. She looks at me and wrinkles her nose before refocusing on the challenge of her wine.

Rick says: 'Ali concurs.'

He drains the last of his drink and offers me another so I say, 'a vodka and diet coke.' He goes to the bar, leaving Alice behind to further contemplate the complex bouquet of her house red. I think of chatting to her but have no idea of what I would say.

I glance at Phil and see he's looking at Elizabeth with hunger in his eyes. I was always convinced that the two of them had a thing in Paris. Someone told me that Phil once confessed his love for her while drunk, and I think: *Well, you'd have to be pretty bloody drunk to confess your love to Elizabeth* then chastise myself for being so cruel. I look over at her and she stares down at her purse.

'Having fun?' I ask, but she doesn't respond.

I struggle to stay cool when Louise walks in and shakes the rain from her umbrella. Her coat is tied in a bow at her waist and strands of hair have been pasted to her cheeks by the weather. I call her name and she walks across the pub and wraps her arms around me.

'How are you? It's so great to see you!' she says into my ear and to the others over my shoulder.

She sits down and rolls her coat off, folds it in two, and places it at her feet with her umbrella and her bag. She reaches for Gary and Phil and disturbs a glass we've finished with, emptying all its ice out onto Elizabeth. Louise apologises with a hand pressed over her mouth. Elizabeth waves it off despite the cold mess in her lap and I subdue a laugh by flexing my fingers under the table.

Rick and I have been alternating our rounds and the sober part of my mind has started slipping away. He's speaking with Elizabeth and Alice now about Portobello Market and seems debilitated by boredom. Phil keeps looking at

Elizabeth and Elizabeth keeps looking at me. I let her; it can't hurt anything. All my attention is focused on Louise. I have her all to myself. I'm mirroring her body language and smiling and frowning in all the right places. I'm turning everything into a question about her. I'm showing her my teeth. I'm tensing my arms by squeezing my legs, my glass or the side of my chair. I'm sitting up straight so she can see the contours of my pectoral muscles pressing against the inside of my shirt. I'm offering her drinks and compliments. I'm brushing against her with my thighs and my feet.

She talks, with no sign of stopping, about how much she misses Paris, but also about the love she has for her new flat in Angel, about London London London and all its many splendors. She says something unfunny and I laugh and pass my fingers over hers before lifting sickly-sweet spirit with mixer to my lips. It's only when I begin to feel as if my many tricks are working and I have a chance of bedding her that someone I don't recognise comes to our table – a tall, broad man in a rugby jersey who Louise introduces as Ben, her boyfriend. I shake his huge hand and he crushes my own within it to prove he's the dominant male. I fake my way through it all and the dumb toothy clutter doesn't leave my face even when he takes her by the hand and walks her to the bar. He gives her rump a squeeze and she squeals and slaps him playfully on a chest which is as wide as the sail of a ship.

I finish the last of my vodka and coke with an enormous swallow and a dry-heave.

I turn to Elizabeth.

'Do you want a drink?' I ask.

I lead Elizabeth down the hallway and into my bedroom. I hear Jack calling out, 'be safe, you two' as I close the door behind us.

She's very shy as she starts unbuttoning herself. She unzips her skirt and can't quite keep her balance as she tugs it over her feet; she stumbles, steadying herself by using my drawers. My CD tower sways and for a horrible moment I

31

think it's going to crash down onto the floor.

I curse at her and tell her to be more careful. She slurs something about how long she's wanted this to happen.

I unbuckle my belt, throw my trousers down to my ankles, and step out of them, entirely drunk myself but still somewhat composed. I stare at the mousy brown roots of her hair where they meet the parts that have been dyed mustard blonde. She slips her knickers over her large thighs, her bruised shins. Her legs are veiny and hairy. Her breasts are blue and putrid.

She gets under the duvet. I take off my shirt and my underwear.

I don't want this ...

I visualise Jess, each orifice an *O* of pleasure. She's backing onto Marcus and letting him bite her hair and twist her nipples and she's screaming with joy; she's coming, she's coming, harder and harder, and then in a beat the image flips and there is Louise straddling the huge member of her rugby-playing lump of muscle and gristle, pulling herself apart, savoring the sweet pain as he enters her.

Elizabeth is slopping drool onto my face and neck and I'm left contemplating how I'm supposed to do this without an erection. More than anything, I just want it to be over.

I picture Jess, then Louise, then I imagine Jess and Louise together, naked and glistening, their hair a fanned-out flame of blonde and brunette that burns as I fuck them with two pricks.

Elizabeth is out of her head. She licks and scrapes me with her incisors and makes the most of the playground of my body, my muscles, my hair, the angles of my form, my face. She says something into my skin. It's almost unintelligible but I think I know what it is, I think I can detect its meaning, and I freeze.

She repeats these three words over and over again as she fondles my testicles, swirls them around: *I love you I love you I love you.*

I slide out of bed, never shifting my attention away from a

32

face that is now wet with sweat and smudged with bad make-up. I stand naked, still limp. Anger overwhelms me but so does an acute sense of desperation. My emotions have been smeared together and picking them apart and separating them no longer seems possible.

I collect her clothes from the floor and throw them at her as hard as I can.

'Get out,' I say.

Her skirt and underwear rest next to her.

'What?'

'You heard me. Get out. Put your clothes on and get out of my bedroom.'

She doesn't move.

I become nothing more than an ethereal bystander that watches my physical form take Elizabeth into my arms, wrenching her from the bed and onto her feet. I have no control as I watch myself holding the skirt in front of her face and screaming at her to put it on. She says again that she loves me through the chokehold of her tears. I watch myself telling her not to be so stupid. She doesn't love me. No one could love such a wreck, such a husk, such a pathetic shade of a man. She's delusional. She's drunk and desperate. She ruins her face further by twisting it up with sadness, saying 'I love you; I love you so much, I always have …'

I watch myself grabbing her and marching her out. I call this poor girl *a stupid slut.* She says she's loved me from the moment she first saw me. I watch myself saying: *The way I look has no bearing on who I am as a person.*

I am nothing. I barely even exist.

I cast her out of the bedroom and throw her shoes out after her and collapse onto the floor in a heap, naked and alone and the furthest thing from lovable that a person could possibly get.

9

I tell Jack I'm thinking about moving back to Paris.

'Why the fuck would you want to leave London?' he asks.

Because London has slid its tentacles too far into me and is playing me like a puppet.

'I'm done with London,' I say. 'London is a dead scene.'

He looks at me. That's all he does. He can see through my pretence. He knows I could never be done with London.

'I don't like the school I'm working at,' I tell him. 'I'm feeling fairly unfulfilled. Things aren't panning out the way I thought they would.'

He waits for me to dig further.

'Also, there's the flat. My bedroom here is way too small. It feels like I'm sleeping in a prison cell sometimes.'

He puts down his mug (inscribed with his name in purple nail polish; a gift from his boyfriend, and spelt without a "c"). He kicks back into the chair and says, 'Mate, you don't know how lucky you are, that's your problem. You live in the centre of fucking *Camden*, and I know a few people who'd kill for a room here. And at least what you do isn't completely fucking soul-destroying, unlike my job. It's well paid too, right? The money I get working at that vegan hellhole is an absolute joke. And as for tips? Vegans, no sorry, *London* vegans – they're as tight as a camel's cunt, man, I swear.'

'A camel's cunt? Are they known to be tight? Is that even a thing?'

He frowns.

'Yeah. At least, I think so. You know – because of all the sand floating around in the air. Their holes would have to be tight to stop all the sand and grit and all the other muck getting inside them.'

'Ah, I see. So all of a sudden you're an expert. All of a sudden you're a vagina connoisseur?'

35

'Well, I don't really know anything about camels *or* vaginas but it does kind of make sense, doesn't it? That they're tight?'

We look at each other for a few moments before we both start laughing.

'Anyway, as I was saying – I've got a hard fucking day-job, especially compared to yours. The money's shit, what I have to do is shit, and it's the polar fucking opposite of what I'd call a *vocation*,' he says.

'But what you don't realise, Jack, is that teaching's hard too. Getting up there and talking, well, *performing*, really, in front of all those people …'

I'm baiting him. Like all actors, he likes to be the centre of attention. It amazes me to think that the job of reciting page numbers and exercises and answers from a crib sheet might actually be a job he'd like.

He runs a hand through his hair from his scalp down to his shoulders and says, 'Jesus, I'd do *anything* for work like that. Especially with my ambition to act getting me precisely fucking nowhere. Do you how long it's been since I was in *Birthday Party*? Seven months! Seven months without a role! Do you understand how painful it is to keep getting rejected? I go for auditions, what, three times a week? I learn the lines, I walk the parts through over and over, get the accent exact, get the mannerisms down, man, and do they call? No, of course they don't. I'd love that job of yours and so would Liu, and he can hardly even speak a word of the bloody language. He'd just stand in front of the students flapping his arms around and shouting, but I guarantee he'd get more satisfaction from that than what he's doing now. I mean, he is so above that fucking job. He's making coffee for ungrateful cockney dicks until *seven-thirty* today. Shockingly low wage plus tips, which he also never gets because of his race or his sexuality or some shit, I don't know. Consider how hard it is for him eking out a meagre living before you start feeling so sorry for yourself. Teaching English the way you do? That's nothing. That's easy. Count my poor Liu's scalds later.

That'll shut you up. That'll stop you moaning. That's *proper* work, my friend, and you wouldn't know it if it pissed in your fucking *eye*.'

'OK, OK, I get your point', I say, and he smiles and takes a sip of tea.

'So anyway, about Paris,' he says. 'What would you do when you got there?'

'Teach,' I tell him, and he laughs. 'There wouldn't be many other options because my French is abysmal. And as you so eloquently put it, it's a noble profession. A vocation, if you will. One can practice it anywhere. The last time I taught in France, I had a pretty awesome time. I have friends that are still working there, really *good* friends, and … oh, I don't know. I can't quite put it into words …'

'Oh God, it's just hit me. I know what this is about now. Speaking of vaginas: it's a fucking *girl*, isn't it? There's a girl over there you're into. Mate, you don't have to go to Paris for a girl. London's full of them. You're gorgeous, you won't have any problems. Shit, you *don't* have any problems. We live on the same floor, remember?'

'It's not because of a girl, Jack. That's not the reason I might want to go,' *(except it sort of is,* I think to myself, *because Jess is both a reason to stay and a reason to leave).* 'I just need a change. You know what London can be like sometimes.'

'Hey, I'm not stopping you. If that's how you feel then that's how you feel. I suppose it'd be good for you to mix things up before you get too old.'

I show him teeth and hope it looks like some sort of smile, no matter how forced.

'Seriously though, Liu and I would miss you if you went away.'

'Aw, thanks.'

'No bother,' he says. 'Be sure to keep me updated with what you decide, but do give it some serious thought. It's a big decision. You'd be giving up your room, your job, everything really.'

'I will.'

'You will what? I want to hear you say it.'

'I'll think about it, Jack, oh wise one, oh sensei, oh camel cunt expert –'

'Think about it? No, no that's not what I said, is it? What did I say? What did I tell you to do?'

'I'll give it some *serious thought*. Fucking hell, what's got into you today?'

'Nothing yet. Maybe Liu later, if he's lucky.'

'Gross,' I say, and grin at him.

'Good man. *Serious thought* is what this situation needs, for sure,' he says as he takes a hair tie from his pocket.

'What's all this in aid of? I haven't seen you wear your hair up in ages.'

'Sweet of you to notice. There's an open audition for *Streetcar* in Dalston tomorrow and as you may or may not know, Stanley's more a of a rugged short-back-and-sides kinda fella.'

'And you're putting your hair up *now* because …?'

'Keep up, mate,' he says. 'What have I told you about getting into character? This is all part of the process.' He rises from the sofa. 'I'm off to give my lines a go so don't mind me if you hear me taking to myself.'

'Gotcha,' I say.

'Oh yeah, and before I go I have to ask: who was the girl you brought back last night? Quite frankly, you can do better than her. You can do *a lot* better.'

'We all have needs,' I say.

'Indeed we do, but who needs *that?*'

He leaves the room laughing and heads into his room. I stay behind for some *Serious Thought* and it consists of only two things: *would it be more painful to see Jess sporadically, as I am now, or to not see Jess at all?*

When I get into my room the first thing I do is check my *LovedUp* profile. I have a message from a girl called *LondonGirl1979* that I read through quickly. I copy and paste

38

my well-rehearsed reply and send it to her because she has a tattoo and a piercing and an overbite.

I click the online tab to see who else is pouring their hearts out into little white boxes and pining for a suitor. Girls of all types stare back at me, wanting to be loved, cherished, and adored. They know all the ins and outs of button presses. They trawl through the desperate men loitering around their inboxes – one click leads to another and another and the shaking of a head and the lapping of tongues against hard white enamel and *PING* another suitor. Loved by a dozen strangers yet still lonely. A week spent fretting over why the messages stop. Questions skipping around their sleep-starved heads at 4 a.m.: *where are you, my darling, and when will you find me?* A part of them must realise the only reason we're on here is to see each other naked. They surely can't be deluded enough to think it would be possible to find a soulmate through social networking. *Go outside*, I want to tell them. *Stand in a bar and announce you want to be loved and I promise it'd take precisely thirty seconds for an orderly queue to form in front of you.*

Nobody on *LovedUp* appeals to me this evening so I log-off and go to the fridge for a beer. Jack's in the kitchen making dinner. He doesn't say anything as I clamber around him, bottle held at heart height, thinking about what I'm supposed to do next.

I end up holding the photo of Jess against my chest in my bedroom, drinking beer straight from the bottle, and staring at a dead spider on my windowsill.

Before turning in for bed I make it to the bathroom with the intent of brushing my teeth and flossing and moisturising but forget about all that when I see the slick yellow rubber of a spent contraceptive clinging to the inside of the toilet – not quite disposed of in the way Jack and Liu might have planned. I take hold of the open end of the condom and lift it. It's heavy with genetics. I'm taken elsewhere by the slight sway of it as I rotate my wrist left and right. I hold onto the rope that binds them together. I pinch its reservoir and watch the white glue inside it creep upwards. All the power of the world is held within this smear; not just the love that sparks between two people but also the very essence of *being*.

I poke it and it pendulums.

The white I have inside myself should be reserved for the one I cherish. It should one day sprout arms and legs and we'll call it Elliott, after Elliott Smith. He'll have Jess's hair and Jess's complexion and Jess's everything, I hope. In fact, the less of me held within his DNA, the better.

And what if it's a girl? What shall we name her then? Louise?   Elizabeth?   Lollipop86?   CitySweets? LondonGirl1979?

I wrap the condom in tissue paper on my housemate's behalf and flush it into the sewer, into the river and far, far, far away from here.

As I'm reading out names from the register, I notice I have a new student – *Sophie Angier*. I wrap my tongue around these syllables as I look over the heads of the Italian accountant and the Mexican housewife and spot this girl in a baggy top with one of her shoulders left bare, her hair worn up in the lazy way I remember from my time in Paris. I start to initiate a brief back-and-forth between us but she doesn't seem to understand much of what I'm saying. I neglect the rest of the class and probe her with stimulants: the quality of French food, Notre Dame in the rain, the happy-hour drinks at the UFO bar in Parmentier, but she can do nothing more than pout.

I write *PAGE 17 Ex B – H* onto the whiteboard once I've given up trying to make a connection with her. The students take out their books and pencil cases. Verbs are conjugated. Synonyms are matched. A hand is raised but it would take much more than that to pull my attention away from the glow of Sophie's skin.

Twenty minutes into the lesson and I feel the vibration of my phone in my pocket. I'm stunned to see it's a message from Jess; this being the first I've heard from her since White's of Covent Garden. It says: '*Soz about the freak-out, everything's fine now, see you soon.*' She hasn't signed off with a kiss or anything. I assume her kisses must be tightly rationed, with Marcus receiving the greater share.

I watch over the students as they continue to work through their exercises. I look at the French girl and inside my skull I'm throwing her onto the words she's been studying, I'm rolling her lacy black panties down her legs and stepping into her and I start getting hard with shards of pain scraping against the inside of my stomach.

I leave the classroom without a word of explanation, walk to the toilet on the floor above, and hide in a cubicle until the lesson is due to end.

At breaktime I find the other teachers huddled together in a group in the centre of the staffroom. Karen the Director stands amongst them, explaining that *everything's going to be all right* and that *worrying would be a fruitless task we shouldn't focus any unnecessary energy on.* I ask Matt what's up and he picks up a marker and writes across the front of an unused photocopy: *INSPECTION – IMMINENT!!*

I make Karen the Director's words disappear by entering the smoking yard. I take out the box of cigarillos I bought on the way to work. I light a stick and tug on it and hold the smoke in the temple of my mouth until the taste of it is plastered onto my tongue. I allow it to leave my body and it rises into the air. I follow it and notice Sophie Angier standing above me on the fire escape. We watch each other smoke before she douses the stub of her cigarette on the metal railings she's been leaning over and retreats into the building.

I walk back into the staffroom, my head still swimming from the smoke and from Sophie. The things I'd do to that girl would shame even the most sadistic of perverts.

Matt threatens to disrupt my wandering libido when he places a hand on my arm and says: 'What are we gonna do? We are so *screwed*!'

Karen the Director bounces around the room, checking in with each of her troops and making lists of all the things we need to address before the inspectors arrive. Rob stands in the corner, as furious as ever. *You need to get laid* I think to myself, before the sad notion that this has never done anything to aid my own cause settles like dust on my mind.

Trudy is visibly disturbed, saying something about everyone being out to get her. She bites her nails before passing them through her wiry white hair and plucking lumps of dandruff from its strands.

I think to myself: *What a sad bunch we are.*

A few minutes later I make my way back up to class and

focus all my attention on looking good for Sophie.

I glance at the papers spread out in front of me and learn then that the sweet little French girl I've been mind-fucking is only sixteen years and three months old.

They stagger into daylight, my troupe of office workers and lawyers and secretaries and architects and chemists. The Colombian boy curls up his lip as he belts up his outer layer against the cold. The Spaniard wraps a scarf around his neck and chin and tugs a beanie over his afro. They don't know how we're able to live like this. I've watched them over the last few months as they've forced hunks of dry, stale ham sandwich and piss-weak coffee into their gullets. I've seen their tanned leather skin turn translucent and wilting beneath the overbearing dullness of the slate-grey London sky.

They each arrive with optimism but are robbed of it by the second day.

The Arabic vet looks pained as he catches the first fat droplets, an ellipsis dotted before an inevitable paragraph of rain.

They move onwards to their respective tube stations, to the waiting masses, to the heaving, steaming cattle, and what makes things worse is that they've learnt nothing and they will learn nothing from now until the day they go home.

With the rest of the classroom emptied out, Sophie remains in her seat. She turns her hair around one of those long ivory fingers as I try to maintain the sexual allure that, as an educator, I must always be exuding.

Once we've put enough distance between us and the school, I let her link my arm. I walk her to the tube station, where we catch two trains to South Kensington. I figure the Parisian in her will get a kick out of the museums; I'm proven correct as the Natural History Museum rises from the exit of the station and the girl at my side whispers what I think are an assortment of French compliments.

She rests against my shoulder as we make our way

towards the entrance. She whispers in awe as we ride the escalator into the hollow shell of the earth and up to a room filled with coloured gems and precious stones.

She looks at me and says something I don't understand.

We walk past the first few display cases. I explain to her what we're looking at, despite not having much of a clue.

She points at all the pretty colours and ignores me.

I rest a hand on the small of her back. I turn away from the peach of her behind and curse at myself.

She puts the *ache* in *teacher.*

We share a pot of tea outside a café across the road from the museum.

'I'm sorry,' I say. 'I shouldn't have brought you here.'

She smiles and pats my arm with one of her mittens.

'Don't you understand? I'm no good. I'm not a good person. Je suis … erm … Je suis nul personne. *Tres* nul personnes. Comprends pas?'

She covers her mouth and hitches up and down and I can see the laughter sparkle in her eyes.

'You are handsome,' she says when her lips are exposed.

'Listen to me; this can't happen. I love someone else, someone I can't stop thinking about. Someone who's already taken, in fact. Fuck, what does she even see in him? Sophie, if you were English, if you lived here, would you go for a man with no personality? What the fuck is it about Marcus? What does he have that I don't?'

She doesn't respond. She's been distracted by the arrival of a woman with a yipping dog. She takes off her gloves before reaching for the mutt and tickling the top of its head. The way she is manipulating it pushes out its tongue. It sits at the mercy of its own rapid panting as spit drips onto the pavement and blooms into the shape of a small black heart.

Sophie doesn't understand my wretchedness. She remains oblivious to what sort of man I am and what it is I'm going through.

I signal the waitress with a heavy sigh and ask for the bill.

44

I mouth the words *HELP ME* as I count out change.

Sweat has spread across the bed. *Daydream Nation* has run its course so now we only have the sounds of each other mock-moaning to fill the silence.

As soon as I hooked her leg over my own and entered her and kissed her forehead and her nose and her eyelid then refocused and saw it wasn't Jess, it was someone else I was nuzzled against, my mood started to sink and my sex-drive began to dissipate and empty itself out, so now I'm reluctantly looking into her beautiful young face, I'm going through the lyrics of my favourite songs, which is pointless and frustrating because I want to subdue my awareness of things but doing so is making me last longer.

I picture Jess to help things along but it doesn't make me excited, it doesn't make me come. It just makes me sad.

I fake an orgasm, separate myself from her and go to the kitchen for a drink of water. I hear Jack and Liu come home, both drunk, and I wait for them to pass the kitchen and go into their room.

I throw a glass against the wall and it smashes.

I return to Sophie and get into bed with her. After an age she falls asleep and I take this opportunity to weep then dream of you, for ever you, *always you!*

11

The next morning, Jack notices the broken glass from last night sprinkled across the worktop and the floor but doesn't ask any questions other than: 'What time is it?'

I take my phone from the pocket of my pyjama bottoms.

'Nine-fifteen.'

'God, so early …'

Toast jumps from the toaster and we both look at it for a second.

'Shouldn't you be at work?' he asks. 'What day is it? I'm so fucking hungover. Liu and I went to The Old Hat in Haggerston and we bumped into Richard and drank and drank and drank and, do you know Richard? We were catching up with him and he was buying us bottle after bottle of bloody awful wine and we bled him dry until he asked us back to his, which we turned down flat because we'd *intended* to go to this party in Peckham with Craig and Charlotte but –'

Sophie's standing in the doorway, bare-footed and gorgeous. She's been enveloped by one of my T-shirts and her hair drenches her. She says 'hi' and steps into the kitchen, fills a cup with water, then slinks off to the doldrums of my bedroom.

Jack watches her closely and when she's gone says: 'Holy shit …'

'What?' I ask, as if I don't know.

'Nothing, nothing. I just never figured you were a paedophile, that's all.'

'Jack, don't be so dramatic!'

'Are you kidding me? Have you lost it completely? She looks about *seven*!'

He claims the toast for his own and takes the butter out of the fridge. I ready a tirade of things to say in my defense that I haven't quite figured out yet.

'She's sixteen, actually,' is all I can come up with.

'Sixteen? Still pretty fucking young, in my book. Does she have daddy issues or something?'

'Leave me alone,' I say. 'I had a bad night.'

He puts a hand to his heart and widens his mouth in faux-shock, pretending to be horrified.

'A bad night? A *bad night?* Oh, say it ain't *so*, my friend. You weren't forced to ... to ... *drink* too much and ... and ... bring a *really really young* girl back to our flat, were you? That must have been so *hard* on you. And don't tell me there was ... there wasn't *coitus*, was there? You weren't forced to have *sexual intercourse* with her, surely? Oh my poor little lamb, my poor, hurt little bird, *I can't believe how awful your life is!*'

'All right,' I plead with him, 'all right, you've had your fun. Stop it.'

He shakes his head in disbelief and giggles as he takes a bite of toast.

I say: 'Let's talk about something else. Why not tell me about your audition? Have you had it yet?'

'You mean for *Streetcar?* It's later today. Shame my mind's so mangled. Shouldn't have drunk so much poison last night. Fucking wine. Why do we do this to ourselves?'

I laugh but it sounds too forced to be believable.

'Regardless of you being such a dick,' I say, 'I wish you well. Let me know how it goes.'

He cocks a thumb to where my bedroom is and says, 'Yeah, you too, salty,' before walking out of the kitchen and back to his boyfriend.

I put two fresh slices of bread into the toaster before sinking into a squatting position, allowing scattered broken glass to nip at the skin of my feet. I collect broken glass in my hands and when I convulse with disgust over thoughts of what I've done, I accidentally cut the skin of my palms.

I bleed.

12

The rain has been relentless for the best part of an hour and I battle through it, dissecting spectral reflections of light cast out from shop windows, creeping ever closer to the graveyard.

The irony doesn't escape me that Highgate Cemetery is where I first faced up to the death of the idea I'd had of Jess and I. We'd been walking across the mossy ground, squinting at Victorian etchings on flaking marble headstones, reading out loud the inscriptions we'd found most captivating when I stopped our tour to tell her I was falling in love with her. My voice was shallow, hushed by nerves, and as soon as the words left me behind I wanted to take them by their ends and ravel them back up. Mourners and tourists moved along the narrow footpaths of the grounds between the graves and slabs and grandiose sculptures and I willed one of them to distract us from the conversation the two of us were bound to have.

Angels covered their worn faces in stone hands as she let my own hand drop.

'Where's all this coming from?' she asked.

I swallowed stale air and felt my pulse quicken.

I said: 'The past few months have been amazing. You can't dispute that.'

'But I have a boyfriend.'

'Then what are we doing here? Why do you even bother indulging me at all?'

I wasn't being loud and yet my voice sounded harsh as it reverberated around the cemetery.

'We've been through this before,' she said. 'We're casual. I told you that when we first started seeing each other.'

'Yeah, well, I suppose I want more than that now.'

'What're you saying?' she asked.

'Isn't it obvious? I want *you*! I want us to be a couple. I want you to leave *him* behind.'

She started getting as agitated as I was.

She brushed hair away from her eyes and said 'I'm sorry, but I can't give you what you want. I'm with Marcus, Marcus is my boyfriend. I couldn't have been clearer about that, could I?'

'Do you really love him?'

I was all too aware of the answer to that question. I didn't need to hear her response.

'You know how I feel about Marcus. I've never hidden that from you. The two of us, you and me, it's … *different*.'

'Different? Different how?'

'Look, do we really have to talk about all this here? Can't we wait until we get back to the house?'

'No, I need to know now. I can't go on like this. And I can't imagine there'd be a better place than a graveyard to drag all this out.'

She folded her arms over her heart, making sure I was locked out of it.

'Well, it's not that I don't *like* you,' she said. 'There's clearly something between us, I know, but Marcus and I have been together since we were kids. I love him and I'm probably going to marry him one day.'

'Jess, how do you think that makes me *feel*?'

'I never thought feelings were a part of this. I thought all this was supposed to be cool.'

'No, it isn't cool. Not any more. I don't think this has *ever* been cool, to be honest.'

'So do you want us to stop seeing each other? Is that it?'

I didn't answer.

'I don't want to hurt you,' she said.

I was silent, the damage already done.

'Come on,' she whispered. 'Let's go. We'll talk about this later, I promise.'

She gestured to take my hand and I became the author of my own destruction when I allowed her fingers to mesh with mine.

Soon afterwards we kissed against a twisted oak tree. I

wanted to breathe all the love I had into her but from the trauma of what had just transpired and in kinship with the strangers buried all around us, breathing was something that now eluded me.

Thinking about the past has made the journey up here evaporate. By the time I get to the cemetery gates the day has dimmed further. A mirage of the two of us walking this path glides away from me, into the fortress of marble and stone, and I follow its trail with my chin on my chest.

Death permeates everything.

When I come across a particular stone that Jess had been in awe of I take the paper and charcoal from my coat pocket, spread the paper over its etchings, and begin to rub. The words come up from behind it like an apparition pressing into it from the marble. It's an altered version of *Do Not Stand at my Grave and Weep.*

It reads:

You are a thousand winds that blow.
You are the diamond glint on snow.
You are the sunlight on a rose
I don't know why you had to go.
For ever loved, for ever missed.

I fold the paper and put it in my pocket. I should frame it and give it to her on her birthday. Maybe that would invert her opinion of the two of us.

I walk deeper into the territory of the dead. I trace the path we once took, take in the statues and the monuments and the tombs and brush past the tree where we kissed. I wade through mud and rain and the disturbed dirt of graves as I chase the spirit of the two of us.

I get to the place where I'd told Jess about my feelings and have to rush through it. I walk past the graves of Karl Marx and Douglas Adams and find myself back at the start of the circuit I have made; the circle now complete.

I hurry to the bus stop, flash my Oyster card, and find the driest seat I can on the bottom deck. I take the stone-rubbing from my pocket. Rainwater has made the words smear and distort, so much so that they are now completely illegible.

13

I stand under the shower and let it heat up my blood as remnants of the cemetery swirl into the drain. My phone vibrates with a message from *Lollipop86* saying she's waiting for me outside Stables Market.

I squirt shampoo into my hair and wash it for the third time. Halfway through flossing I stop to ask myself: *what are you doing?*

I walk into the living room and find Liu concentrating on picking the skin from a blister on one of his hands. He's lying on the sofa with his head in Jack's lap.

'Ask me then,' Jack says.

I stand in front of him and frown.

'Ask you what?'

'Don't you want to know if I got the part?'

I look at him and he stares back at me.

'Erm, hello? I had the audition today? Fuck, don't you listen to *anything* I tell you?'

I sigh and say: 'OK, Jack: Did you get the part?'

'I didn't, but thanks for asking. I was shafted once again. You know, there was a guy there that actually looked like Brando? Not the spit of him, of course, but more so than I do. It made me think I should get a haircut. I reckon I should join a gym or something too, maybe even go whole-hog and give up the booze and drugs and cigarettes.'

'That ain't you, Jack,' I say as I sit down. 'You wouldn't last five minutes.'

He laughs and says, 'Damn right it isn't. Thing is, I'm so overdue a break, it hurts. When oh when will I catch my fucking *break?* I gave a great audition. I *smouldered*, mate. I would've fucking *slayed* if I'd got the part.'

'Better luck next time, I suppose.'

Jack looks down at his boyfriend.

'How about you, babe?' he asks. 'Do you think I should

change who I am just to get ahead? Go tee-total? Chop off my hair? Turn celibate too, perhaps?'

Liu doesn't respond, probably because he's not able to follow much of what's being said. Jack smiles warmly at him and picks up one of his hands to kiss it. He pauses with the hand in front of his face.

He extends it towards me and says, 'See what I mean? Look at the state of that. What did I tell you about *real work*?'

'Yeah, must be painful,' I say, but if it is Liu doesn't show it. Jack kisses each burn mark, careful not to irritate the injuries further.

I go to the hall to put on my jacket, checking the hipflask I keep in my inside pocket is full. Before I disappear for the evening Jack says, 'You look nice. Special plans?'

'Not really, mate,' I say as I open the front door, 'but don't wait up.'

It's quarter-past eight when I get to the market. *Lollipop86*'s been standing in the cold waiting for me for forty minutes. She's wearing a raincoat buttoned up to a furry leopard-print scarf. Her hair is parted in the middle with a few strands left hanging over her eyes. Her lips are painted plum.

All I really see is the grotesque death-mask of her come-face.

'You look amazing,' she says, and I thank her.

I walk her towards the Lock Tavern. She starts bringing up all the texts she's been sending and asks why I haven't been replying. I distract her with questions about her job and the new show she's in and where she bought her cool new coat and she's flattered enough to forget how inconsiderate I am.

I'm so good at being a bastard – a realisation which does nothing for my mood.

I order her a dry white wine and a double rum and coke for myself, feeling acrimonious towards her just because Jess likes dry white wine too. She sips at it and prints her lips onto the rim of the glass.

A spot at the far side of the room becomes available and by the time we've made our way to it I've finished my drink and have to go back to the bar to order a fresh one. I ask for the same again but with less ice.

Before returning to my date I carefully unscrew my hipflask to transform my single rum and coke into a quadruple.

Her words are softened by the rhythm of loud electronic music so she has to lean in against me, putting pressure on my upper thigh, and despite my indifference I start getting hard. Jess appears in my thoughts and I try to get rid of her but she isn't going anywhere. I could grow to like this *Lollipop86* girl if it wasn't for the Jess in my head always insisting on having her say.

I nod and smile and *yes, yes, yes, I know, yeah,* and she's getting more and more animated but I can't understand what she's talking about, not really, and *oh really, yeah, mmm, yes, yes, you're spot on, that's true, that's so true ...*

She goes to the toilet so I pour more hipflask rum into my glass. The moment she returns she takes up the monologue she left me with and continues to pursue it. I get more and more drunk as I continue thinking about Jess and reflect on how much of a monster I am, how terribly I've treated Elizabeth, how I've had sex with a sixteen-year-old-girl put in my care, and when it all starts bringing me down I sink the rest of my drink, buy *Lollipop86* a large glass of wine, and treat myself to a Long Island Iced Tea because it's the most alcoholic thing on the menu.

At the end of the evening I crawl out of the bar and she picks me up and supports me under my arms. I give her vague directions back to my place and she's able to carry me to my building. She takes my key and opens the front door and we climb up, up, up, for ever, for ever, until we reach my flat.

I trip through the hallway, thankful that Jack and Liu aren't in because I'd hate for them to see me in such a state so many times in one week.

We find our way to my bedroom and do we fuck? I don't know.

As soon as I regain a sense of self, I ask her to leave.

14

I initially opened my laptop to start typing formal lesson plans ready for the school inspection (*Exercise, A, Exercise B*) but now I'm considering tapping out something more *existential.*

I type *I dream of you each night* into the emptiness of the blank page. I'm tired of waking up sad. Last night I dreamt we were in bed together and it soon became apparent I was dreaming because the layout of her bedroom wasn't quite right, so I looked into her face and said *I love you Jess, remember this tomorrow morning please please remember* and when I woke up and realised where I was it was like being hurt by her all over again.

I follow what I've written so far with a series of dots, then the word *fuck*, and when I read it back it looks like this: *I dream of you each night ... fuck.*

I save it as *Jess#1* and take a drink of wine.

Writing never used to be something that eluded me. Somewhere in my Dad's house is a box of books with a bunch of my writing inside, from a time before Jess became all that mattered. Back then *(for ever ago)* I would travel as much as I could and note down thoughts and feelings of the places I discovered – the adventures of my youth.

I spin the globe I usually keep on top of my wardrobe. I watch Italy come and go and recall the motion of the train as it carried me from the casinos of San Remo to the Duomo of Milan. I had all my possessions *(clothes, sleeveless novels, bags of grass)* stuffed into a bag balanced on an overhead rail. I'd write a few words about the landscape rolling by the window and every so often I'd look up at the girl sitting opposite me, trying to get her attention.

At times, I'd catch her peering at me over her magazine.

I left the train and followed her to a café not too far from the station. I read and revised my writing over an espresso and a pastry while she sat at a nearby table, attempting to figure me out. I was young. My skin was olive-brown from an aggressive Italian summer.

I looked good and so did she.

It wasn't long before I made my way over to her. I ordered two cups of coffee as I sat down, using broken fragments of the language I'd picked up since landing a month before.

I smiled at her, my teeth bright-white. I held her hand and shook it.

Her name was *Catherine.*

We took the train east until we neared Venice, sharing a bunk on an overnight train. We booked ourselves into a campsite a bus ride over the bridge from the island. It had a hot tub and a bar that stayed open until six in the morning. We didn't see much of the old town for the first few days; we lay half-naked on scorching hot stone, drank bottle after bottle of lukewarm beer and made love sweating on the floor of our tent, always with a pre-rolled joint ready to be smoked somewhere nearby. She'd go for a soak every so often and I'd lie on my front and write. I'd outline details of the way the air shimmered above the water and how her skin glowed in its suds.

When we finally made it to Venice, we sat on the patio of a restaurant just off the Piazza San Marco. The food was drab and overpriced but it was of no concern to us; we knew that as soon as we were done we'd take each other's hand and run, deep into the throngs of people standing outside the cathedral.

She took lots of photographs and I wrote down everything that happened.

We dropped by Florence and found it boring, riding to Rome as soon as we could. There we stayed in a cheap hotel and fucked below an oil painting of the Holy Mother.

I held her against my lips under an umbrella on the Spanish Steps. We climbed the Vatican. We splashed each other with water from the Trevi fountain. Afterwards we used the ridges of a radiator to open bottles of beer and she let chocolate melt on her before asking me to remove it with my tongue.

She bought a couple of postcards. I was to write her a note about how beautiful and funny I thought she was. She told me she'd do the same about me on the other postcard but when we exchanged them I saw she'd written nothing. She'd just drawn a picture of the two of us spooning on the bed of our hotel room.

On leaving Rome we caught a train to Napoli, where we stayed in a twelve-person dorm in a shitty hostel to save a few euros. Running our hands over each other's bodies when night fell was made even more exciting by the presence of strangers.

A few days later we travelled towards Bari but were kicked off the train for not paying full fare. I stole bread rolls from a market stall and bottles of wine from a supermarket.

We ate and drank and slept in the street, held against each other when the sun went down.

The next night we snuck into an overnight carriage and were taken further south. The train terminated near the tip of the boot but we hung around the station until the next one arrived, which pulled us onto a ferry bound for Sicily. We walked to the top deck to watch the day break and I held her hand and waited for mainland Italy to disappear.

We couldn't find anywhere to sleep on arrival so we spent the first night lit by the moon, making love on sand almost as white as the pages of my notepad.

I hitched us rides across the shoreline from Messina to Palermo.

I paid for a hotel room and an expensive meal for the two of us because I knew that before long our trip would come to an end.

I wrote her a letter and hid it in the pocket of her backpack but she found it two days later.

We drank bottle after bottle of wine and screwed on beds with cotton sheets.

The last day we had together was on a beach in Trapani. We rested beneath an umbrella that shielded us from an overbearing sun. We talked each other through chapters of the books we'd collected from the lobbies of the hostels we'd lodged at. At times we read aloud, accompanied by the shushing of waves as they lapped at the sand in front of us.

In the end I decided it would be less painful to leave her, rather than to watch her leave. I wrote her a short note while she swam, slipped it between the pages of her book and took a bus back to our hotel. I collected my things for an onward journey to Croatia and whenever Catherine came to mind I focused on the fact that this was no doubt for the best. We had no realistic future together. There was no reason in prolonging the pain of parting or making our goodbyes any worse than they needed to be.

I left both Italy and her behind haven't seen either of them since. Regardless of my current state, I sometimes like to fantasise that she's still walking the length of the beach in Trapani and calling out my name, then wonder with some despair whether I'd ever want to be found by anyone other than Jess.

15

Rob tugs my arm as I'm walking past and says, 'In my office.'

I follow him reluctantly into his lair of old documents and forgotten ink stains. I sit down and drop my bag at my side. He lands in his chair then lowers it so he can prop his elbows on the desk.

'We've got something serious to discuss, so you'd better get comfortable,' he says. 'I want you to know that everything you're about to tell me will go on record.'

'There's a record? This sounds like a police interview. Do you want me to put my hand on a grammar book and swear to tell the truth the whole truth and nothing but the truth?'

He burns red with anger and it gives me a strange thrill to know I can get under his skin this way.

'Trudy told me she saw you leaving work the other day with a student. I think it was …' He pretends to look through a few of the papers on his desk. '… Ms Sophie Angier?'

I resist gifting him with any sort of reaction because to show weakness in front of this psychopath would be a terrible error.

'Oh, that. Is that what you wanted to talk to me about? That was nothing. We were just walking to Tottenham Court Road together. We both take the Northern Line home,' I say.

'Is that right?'

'That's not against the rules, is it? Walking in the street with students? I thought natural English conversation in an open environment was good for their development. Isn't that what you told me once?'

'This is different. You know we're against any kind of social contact between teachers and students outside of the social programme,' he says. 'It's not worth the aggro it causes, especially with younger students when their parents find out.'

Younger students ...

'I haven't done anything wrong.'

'You haven't?' he asks. 'Are you absolutely sure?'

He grits his teeth in an odd smile and I start to wonder how much he knows.

'Yes, I'm sure. Of course I'm sure,' I tell him unconvincingly. 'Trudy's just causing trouble for no reason, yet again.'

He starts pointing at me with the staff of his index finger.

'You listen to me, and listen carefully. If I ever find out you did something with that girl, I'll be on you straight away. Do you understand what I'm saying?'

'Sounds inappropriate, Rob. Are you sure you're OK with that being *on record?*'

'I don't want you going anywhere near students when not in class. Am I making myself clear?'

'Perfectly,' I say, 'although I still don't really get what all this fuss is about.'

'You do know we have a school inspection in a few days?' he says.

'Yeah, what about it? What's that got to do with anything?'

He looks fit to burst when he says: 'If you do anything to mess this up for me, I swear to God I'll … I'll *end* you.'

I let him tremble for a few moments before making a show of looking around at the bedlam of his office and saying, 'Well, maybe it's not me you should be so worried about. Can I go?'

I think about giving Trudy a look that shows I know she's betrayed me but when I see her hunched over three open books I figure she's probably hurting enough. I rush through the staffroom and out to the smoking area.

At one point Sophie pokes her head over the railings of the fire escape. I don't look up after first noticing her but I can feel her watching me as I smoke and I find myself trying to telepathically shoo her away. She isn't in the classroom when I start the next lesson so perhaps it works. I'll have to bear this in mind for the next time I want to shake off unwanted attention, and as most attention I get is unwanted this could turn out to be a most invaluable tool.

16

I walk into the living room and find Jack in a heap on the sofa. I'm disturbed by the state of his face; sopping wet and contorted into odd shapes.

'Shit, are you all right?' I ask.

All he can do is let out a long wailing sound that sounds ever so slightly like: *Liu ... Liu ... gone.*

I wrap an arm around him as he gets out what he wants to share with me. Liu's left London to return to his father in China and isn't coming back, a circumstance detailed in the poorly written letter Jack now holds against his chest.

I go to take the letter from him but he's gripping it too tightly.

'I love him so much!' he says. 'It hurts so much!'

He buries his face into my neck.

I stroke his lithe back and say 'I know, mate. I know exactly what you mean.'

The next morning, we sit in the living room wrapped in dressing gowns and watching daytime television, drinking cold tea, smoking cigarettes and joints, and ingesting MDMA through our nostrils in an attempt get happy.

Jack lifts his head as if to say something then lets it drop again.

I told him about the problems I'm having with Jess. He let me soak him with my sadness and then he did the same to me, he wiped himself all over me, and having the chance to express our anguish lessened the weight bearing down on both our hearts, but only slightly.

My phone rings. It's Karen the Director. I answer and tell her I'm feeling worse and I might not be in work tomorrow either. She says *oh OK* and asks what Rob should be doing with my students (he'll be *furious* about this) so I say pages seventeen to infinity and she says *what* so I say pages seventeen to twenty-three. She thanks me and wishes me a speedy recovery and reminds me again about the inspection.

I let the phone drop to the floor and go to offer Jack a fresh cup of tea but can't find the words I'd need to do so.

We sit and bask in our collective misfortune. We are in pieces.

I have my laptop open and I'm clicking refresh on my *LovedUp* profile every few seconds but no new girls are checking me out. I'm going through a dry patch, and what I wouldn't give for a hug from a woman. I send *Lollipop86* a text asking if she wants to come over when she finishes work but this is the third text I've sent her in three days and it's getting less and less likely she's going to get back to me.

Jack and I don't shift until the moon has risen, not even to eat – not seeing the point in sustenance, no longer relating to the idea that life is worth living. Time consists of constricting seconds and minutes and hours of wanting the ones we love at our sides.

We decide to go our separate ways only when the last of the wine has disappeared. We embrace like brothers before retiring to the epicentre of our agony, being the bedroom and the bed.

At around three in the morning, I lie awake and listen to the sound of crying coming through my walls. The dream I had about Jess remains fully formed in my mind and I can recall every moment of it with very little effort. I hate how adamant my brain is that I shouldn't just put all this to rest. I can't let go of her, despite how apparent it is that I'm not the one she wants.

I look around the room for something to do. Masturbation is always an option, although last time I started sobbing as I climaxed because I missed her hand.

I read from *War and Peace* but can't recall the sound each letter should make.

I sketch Jess's face on the novel's title page. I've never been much of an artist so the finished product looks like the distorted version of the Jess I see when sleeping – a hideous nightmare, in other words.

With daylight poking through my bedroom window, I walk into the lounge in nothing more than boxer shorts and a Reuben T-shirt. Jack is sitting on the sofa watching television. He hasn't shaved and is covered in bristles. His hair is greasy and toxic.

He clutches the letter Liu left behind, his hand stiff with the rigor mortis of a dead relationship.

'Do you want to talk about it?'

The moment I ask the question he says: 'I don't want Liu to fuck anyone else. It hurts so much to think about but I can't stop myself.'

I approach him and bring him against my hip and rub his arm.

'Come now, mate. We'll get through this.'

'I don't think we will, though,' he says. 'I honestly don't think we will. The thought of him with someone else makes me want to chop my fucking head off. It makes me want to stab myself in the fucking chest …'

Through this topic of conversation he's making me think of Marcus hanging out inside Jess, inside my favourite hang-out spot, which depresses me further.

'If I don't hear from him soon,' he says, 'I can't be held responsible for what I'll do.'

'Promise you'll come and get me before you do anything too heinous?'

He doesn't say anything more, he just weeps into my hand. Jack has become a stranger overnight. I'm used to him being buoyant and cocky and to see him in any other way demonstrates how very severe this situation is.

He wipes his eyes with my fingers and says, 'I just want to be *loved!*' and I think: don't we all?

We've finished most of the third bottle of wine of the afternoon and now we sit slumped on the couch with Bon

Iver playing as the soundtrack to our misery.

'Cunt,' Jack says.

'*Fucking* cunt,' I add.

As we surrender ourselves to the music and to the alcohol in our blood he presses his lips against mine. I'm drunk enough to leave my own lips limp – he parts them with his teeth and pushes his tongue against my tongue and we remain like this until the album ends.

We separate and look at each other, surrounded by silence.

'Fucking *camel's* cunt,' he says, and we both start laughing, and no matter how brief it may be it feels good to laugh again.

We have an evening planned that involves spaghetti bolognaise on the sofa and the devouring of one of Jack's *ER* box sets. The curtains have already been closed and a few joints rest on the windowsill waiting to be smoked.

Over dinner, Jack asks if I've ever heard of something called *Grindr*.

'It's basically Facebook for gay sex,' he says. 'It's a pretty radical concept.'

I decide not to tell him about *LovedUp* and that it's basically Grindr for straight people because then he'd have the suspicion I was a member.

'Sounds good, if you're into that kind of thing.'

'Which I am, as you well know,' he says, but it's as if he's kidding himself.

He twirls spaghetti around his fork and pulls it into his mouth and spots of tomato sauce fall onto his favourite ribbed-white T-shirt. He stares down at the mess then looks at me and makes *oink*ing sounds.

'You took that well,' I say.

'Yeah, well, fuck being such a miserable bastard, Oh, and fuck Liu, too. If he's willing to leave me the way he did, with a fucking *letter*, then he's honestly not worth my attention. I'm not gonna cry for him any more and I'm not gonna moan like a little girl about getting a bit of fucking red on my T-shirt. What's the point?'

He sounds angry when he follows this with: 'life's too fucking short.'

He inadvertently brings to mind the way I abandoned Catherine on the beach in Sicily with only a note as explanation. This causes me to prod a pepper with my fork a little too hard.

To divert my train of thought I say, 'So, which season of *ER* do you want to start with? The new class? Or do we treat ourselves and delve way back into *The Clooney Years*?'

He looks at me as he considers an answer. He looks down at the plate in front of him, across at the TV, then at the phone that rests on the arm of the chair next to him.

He drops the plate onto the floor and stands up.

'Where are you going?' I ask.

He picks up the phone and says, 'I don't know yet.'

'What about the spliffs? What about *ER*?'

Before leaving to get ready for whatever he has in mind he yells '*Fuck ER*!' straight into my face, spraying me with spit.

I pick up my guitar and swear to myself I'm not going to put it down until I've wrung something from it that's worthy of how I feel. I start playing the few chords I can transition between and I let this disgusting tuneless catastrophe penetrate the rotten air of my room.

I sing whatever and it's all about her.

I record a rough demo of what I've come up with and when I play it back I'm so sickened by what I hear that I throw my four-track across the room.

It bounces across the floor and comes to a stop at the door that Jack is now holding open.

'Everything OK in here?' he asks.

I burn with embarrassment and rest my guitar on my bed.

'Yeah, fine. I'm just writing a song.'

'I can see that,' he says with a sad smile. It's obvious he's been crying again and I can tell how drunk he is by the way he's propping himself against the doorframe. 'Going well, is it?'

He blows cigarette smoke into my room and it mixes with the odour in here.

'Not too bad, thanks. Never mind that though, Jack – are you OK? Where've you been? Do you fancy smoking those joints now? I've been saving them for –'

'I'll leave you to it then,' he says, cutting me off. Almost as an afterthought, he adds, 'By the way, this is Amar.'

A young Indian man hovers at his shoulder and waves at me so I wave back. Jack hooks him out of sight and closes the door behind them.

I retrieve the machinery of my four-track and press its guts into its shell like I'm an action hero easing the intestines of a fallen comrade back into a reluctant midriff but they won't stay put, it's broken, it's fucked.

I swear at my reflection and tell myself I have to *calm down.*

I slide the plectrum under the strings of the guitar and force it into my wardrobe. I remove my clothes and lie naked on my bed in the dark.

My phone vibrates with a text from *Lollipop86* apologising for not being in touch over the last few days. Someone she has a history with has come back into her life and she mentions it'd probably be best if we didn't see each other any more because she's feeling *a bit confused.* I hit reply and type *Ah, someone from your past has come back and now you're feeling "a bit confused." Good luck with all that.*

I set my alarm for six-thirty, determined to make it into work tomorrow because if I don't then I won't be able to afford alcohol and alcohol is important. I don't get to sleep for an age, partly because of thoughts of Jess, partly because of the sound of a headboard rattling against the other side of my wall.

17

Sophie hasn't picked up her pen all lesson. Another student gestures to ask a question but I ignore it and rub *Ex 30 – Ex 36* from the board, replacing it with *Ex 37 – Ex ??*

The notes Rob left me detailing the last few lessons he taught on my behalf while I was "ill" fill me with horror. On Tuesday he held an intensive grammar workshop focusing on the use of the past, present, and future perfect tenses. On Wednesday he spent three hours dividing the class into groups and assigning them each a part to play in some sort of overly elaborate roleplaying exercise.

As I'm reading through bullet points of the homework he set, my phone starts ringing.

Jess is calling.

I don't bother to excuse myself before walking out of the classroom.

'Hey, how're you?' she asks.

'Fine.'

'Marcus is away for the night so get here at eight, OK?'

'OK.'

She cancels the call and I return to class, where Sophie sits and licks her lips.

'It's the inspection tomorrow, don't forget,' Karen the Director says.

The photocopiers are now both jammed and the printer is still out of ink. So much needs to be done. People are drowning in piles of paper. Staples spring from fresh puncture wounds. Rob surveys this carnage from across the room – he's staring at me like he wants me to join in with all the madness but I won't give him the satisfaction.

I look back at my boss and watch her as she fidgets.

'I know Karen, yeah. Everything's under control.'

'Are you sure? Because you haven't shown anyone your

lesson plans yet. We're supposed to go through them together before the inspectors arrive to make sure they're up to scratch.'

'Sorry, but I've been off work, haven't I? I was ill. Nervous about the inspection, I reckon.'

I hesitate long enough for her to start doubting me.

'I have a doctor's appointment, so I'd better go.'

'Could you come with me to the office for a few seconds first?' she says, and I have no choice but to follow her. I feel sweat start to collect on my chest and under my arms and as I walk past Rob I have the almost overwhelming urge to thrust a pair of scissors into his temple.

I stitch my fingers together and place them in my lap. I maintain constant eye-contact to divert her attention away from my appearance. I didn't iron my clothes last night because I was too depressed to do anything productive and my trousers reek of coffee from an accident I had during break. The time I've spent wallowing with Jack has lowered my standards to the extent I'm almost embarrassed to be seen in out in public. If Jess was to ever admit her love for me, I'd have an expensive suit tailor-made and I'd wear it every day. I'd polish my shoes to mirrors and the creases in my shirt would be sharp enough to slit a throat, but as things stand, why bother?

Karen the Director picks up a folder with my name printed on it and starts taking my old lesson plans out of its centre. She catches a yawn before composing herself.

'Is this all you've been doing with your class? Exercises from the textbook?'

She holds up the papers with my writing scattered across each page, penned in a hurry in a haze of desperation as the end of each day drew nearer.

'Isn't that what we're supposed to be doing?'

She fans the documents out on her desk and starts to say 'well, yeah, but ...' then loses me under a pile of heaving rancid bullshit, all connected to the inspection, all laid out especially for its arrival. She doesn't care, not really. She's always known what we as teachers were all about. The Inspectors are getting their claws into everything and I loathe them already; *THEM*, with their clipboards and agendas and fucking *opinions*.

'… Do you know what I mean?' she asks.

'Yeah, yeah, sorry, I see what you're getting at.'

'Rob's been doing some great things with your class while you've been away. Have you read through the notes he's left you?'

'I have. I agree. It's really great stuff.'

'I'd like you to carry on like that,' she says. 'The Inspectors love to see a bit of variety in the classroom.'

'Sure. No problem.'

'Good. So, can I quickly see your plans for tomorrow? The ones you'll be using for your observed lesson, I mean …'

'I don't have them on me,' I say, when in fact I don't have them *anywhere*. 'Can I e-mail them to you later?'

She tucks the paper back into my folder and puts it away.

'Make sure you do. This inspection is very important, more important than you might think.'

I get up to leave.

'Relax, Karen,' I say. 'I'm on top of it, I promise.'

I pass through the insanity of the staffroom and retreat outside, avoiding any form of interaction with the students gathered there. I put my head down, select Slayer on my iPod, and pummel my brain with it, turning it up as loudly as it'll go, and when I'm about fifteen feet from school I forget all about the inspection and start to lose myself in thoughts of Jess's favourite sexual positions.

73

18

The shirt she likes lies on a stack of other soiled and stained clothes in the corner of my room. I pick it up and turn it around, turn it over, lift up its sleeves, and feel dejected.

I drop it onto the pile and take a V-necked T-shirt from the bottom of my drawer. I make a sweep of my desk and place the ashtray and empty cigarette boxes and cups and glasses and plates and plectrums and laptop and headphones and styling wax onto the floor. I plaster the shirt across its surface and set the iron to heat up as I go to the bathroom to shape the hairs on my face.

I don't know why but I'm shaking.

I go to the kitchen to pour myself a shot of rum and light a cigarette. The flame flickers and I can't hold it steady.

I tell myself to *breathe.*

Jack comes home shortly afterwards with a scrawny figure clasped against him and I welcome the distraction, no matter how short-lived.

'This is Min-jun,' he says.

'Hello, Min-jun,' I shout as his door slams closed.

I open my mouth to speak but she doesn't give me much of a chance – she reaches for me and pulls me inside and makes me hate everything, makes me despise all other people and individual grains of sand on beaches a thousand miles from here, makes me hate life, hate death, hate empty Coke cans rattling along despicable streets I've never walked down, hate stars in the sky that are pimples on the blackened bruised face of an infuriating god, and gardens are now graveyards, and flowers are puss-covered cancer sticks blooming with picked-scab petals; I hate all else because she is so beautiful, she is so gorgeous, and I walk into her home and throw myself around her, kiss her with violence, throw up all my love into her mouth, invade every centimetre of her with my hands and

I hate my hands, my arms, I hate every hair on my head, I hate the written word, voices, shapes, colours, I hate all things but I love her, how I love her, I love her unconditionally.

She takes me through the hall, all the way to the bedroom. She steps back and slides the T-shirt over her head, unbuttons her jeans, and shimmies out of them. She stands wearing white cotton knickers and a necklace with red stones that loops around her neck and drip-drips down between her breasts. She goes for the bottom of my shirt but I stop her. I look at her. I just let myself look at her for a few moments. I use my nose to breathe her in and hold her in and let her circulate.

I kiss her forehead, then her nose, then her lips.

She stretches out on the bed but I don't feel excited; I merely feel this love, this disease that eats away at me, and I hope I'll remember this moment for ever, her body extended, her skin, her body, her bed, all mine, for now, all mine.

I stand in the bathroom holding the condom in front of my face and for an absurd moment I consider taking it home with me.

I drop it into the toilet and flush. I stare at my reflection and smile at myself. This is the only place in the world I feel as if I belong – in her house, in her bathroom, in her dressing gown, with the taste of her body fresh on my tongue.

I walk back into her room. She has a thin sheet draped over her bottom half. She's holding her phone and tapping something into it.

'You OK?' she asks without looking up.

'Definitely,' I say. 'That was awesome.'

'You didn't flush the condom, did you?'

'Nah, I wrapped it in toilet paper and put it in the bin.'

'Did you empty it into the toilet first?'

'Yeah.'

'Good boy.'

I let the towel I've wrapped around myself drop and I

climb onto the bed. She sweeps the cords of her hair over her shoulder so I can kiss her neck.

'Sorry, I'll be with you in a minute,' she says as I rub my erection against her thigh.

The air holds undertones of a summer fruits joss stick, lit to nullify the scent of our lovemaking. The soft light of a dozen tea candles illuminates a Sublime poster tacked over her bed and an Ikea case filled with battered paperbacks: *Dracula, The Life of Pi, 1984, Sputnik Sweetheart, The Dharma Bums, The Secret History, Rules of Attraction*; a CD rack has The Cinematic Orchestra and Nirvana and The Smiths and The Cure held between its ribs; a metal tree covered with bracelets and beaded necklaces stands erect on a dressing table dotted with make-up boxes, closed clams of blusher, perfumes, mousses, powders, and a silver tray of birth control pills of which I'm Thursday.

This is the girl I love ...

I rest a hand on her back to search for the movement of her blood.

She puts the phone down after it pings confirmation of something I'd rather not know.

I kiss her and stroke her hair and when I enter her once more I feel like I die a little bit.

19

She made breakfast and a cup of strong coffee and painted her face as I ate. When we parted ways at the end of her street we hugged but didn't kiss; she said *see you soon* but we didn't make any solid plans. I'm worried it's going to be a while before she lets me over again and I torture myself by thinking of Marcus coming home and getting into bed with her.

I alight at Tottenham Court Road. I step into the slipstream of a thousand commuters and let them transport me through the barrier. It's early so I buy a coffee and a pastry from a small Italian café. The girl working at the counter normally flirts with me but this time she serves me straight-faced and I think I must be doing myself a disservice today. I check my reflection in the back of a teaspoon to fret over how I look. I rake through my hair and splash myself with water taken from a bottle someone left on the table next to mine.

I stagger out of the café work-bound.

When I'm almost at the entrance of the school it dawns on me that today's Inspection Day and I spit the word *fuck* through gritted teeth.

I pick up a book and thumb through it, not knowing what I'm looking for. Other teachers clip together wedges of paper and cut-outs and laminated flashcards and I start to wonder to myself what it is I do with my time. I sit down at a computer and click through folders and files and slideshows, waiting for a flash of inspiration.

Karen the Director clears her throat and when I look up I see a man in round wire-framed glasses standing at her side. He's looking at the watch on his wrist and up at the clock on the wall and with deep concentration and rabid intent I will him to burst into flames.

The Inspector follows me to my classroom, where Sophie plays with her hair and pretends not to care when she smiles at me and I don't smile back. She still appears captivated by me. I figure it's because to her I'm somewhat exotic – a part of English culture she can take home in her loins.

Attendance is taken as The Inspector slides the gnawed tip of a red biro across his cheek. I mispronounce some of my student's names to waste time. I run through the years I've spent as a teacher and can't fathom how it is I got this far – I can't recall anything I've ever done in this capacity aside from dictating page numbers and willing time to go quicker.

I choose a name at random from the register and say 'Rodrigo. How are you today?'

He looks perplexed.

'I fine, teacher.'

'Good. Good …'

I recite another name and ask the same question.

'I OK, teacher, thank you. And you?'

'I … I'm fine, Silvia. I'm good, thanks.'

The Inspector writes something as sweat drips from my armpits.

'Right class, everyone stand up.'

They scrape their chairs back and wearily do as I instructed. I pick up a stylus, let it drift across the whiteboard, and only realise I've written *talk about your favourite thing* when I take a step back to assess my handiwork. They look at each other and in my head I'm screaming: *please do this for me. I know we did this exact same lesson for Karen's observation but please don't point that out, please, please don't let me hang myself in front of this suit, in front of this monstrosity …*

The Inspector rattles the pen against his leg, jots something down and I think: *choke on it, you loathsome fucking rat!*

To break the stalemate, Rodrigo approaches Olivia, a barrister in her home country, and says, 'So, what you favourite thing?' She looks at me for influence, her bottom lip quivering, before turning to him and saying 'I like the music, what you favourite thing?'

I look at The Inspector and he writes something in blue ink, which he underlines not once but twice. I manage to make this exercise last for thirty minutes by switching various words on the board and telling the students to alter their answers accordingly. Afterwards The Inspector clicks his pen closed, straightens out his papers, and offers me an unreadable expression before leaving.

When I'm sure he's gone and not coming back I tell the students to take their seats and to open their textbooks to page ninety-eight.

I press the cotton of my shirt against the parts of my body that are the wettest.

I check my phone and am dismayed when I find no messages, no missed calls – no Jess.

The Inspector returns a few minutes before the lesson is due to finish. He motions for me to approach him, so I tell the students to carry on with whatever they're doing and walk out of the classroom.

'We need to go through the feedback I have for your lesson.'

'Yeah, sure, no problem.'

'Do you want to let your students go to break so we can use your classroom? I know you have lessons to prep and I have other people to observe so we'll get it all over and done with now, if that's OK with you?'

'Sounds good.'

I tell the students to pack away their things. They don't understand what I've said so I point at their bags then towards the door and they sigh with gratitude as they close their books.

The Inspector walks in and collects a chair. He brings it to my desk and sits on it facing mine as if he's about to put me through some sort of interrogation.

Rodrigo walks past and wishes me a good day; a

pleasantry I haven't got the decency to return.

'Be with you in a minute,' I say to the Inspector, right before Sophie approaches and presses a hand into my crotch. She smears her tongue across the side of my face and says, 'See you later, teacher.'

The Inspector opens his mouth in shock.

I watch Sophie walking towards the door and before she's out of sight she looks back at me and winks and I think to myself: *clever thing ...*

I leave school with papers and books clutched against my chest. I navigate my way through students that are smoking and speaking in any language other than English.

I hear Rob screaming my name as I roll the headphones over my ears.

I walk towards Camden. I fill up a bin with all the things I'm holding. A few of the books won't fit so I have to bend and twist them before shoving them in.

I reach Regent's Square, find a spot on a bench and take my phone out of my pocket. I have a new message – not from Jess but from Louise; she of the hourglass figure, the object of my obsession during my time in France. It reads: *Hi guys. I'm moving back to Paris (I missed it too much!) so I'd like to cordially invite you to an evening of frivolity, tomorrow night in Hoxton Square. It'd be lovely to see you all before I go!*

The text I send back is simply one of confirmation: *I'll be there.*

I start thinking about what I'm going to wear as I continue the lengthy walk home, turned uncomfortably numb by just happened at school.

Jack makes no apology when I walk into the kitchen and find him sitting on the worktop, making out with a middle-aged Japanese man in a pin-striped suit. I take a beer from the fridge, open it with my teeth, and drop the top into the sink before heading into my bedroom. Jess hates it when I do that. She worries that one day the bottle top will bring my teeth with it.

I drift off to the music of Elliott Smith and when I wake up the sun's gone down. I check my phone and find I have a text from Louise *(great see you tomoz at 8 don't be late!1!1!)* but nothing more.

I put my headphones on again to drown out the sounds of sex coming from the next room over. Everything hits me at once and I scream expletives into the bosom of my duvet, swearing vengeance on the little bitch known as *Sophie Angier*, refusing to acknowledge that none of what happened was really her fault. I was careless and stupid and governed by my own selfish sense of entitlement.

I go through the inbox of my phone to double-check a message from Jess hasn't flown in under the radar. I think of her and recoil at the pain that grows in my stomach. I click through old messages from her and realise there aren't as many as I thought.

I inspect each picture I have of her and it feels like ripping stitches out of a fresh wound. I linger on a particular photograph of the two of us taken in her bed, still flushed red from making love, and with a sudden surge of effort that sadness brings I'm able to delete it.

I go to my contacts list with the intention of speaking to *Lollipop86* but she doesn't pick up. I leave a voicemail message explaining how sorry I am and that I want nothing more than to be her friend.

She doesn't return my call, she doesn't send a text.

I go to bed to sleep at quarter to eight.

20

Louise texts me with the address of the bar we're meeting at tonight. I start fantasising about her skin and her legs. Every time Jess appears in my mind like some kind of bloodsucking arachnid I picture a huge *STOP* sign and divert my attention elsewhere; to Louise's chest, to her tongue, to her legs, to considerations of what it is I'm supposed to do next.

I roll a fresh spliff on the bedside table and smoke it in honour of my first day of unemployment.

I enter the living room and find the same Japanese man from yesterday with his head in Jack's lap, in the exact position that Liu once occupied.

'No school today?' Jack asks.

'No school any day. I got fired.'

The Japanese man flinches when Jack starts applauding.

'Oh, bravo!' he says. 'Good show, old chap! Good show!'

I bow.

'Let me guess – fallout from the little girl scandal?'

'Sixteen, Jack,' I remind him. 'And yes. Happy?'

'Very,' he says, and starts laughing. 'Wanna see if I can get you a job at the café?'

'No, no, no,' I say. 'I'm not into that.'

'Well, nobody's *into that*, mate, but it has to be done!'

'I just want the world to leave me alone …'

'But the world doesn't work that way, does it?' Jack says. 'You should know that by now.'

'God, you can be a real dick sometimes,' I tell him. He pretends to be offended by what I said but he can't stop grinning. 'I'm going back to my room,' I say, and Jack says 'wait a second, don't you want to meet …'

He looks into the Japanese man's crown.

'What's you name again?' he asks.

'Ken.'

Jack looks back at me.

'Don't you want to meet Ken?'

'Hello, Ken,' I say, and Ken salutes.

'Right, I'm off to my room,' I tell them, 'and I don't want to be disturbed.'

'Reading you loud and clear, mate. And congrats again on your outstanding achievement!'

As I'm walking through the hall Jack starts bellowing 'School's Out'.

I button up a fitted shirt. I smear tight jeans over my legs and tug at my crotch so it isn't as noticeable behind the denim.

I tie up my Cons and slide on my suit jacket.

Louise and her group aren't there when I arrive so I order a pint of Camden Hells and sit at the bar reading a copy of the free music newspaper taken from a pile near the entrance to the gig room. I check my phone frequently but because of the mental *STOP* sign I've erected I don't know if it's in anticipation of contact from Jess or from Louise.

The sudden idea Elizabeth might be joining us tonight causes me to drive my glass down hard onto the bar, drawing the attention of the dreadlocked barman away from the lemons he's been slicing. After feeling Jess slipping further away and losing my job in such a spectacular fashion I doubt I'd be able to deal with the tri-factor of also absorbing Elizabeth's flatulent emotion on top of all that, so I order a shot, swallow it, and leave.

I send Louise a text wishing her a safe journey to Paris and offering an apology that I won't be able to make it tonight. Instead of catching the tube or the bus home I decide to walk, struggling against the cold, fighting a strong wind, and it takes me over two hours to get there.

21

Our landlord has indicated a desire to root out a new housemate to take Liu's bed. I have a few smokes with Jack in an attempt to pacify him; he bites his nails and winces at the harsh reality that the spirit of his ex-lover is to be exorcised from our flat.

'It's the finality of it that's bothering me more than anything,' he says. 'How can another person sleep where Liu used to sleep? It seems so wrong.'

I hook an arm around him in a pathetic gesture of companionship.

'I know he's gone but if he was to ever change his mind, we couldn't both sleep in a single bed,' he tells me. 'It'd drive him mad. He likes to sleep like a starfish.'

He laughs but it's short and bitter and blunted further by the thumb he holds between his teeth.

'I miss him like you wouldn't believe,' he says, and although I've heard him say it a hundred times before now, I haven't yet worked out how it is I should respond.

We share a final teabag before Jack heads to the room he once shared with Liu to get ready for another day of work at a place he hates. He closes his door with one hand, his other hand resting on Ken's buttock.

Jack looks over his shoulder at me before the two of them leave. I surmise that everyone has their own way of dealing with things, and that he and I have more in common than I ever thought we had.

I'm alone with no distractions so I cave and send Jess a text asking if everything is OK. This gives me such an adrenaline rush that I return to my room, put on a pair of shorts and a band T-shirt, strap on my Converse, and leave the house running. I keep time with the beat of Factory Floor as I head towards Primrose Hill and Regent's Park. I have to stop every few minutes to hold my sides and take in jugs of oxygen. My calf muscles become the foundations of a pain that passes through my body.

I reach the park and jog along the paths that dissect it. I see the top of a camel's head in an enclosure of the London Zoo on my right and, a few metres further on, a group of boys kicking around a football. I run past a couple of girls sitting on a bench and I speed up in front of them and flex each muscle. They look at me with disdain because I'm puffing out air and I'm covered in sweat.

I stop at the drinking fountain and cool myself down with stagnant water from one of its concrete pools. I check my phone: no reply from Jess, but a message from the landlord saying someone's coming to see the room in the next few hours.

I keep running until I'm sick into a flower bed.

After getting home and napping for a few hours I'm woken up by a rattling at the front door. I open it in my pyjama bottoms.

'Hey. I'm Dom. Is this the flat with the bed for rent?'

'I suppose it is,' I say. I step aside to usher him in and he immediately starts scrutinising the place; the pictures we've stuck to the walls of the hallway, the pile of shoes we never wear stacked next to an empty newspaper rack. He enters the bedroom he'll potentially be occupying with Jack and takes in both halves of it – one half filled with nothing more than a stripped single bed and a torn *Katekyo Hitman Reborn* poster, the other stuffed with piles of clothes and ashtrays and DVD cases and drained wine bottles. Jack must've separated the beds after Liu left, although I don't know why – sharing a single bed with all the men he's been bringing back can't have been too comfortable.

'It's an awesome area,' I tell Dom with zero enthusiasm. 'You know. Camden. It's Camden. It's great.'

'Yeah, that's why I'm here. What about the rent?'

'Well, you'd be sharing the room with my housemate,

Jack. He sleeps there,' (I point to the unmade bed sprinkled with empty bottles of nail polish and rolling papers and transparent sachets coated with white powder), 'and you'd sleep over there. It basically halves the rent so it'd be three hundred a month each, all included. Quite cheap for Zone Two, I'm sure you'd agree.'

'What's Jack like?'

'He's great. He's in and out all the time. He works in a café but wants to be an actor. He's a good laugh, chilled out, friendly, gay …'

'Gay?'

'Gay. Do you want to see the bathroom?'

'Nah, no need, mate,' he says. 'So, what do you two do for fun?'

'Just normal things, I suppose. We drink, we smoke, we watch TV.'

'Do you party?'

'What?'

'Do you, you know, party?'

'If by *do you party* you mean do we take full advantage of living in Camden then I'd say that yes, we do.'

'Right,' he says. 'So I think I'm interested.'

'Cool. You have the number of the landlord, yeah?'

'Yeah, I've got it. I'll probably give him a ring later. Cheers for letting me see it.'

He goes to leave and I call after him: 'Wait – are you *sure* you don't want to see the bathroom?'

He doesn't respond. He lets himself out and I'm left standing in the hallway, positive I'll never see him again.

The sound of a car approaches and I duck down behind a skip on the other side of Jess's road. They get out of it together. He looks wooden and lifeless, she looks incredible, and they meet each other in front of the car and take each other arm-in-arm and let themselves into their home. They turn on the light. I watch them in the kitchen putting away the contents of one of the bags he was holding. She pecks him on the cheek

89

and walks into another room, so I'm left watching Marcus. I study his every move and over and over I'm cursing because it should be me in there, it should be me putting away her shopping and spending most nights in the comfort of her arms, rather than sporadic nights that hold no worth.

My phone starts ringing. It's our landlord. I answer the call and spit *not now, Ahmed!* into its receiver.

Marcus finishes what he was doing and the light goes out so I head back to Camden, back to my shitty life, back to my own meagre existence. Jack tries to talk to me when I get in. I offer him monosyllabic answers before heading into the warzone of my room.

I don't bother checking my reflection.

I lie down on the clothes on top of my bed and hold a pillow over my face.

22

After a breakfast of champions consisting of stale bread burnt and a tepid can of lager found hiding under the kitchen sink I take my laptop to the lounge, turn the TV on, and mute it. I open a new document, resisting the urge to sign in to *LovedUp.*

I type: *I've tried in vain to drop this thread and let it all unravel.*

I start thinking I could craft the finest novel of my generation, a single line a day, but it'd take two hundred years for me to finish it …

I delete what I've written so far and replace it with *PLAN OF ACTION* in capital letters. Beneath this: *Number One,* then *Drink/Smoke/Snort Less.* I feel as if I have control but that might be just a trick of the mind caused by too many mind-altering substances.

What else?

I want to travel the world with my music. I want to write an account of the lifestyle of a down-and-out, an alcoholic who barely hangs together. I want to paint a bowl of fruit (an assortment of life that will never rot), call it *JESS AND I,* and sell it to the Tate, and it's at times like this I wish I had talent, any sort of discernible talent at all.

On TV I watch a fetching young doctor sitting beside a bed-ridden blonde. The camera cuts to a close-up of the girl and she immediately looks away from me.

I could travel and teach English. I could go to any country I liked, but how far away from Jess would I be willing to go if it came down to that?

I write *Find Employment* next to *Number Two* and then: (*preferably close, preferably not teaching.)*

Would Paris be an actual option, or am I just kidding myself?

I lift the beer to my chin, remember *Number One* then put

it down again.

For *Number Three* I write: *Win over the girl I love.* I stare at it for a long time before deleting it. In its place I write *Get Help* then delete that too, before I even have a chance to read it back.

I watch the doctor as he leaves his patient to weep in isolation in her hospital bed. I wonder to myself what she's just been told.

I write in big letters: *AT LEAST I HAVE MY HEALTH!!!*

I wait for the show to end and when the credits have rolled I finish the beer and roll a joint. I leave the house in an altered state with no idea of where I'm going and don't stop walking until I'm in Hampstead. I make a pass through the lanes of a book fair, where I am the only customer under retirement age. I trail an index finger across broken spines, scanning titles and names of authors I've never heard off, and stop when I get to a book by Murakami because he has always been one of Jess's favourite writers.

I pick up a coffee on the way to Hampstead Heath and when I get there I find a bench to sit on. I sip at my drink and watch birds landing on the water. A dog circles my feet to investigate my presence here. I give it a shove with the outside of my shoe and its owner calls out a feeble *hey*.

The coffee does nothing to increase my energy levels so instead of venturing further into the womb of trees and mud and dog walkers and people who know how to live and act and behave like people I walk back the way I came, nursing the pain in my thighs. As I approach Chalk Farm I see Jess leaving a craft shop with a man that isn't Marcus. She's wearing a short leather jacket and grey leggings. He's wearing a denim jacket and skinny jeans ripped at the buttocks, enough for the dark blue of his boxer shorts to be visible through the tear. A dense black moustache skirts his upper lip. He is thin enough to be threatened by a sudden gust of wind.

I follow them as best I can on legs still destroyed from the run in Regent's Park. They stop at a gelateria. I watch her tongue lapping at a plastic spoon from the vantage point of a slope on the other side of the road.

She doesn't have to pay for what she's had. She's treated to it by the man in the denim jacket.

I get ahead of them by jogging. I have to grit my teeth against the stiffness in my calf muscles. I reach a position where I can watch them face-on as they walk the steady incline of Haverstock Hill. I pretend to inspect the window of an antique shop as they draw nearer. The volume of her voice increases; my heart beats quicker and quicker and sweat starts soaking my back.

They get near enough for me to notice that Jess's companion now has thick cream covering the ends of his moustache. I turn to them. Jess frowns as if trying to place who I am and Monsieur Moustache slurps the top of his cone as he looks me over.

'Hey Jess,' I say pathetically. 'Haven't seen you around here for a while. What're you up to?'

'Nothing much,' she replies.

There are a few seconds of uncomfortable and awkward silence, the words *who is that man you're with?* stuck in my throat.

'It's a bit cold for ice cream, isn't it?' I ask.

'It's a sorbet that Jess is eating,' Monsieur Moustache says. The two of them look at each other. 'This one's ice cream, though. Do you want a little taste?'

He holds the cone out to me and I stare into the indentation his mouth has made. I switch focus back to Jess and she's wearing a delicate smile that I fail to make sense of.

'No. No, you're OK, mate. Thanks though,' I say.

I'm tempted to grip onto his arm and force the ice cream into his face, into his moustache, possibly even choke him with shards of wafer, but I somehow hold my shit together.

'Too bad,' he says, and takes another lick. 'It's really quite good.'

Awkwardness applies pressure to our circumstance. Jess

tweaks her companion's free hand and says, 'We should get going, I'll see you soon, yeah?'

'Yeah,' I say, massaging my wounded heart. 'Yeah, you will. Hopefully.'

The first thing I do when I get back to the flat is go to my wardrobe and rip all the clothes from their hangers. The shirts, trousers, belts, sweaters, cardigans, and coats fall to the floor and I mindlessly tread all over them.

I pick up an old cup of tea and empty it out onto the fabric and leather.

I sit on my bed and tend to the pain in my legs and attempt to calm myself down with the consideration that, in all honesty, he was probably just a friend of hers.

I smoke a cigarette, looking around at the carnage I've created. The walk to Hampstead and the pursuit of Jess *(the ever-lasting pursuit of Jess)* has once again rendered me exhausted so when I'm done with the smoke I rest my head on my pillow, close my eyes, and sleep. All I'm able to dream about is her and Monsieur Moustache fucking on my bedroom floor, using the ruined clothes I once loved as blankets and sheets.

23

I hear a scream. It's guttural, wild, and coming from the room next to mine.

I hear a thud and the screaming stops.

'Jack?' I call out to the darkness.

My voice is strained.

'*Jack?*'

I sit upright.

I don't know what to do.

I take a fork from a discarded dinner plate at the foot of my bed.

I don't know what to do!

I'm petrified.

What time is it?

I hear a knock.

'Hello?'

Another knock, this one more urgent.

'Open up, it's Jack.'

I creep over the debris scattered across my carpet.

'Jack? Is that you?'

'*Yes! Yes, it's fucking me, it's fucking Jack, open the fucking door!*'

Jack's wearing my raincoat and a pair of dark-blue jeans and I can tell this by the glow of a streetlamp bleeding through the pores of the blinds in the kitchen. He's holding the wrist of a stranger cowering behind him.

'Jack, what's going on?' I ask.

'You tell me. I just got in. What the *hell*, man?'

I look to his companion for answers.

'This is Sun Jin.'

'Hello, Sun Jin,' I say.

Sun Jin doesn't respond.

'What are we gonna *do*!?' Jack pleads.

I don't say anything. We each focus on his room.

'See who it is,' Jack says.

'Are you serious? It might be a crackhead or something! I'm not going in there! Jesus, that scream …'

We look at one another for a few uncomfortable moments. Jack mouths the word *please* and indicates his latest acquisition with the rotation of his eyeballs.

With no warning the handle turns on its own and the door opens and the three of us cry out at the figure standing naked and scratching at the matted hairs on his chest. 'Guys, could you keep it down?' he says. 'I'm sleeping in here.'

Jack looks at him, still shaken, and says, 'Who the fuck are *you*?'

I feel foolish when I have to say: 'Jack, Sun Jin, Dom … Dom, Sun Jin, Jack.'

Dom explains that he's prone to night terrors. He was dreaming of something nameless and fell out of bed. Jack grits his teeth through it all – he offers Dom a cigarette but Dom doesn't accept, just wishes us a goodnight and makes his way back to bed.

Jack looks at me like he wants to rip me into confetti and even Sun Jin is scared by it.

'You'd better leave,' Jack says to Sun Jin. 'I'll call you tomorrow.'

When he's gone Jack drills an angry stare into me and grunts: 'You *cunt*!' He pushes me and I fall against the wall. 'Don't you think you should've told me some fucking random was taking Liu's bed?'

'I didn't know anything about it!'

'*Don't bullshit me!*'

'I'm not! He came round a few days ago, said he might be interested in the room. How was I to know he'd move in so quickly?'

'Of *course* he'd move in quickly! This is Camden, remember?'

He pushes me again and I hit my head hard against the wall.

'Could you stop doing that?'

'I can't believe this. Where's Liu? Where's my Liu? Who's the stranger sleeping in his bed, on his pillow? God, Liu, where *are* you?'

'Mate, Liu's in China. He dropped you like a fucking stone then left, remember? I know it's hard but someone had to take the bed eventually. We talked about this the other day. It sucks. I'll help you in any way I can, but you have to stop freaking out first. Can you do that?'

He slides down to the ground, sad and drunk. I start stroking his hair and he lets me do that for a while before grabbing my hand and throwing it away.

He sobs and whispers over and over again: *Liu, Liu, Liu* ...

I go to the kitchen for a rum and coke. I offer the drink to him but he doesn't acknowledge it so to steady my own nerves I tip the glass back and drink it myself.

'I'm not ready for this,' he says. 'I don't think I'll ever be ready for this.'

'Look, you have to move on,' I say, and it is so ridiculous that this is coming from me. 'There's nothing more you can do. Face it: Liu's gone and he isn't coming back.'

He aims his red eyes at mine.

'Fuck you! Fuck you! You have no idea how I feel. I want to die. Kill me. Get out a breadknife and cut my throat, I'm begging you.'

'Calm down, Jack. Take a few deep breaths and try to calm down ...'

'Why didn't you just *tell* me this was happening? I didn't even know someone came to see the room, and now someone's fucking *moved into* it! So I'm supposed to, what, keep my mouth shut and sleep next to a stranger?'

I say: 'After the week you've had, you should be used to that by now.'

'What's that supposed to mean?'

'I dunno, Jack. Maybe we should ask Sun Jin? Ken? Min-jun?'

97

He stands up suddenly and comes at me. He gets me in a headlock and twists me onto my knees, saying, 'You bastard! You bastard! How fucking *dare* you say that?'

'Dom's moved in and there's nothing we can do about it now,' I say into his arm. 'Stop it! You're choking me!'

'Good,' he says, although shortly after he loosens his grip and wipes tears from his eyes.

He points at me and says, 'This is the worst thing you've ever done.'

'What did I do?'

He doesn't respond. He stares silently at me before letting himself into the room he now shares with Dom. I consider reminding him I'm his closest ally and I know more than anyone else what it is he's going through, but adrenaline prevents me from speaking further.

I walk to my room and get into bed. A few moments later, smearing itself all over the sound of Jack's persistent sobs, I hear Dom screaming again.

24

The next morning, Dom steps out of the kitchen to intercept me.

'Hey, how're things?'

'Not too bad,' I say, clawing at the keys in my pocket.

'Sorry again about last night.'

'Don't worry about it. It's quite funny. We had no idea you were moving in, so were a bit shocked to find you here.'

'Yeah, I gathered that. The strange thing is the landlord said I could move in whenever I wanted to. Didn't he tell you I was coming? When I let myself in and didn't find anyone here I thought I was alone. I called out your name and everything …'

'Doesn't matter, Dom. Don't worry about it,' I say. 'I do wish Ahmed had told us you'd be getting here so soon, though. It would've made the transition a lot easier.'

'Yeah, I think I know what you mean. I'm not getting much of a positive vibe from my new roommate – he seems pretty pissed off with me being here. Is he OK?'

'I'm sure he will be eventually,' I tell him, convinced what I'm saying is far from true.

'What's wrong with him?'

'Well, it's a long story. It's not you that's the problem, though, not really.'

'Are you sure? It's just that I heard him mention something about a guy called Liu living here and I remember you telling me he was gay, so I just thought … you know … I don't want to tread on any toes …'

I rake nails across my arm; edgy, itching to leave.

'I shouldn't get into it, mate. It's not my place to talk about what Jack's going through.'

'But the two of us are sharing a bedroom now, aren't we? It doesn't get much more intimate than that. If there's any sort of problem or issue that needs sorting out between us, I'd like to know sooner rather than later.'

'Why not just ask him yourself when he gets home from work?' I ask.

He takes me by surprise by pulling back his lips and grinning.

'Yeah, I might do that, actually,' he says. 'It'd be a good bonding experience.'

'Do whatever you think's best,' I tell him. 'Anyway, I'd better get going.'

'Where you off to?' he asks, and as I have no clue I say, 'to The Black Heart. I'm catching up with an old friend.'

Even if I had a plan, I wouldn't want Dom to know what it was.

'Sounds cool,' he says. 'I've never been there before.'

He stands watching me and sipping from the mug that Liu gave Jack, no doubt waiting for an invitation that will never come.

'Well, have a great time,' he says.

I stare at him for a few moments, thinking: *if only that was possible.*

After cancelling an incoming call from school, I invite The Fall deep into my ear canals. As Mark E. Smith snarls about *repetition* I walk the same path I've taken a thousand times before. I feint left and right at the feet of every tourist and curse under my breath when I'm delayed by a Spaniard holding out a smartphone to snap a picture of a market stall. I think about picking up an espresso but the queue to the café is snaking out onto the pavement so I power on, aiming for the river.

I skim myself across the green fringe of Regent's Park and step into the pandemonium of Oxford Street. I smile at a girl but she doesn't smile back and I figure I must be losing it (whatever it was that I had). I examine myself in a shop window and can't tell either way because my reflection is so distorted.

I cut through Soho and stare at all the sex. I wish my prick would shrivel up and fall off. I wish I was asexual because it would change my life in so many ways, and all for the better. Naked girls are destruction, they're pink leeches that feed on my humanity and I don't have enough to spare, not any more.

I twist and turn through Trafalgar Square, swearing at all the fucking *people*. I walk towards the river and when I get there I drape myself over the railing and gaze into its depth, thinking: *why did I even come here?*

I watch the London Eye as it rotates. I look across at Big Ben and wait for it to chime.

I close my eyes and count to a hundred and when I open them again I realise nothing has changed, not one single thing.

I hurt all over from the run I took a few days ago. I can't put up with the pain in my legs any longer so on the way home I walk to a shady-looking massage parlour on Romilly Street. The noise from the bell above the door brings a woman in what looks like a white lab coat through a beaded curtain to see to my needs. She takes me to a different room that's warm and dark with a steel bed set up in the middle of it.

In awkward English she tells me to wait and when she leaves I remove my jacket and shirt and tie and shoes and socks and jeans and I get into place on the bed in just my underwear. The girl that is summoned to my side has the figure of a young boy but long hair tied-back and centimetres of makeup obscuring the scales of her acne scars. She gives me a towel and points at my crotch so I remove my underwear in front of her, not hiding my nakedness, and wrap the towel around my waist. She observes this as if this is what she's had to deal with a thousand times over. She's as bored by my cock as I am.

I place my face into the headrest and watch her painted toenails wriggle as she rolls her hands together and spreads them across my lower back. She applies pressure to the thin layer of fat I've accumulated there and pushes it upwards, kneads it loose, fingers my skin, and thumbs my bones.

She presses a palm into my spine. She cracks my neck.

She massages my thighs. She digs into my calf muscles and *squeezes*.

She relieves some of the pressure from my skull. She loosens some of the tension from my nerves. She turns me over and of course I have an erection so great that I feel faint.

She manipulates my arms and my hands. She rubs my chest.

She removes the towel and touches the end of my dick.

'You want?' she asks.

'No,' I say, but she does it anyway.

25

I enter the flat late with a girl on my arm that I plucked from whichever bar I ended up in. I take her to the living room with the intention of consuming any drugs Jack's left behind but instead of his drugs I find Jack himself, shivering in the armchair, covered with the throw we sometimes use to hide stains accumulated during the time we've lived here.

'Who's *that*?' Girl says, and not quietly. She laughs as she pets him, flicking strands of his hair around with her fake nails. I *shush* her but it makes no difference. He's riled awake by her prodding at his cheeks and he stretches the tendons of his neck to get away from her.

'It wakes!' she says.

Jack responds with: 'What the fuck?'

'Jack,' I say, 'what are you doing out here? Why don't you go to bed?'

'Fucking Dom … won't stop … fucking *screaming* …'

'It speaks!' Girl says. 'But what does it speak of? Who is this *Dom*?'

'Housemate,' I say, then to Jack: 'did you try waking him up?'

'What would be the point of that?' he asks, to which I don't have an answer. He'd just fall asleep and scream again.

'You're cute,' Girl says to Jack. 'You know, I'd let you both fuck me if you wanted to,' and her laugh is shrill enough to make me grind my teeth and for Jack to bring hands from under the throw to cover his ears.

'Not interested,' Jack says when she's done. 'One: I like blokes. Two: you're fucking *awful*.'

She looks to me for support but I can only manage, 'Hey, he's right: you *are* fucking awful,' so she storms out and slams the door behind her.

'Got any drugs, Jack?' I ask, and as he reaches beneath his makeshift blanket to produce a sachet of cocaine and a rolled note he says 'I have no idea where you find these troglodytes.'

I smile and say, 'Does this mean you're talking to me again?'

He remembers our predicament and his face goes sour.

'I'm gonna give you this snuff, then I want you to leave me alone. Is that cool?'

'Jack, I –'

He stops me with a raised hand and says, 'Mate, don't bother.'

I spin the globe and watch the world pass me by. It makes me think of Catherine, of where she is now and what she's doing. Married, no doubt. Possibly with child. That's what happens to everyone.

I fetch a pen and a notepad from one of my drawers and start writing, still eager to recapture the hunger I once had to produce something, *anything,* of substance.

Cocaine writes this poem:
My heart is an ink-pot
I dip my cock in
to make bad art with.

26

After Jack has left for the day, I think about attempting to reason with Dom. I want to ask him to stop playing his music so loudly, to stop leaving pubic hair sprinkled across the bath, and screaming when Jack and I are trying to get our heads down, but all of these things are just what makes Dom who he is.

It's impossible to change a person; I know that first-hand from the experience I have with both Jess and myself, so rather than confronting him I decide to take the tube into town. I leave my CV with a hundred receptionists and school directors and teachers and a thousand fast-food restaurant managers and waitresses and recruitment agents. I consider leaving a few at various pubs, bars, and clubs but decide against it, as working in one of those places would surely spell the end of me. I would be too easily tempted to put everything I found behind the bar into my mouth.

I back walk home along Oxford Street, past Great Portland Street station, and across the planes of Regent's Park.

I get back to Camden and fantasise about setting all the tourists on fire.

I find Dom in the living room watching TV and smoking. He offers me a cigarette which I take and I let him light.

'So, how are you and Jack getting on?' I ask, as nonchalantly as I can. 'I mean, have you two even had a real conversation yet?'

He blows smoke out through a smile.

'What are you saying?'

'Well, I don't want to interfere,' I lie, 'but I think you two have a few things you should straighten out. I found him sleeping in here the other night …'

'Yeah, and that was his choice. I've been perfectly nice so

far, haven't I?'

'I suppose you have, but –'

'Dude, I know I'm a strange one to live with. You're not the first person to point that out, which I can only assume is what you're doing now. But if you got to know me, you'd find me to be totally amicable. Example: enjoying your cigarette?'

'Just speak to him,' I plead. 'Get this sorted. You're supposed to be sleeping in the same room, for fuck's sake. You need to set down some ground rules or something.'

'Did he say that?' he asks.

'No, it's only my opinion. I'm just an impartial observer –'

'You're a drag, is what you are,' he says, turning up the TV, suddenly taking an interest in current affairs.

I read my cocaine poem with fresh eyes, rip it into pieces, and drop it in the bin. I sneak into the living room when I hear Dom pissing to retrieve the rest of the drugs we keep under the sofa. I sniff them all up and put on a record, stepping over the notepad that's spread out on the floor like a dead bird. I don't have anything to give the world and I'm dried up in every way imaginable.

The album I'm listening to approaches its final track and I pretty much think I'm on my last groove too.

Jack comes home. I enter the hall to talk to him but see that Dom's thought of doing the same thing.

He says, 'Jack, I think we need to talk,' as they walk into their room together.

Shortly after the door opens and Jack reappears and goes to the living room. I converse with Dom about what happened and all it takes is for him to shrug his shoulders and say 'I tried, didn't I?' for me to know we have a serious problem.

27

Dealer and Lookout sit beneath a tree by the side of the canal. I wait for them to offer drugs but they don't bother. I don't know why. Normally they're pretty vocal about what they have in their duffel bag. Perhaps they're wary of patrolling police officers, three of which I caught sight of on the way here.

I call Jack's phone and ask him what I should do. 'Can't Lover Boy help you out?' he says, and it takes a few moments for me to realise he's referring to Dom.

Talking with Jack has recently become an impossible task so I hang up and go to the off-licence instead. I leave with nothing because I don't have my wallet or any cash to pay anyone with, and even though I'm here most days they still don't trust me enough to offer store credit.

I return to the flat and am taken aback by the mess Dom's created in the kitchen – glasses and bottles and orange peel and rolling tobacco and ladles and wrappers and rags and dirt, all over the place. He stands there squeezing half a lemon into Jack's punchbowl, his white vest spotted with a kaleidoscope of stains.

He yells over the noise of pulsating techno music escaping from the CD player: '*We're having a party tonight!*'

'Have you discussed this with Jack?'

'No. Should I have?'

'Maybe.'

'I'm paying rent too, you know. This place is as much mine now as it is yours and Jack's.'

'Just give him a call and let him know, would you? It wouldn't hurt anything.'

I write down Jack's number to make sure he has it. He takes it from me and slips it into his pocket.

I hear his voice joined by another's an hour later from the safety of my bedroom. They laugh and clink glasses and bottles together. They turn their terrible techno up louder and I consider cancelling it out with The Cure in the vain hope they'd appreciate how clever I was being.

I roll myself another smoke. I open my door to a stranger asking if I have any drugs and as I'm holding a stick of the stuff I have no choice but to shrug and hand it over.

Before long our flat has been invaded by at least another twelve people, all of them men, and they clutter up our space and mess with all our precious things. I barricade myself in my room by shoving a bag of laundry up against the door but Dom still manages to jostle it open.

He pokes his head in, says, 'Come on – we're having a party out here!' and throws me a beer.

I concede to defeat and follow him to the kitchen, where one man inhales from a bong and another cuts lines of coke out on my chopping board. The reveler I gave my last joint to is now smoking one of his own and I can tell by the way he's shielding it from view that he doesn't want to share it.

Dom gives me a glass of punch so now I have two drinks. I absorb the punch first and it tastes of weed killer and bleach and impending regret.

We absorb as much alcohol as we can find and consume all the drugs we manage to get our hands on. Things get blurry later as I start the unending journey back to my bedroom.

Jack arrives clutching a bag of take-away.

'Hey man,' I say, but the sound of my voice is hidden behind the cloak of the music.

'What the fuck is all this?'

Dom approaches and answers on my behalf: 'We're having a housewarming party. What are you drinking?'

Jack doesn't answer. He looks at me and says, 'I need to have a word with you.'

'Yeah, of course.' I finish off the joint and drop its entrails onto the floor. 'Let's go.'

I think we were bound for either his room or mine but as they're both occupied by groups of inebriated men we go to the stairwell instead. I have to focus on each step I take to make sure I don't lose my footing.

We get to the floor below and I can already feel the hate coming from him.

He says: 'I want that dickhead out of our house as soon as possible.'

'Mate, be reasonable,' I say. 'It's not up to me who stays and who goes, is it?'

'Why are you taking his side?'

'His side? I don't know what you're talking about.'

'Oh, you know *exactly* what I'm talking about. I'm talking about the line that's been drawn – I'm on one side and Dom's on the other. I can't *stand* the guy. It's either him or me. It's up to you. Who do you want to carry on living with? It's not complicated.'

I look at him as I consider a response but I'm having great trouble focusing. The whole building is turning around me.

'I honestly thought we were close,' he says, 'but this proves I was wrong. Shame, really. I used to think you were kind of cool, in your own way, but now I'm not so sure …'

'Don't be so melodramatic, Jack. Come back to the party. I promise all this will all look better in the morning.'

He laughs bitterly and shakes his head.

'You've changed. I'm serious. You're no friend of mine, not any more. I mean, look at you. You're a complete state. You're fucking pathetic. I don't know where you're at. I don't know what you want to be. Who are you supposed to be? Jesus, who *are* you? Have you ever given it any thought at all?'

'Don't. Please, don't do this.'

He points at me and says, 'Seriously, if he's not out of here by tomorrow morning, that's it.'

'That's what?'

'That's it; I'm gone, and you two can live in total chaos for as long as you like. You can drink and smoke and snort as much as your little brains can handle.'

'But you and I aren't angels ourselves, are we?' I say.

'Has there ever been a day when we haven't been drunk or stoned? We've been living in squalor for almost a year now!'

'Yeah, but not to that extent.' He indicates the party that's raging above us. 'That's something else, that is. That's off the scale.'

'Well, that's not Dom's fault,' I say. 'What do you expect from living in Camden? It's all part of the *experience*. Parties like this are the reason why we moved here in the first place, aren't they?

'I disagree. We're getting too old for this sort of shit. When I come home, that's precisely where I want to be – *home*. Not in the middle of a fucking rave or whatever.'

I laugh at the word *rave* but only because I thought he said it as a joke. When I realise he's being serious I wipe the grin from my face.

'It isn't just Dom that's pissed me off, though,' he says. 'It's *you. You're* the one who's betrayed me, not him. The fact you *knew* what I was going through and you *still* had the audacity to bring someone new into our home without telling me first? Talk about rubbing it in my face. I'm tired and worn out and I'm losing my looks and all I want is to act and be happy. With Liu gone and that prick fucking everything up, why should I stay? What would I gain from living here much longer?'

'Just so we're completely clear, I'm not responsible for any of this,' I tell him. 'The landlord wanted another tenant. Dom came over to see the room, and afterwards … It just sort of *happened*. We both found him here at the same time, don't forget. It was a surprise for both of us.'

'It was a *complete* surprise for me, yeah, because you never told me about him visiting the flat in the first place! You should've lied and said the bed wasn't available. That would've shown you were in my corner, but you're not, are you? You never have been, not really. We're just friends by circumstance. You've never had my interest at heart, not really. I can't believe you didn't consider I might not want someone moving into Liu's bed so soon after he left. A true friend would've acted differently.'

'You're mistaken,' I say. 'I'm not your enemy, mate. Think about it for a second –'

He stops me and says, 'I don't want to hear it. Get rid of Dom, or I'm out of here for good.'

He turns and heads down the stairwell. As he goes I scream after him: '*But Jack, we're going through the same shit!*'

Once I'm sure he's left and isn't coming back, I return to the party. I don't manage to extract any more enjoyment out of it because the same three words Jack said to me are repeating over and over again, I can't shake them off regardless of how much I drink, smoke and snort, and these three words are: *WHO ARE YOU? WHO ARE YOU? WHO ARE YOU? WHO ARE YOU? WHO ARE YOU? WHO ARE YOU? WHOAREYOUWHOAREYOUWHOAREYOUWHO–*

I lie on my bed and the whole room is gyrating.

I pick up my phone and call Jess.

'Jeeeeeessssssss,' I say. 'Jeeeeeeessssssy Jess Jess Jessssssss.'

I hear her breathing.

'Does he have a big dick, Jess? Yes? Yesssss, yesssss Jesssss Jessssss Jess Jess, enjoy that big cock, Jess, you enjoy that Jessy Jessy Jessss, I'll be waiting for you Bunny, Bunny Rabbit, I'm here and I'm loving you so *intensely*, baby, I love the way you're put together baby Bunny Bunny, love you love you *love* you sweetness, am I your sweetness, Jessy Bun? When he's not there I am, aren't I? Oh yeah we fit, you know, we fit so *good* Jess Bunny Bunny girl girl girl, love you love you *LOVE YOU, BUNNY!*'

I hurl the phone at the wall and when I pick it up again I find the screen is cracked but Jess remains on the line. I say 'hello?' and she says: 'you need to get a grip.'

Then she severs the connection we had and I'm much too out of it to feel anything.

111

28

I'm woken by my phone vibrating. I slide it open expecting it to be a message from Jess. It isn't. I tell myself *I told you so* yet still feel pinpricks of sadness creeping into all of my organs.

It's *Lollipop86,* saying she misses me, which makes me sink further into myself.

I take my wallet out of my jacket pocket. I click through a few links on my laptop and buy a ticket out of here. I know it's a rash decision but I can't help myself. I need to get away. I need to clear my head.

No job, no friends, and no girl ...

I lie on my back. I put on a smile and hold it there, hoping it tricks the rest of me into feeling some sort of contentment.

I throw a few things into a bag – clothes, passport, the secret photo I have of the girl I love.

With that done I stand naked in front of the mirror, thinking: *WHO ARE YOU?*

The flat remains a mess despite my best efforts of sorting through the debris of last night's party. I'm forced to kick a matchbox and several cigarette butts under the radiator before letting Dad in.

'All right, son?'

'Yeah, not too bad.'

'Here we go again!'

'What can I say? I've got the wanderlust.'

'Are you sure you have somewhere to stay when you land?'

'Yes, Dad.'

'And you have a job lined up, too?'

'Yes,' I lie. 'I'll be fine,' I lie.

We walk into my room. I can tell he's troubled by the lack of objects boxed up and ready to be stored in his basement.

'Is this all the stuff you want me to take back?' he asks.

We both stare at the pathetic collection of containers lined up on my bed.

'Yeah, if that's OK.'

'Of course. Shall we go out and get a drink first, though?'

A drink is the last thing I want with Dad sitting opposite but to get him out the flat I reluctantly agree. I walk him to the Lock and he looks amazed by all the life around here. We dodge clusters of people, never able to walk in a straight line. When we get to the bar he asks for a cola but I can see how restless he's getting smelling hops and lingering on fluorescent alcopops held in the hands of hipsters.

He's hypnotised by at all the droplets of condensation sticking to my wineglass.

'When are you setting off, then?' he asks, watching closely as I drink.

'My flight's at five-forty tomorrow so I'll leave the house at about midday. I want to make absolutely sure I'm on that plane.'

'What's brought all this on? You told me everything was going well for you here.'

'It is, Dad. Well, it was.'

'Haven't you travelled enough? You're getting older now. You're what, twenty-nine?'

'Twenty-eight.'

'Twenty-eight, then. By the time I was your age I'd married and had a kid.'

He lifts his glass to sip from it and I can tell how disappointed he is that it isn't alcoholic.

'I must be built differently, I suppose,' I tell him. Marriage is a topic I don't want to dwell on and any subject relating to Mum is too painful for me to address, so to move us along I say, 'How've you been then, Dad? I haven't seen you in ages.'

'Good question. My back's been killing me, so there's that. And work's been a bastard recently, but really, when isn't it?'

'I know what you mean,' I say, as if still employed. 'Speaking of work, before I forget – I don't suppose you know where my old shoebox is, do you? The one with all my writing inside?'

'What shoebox?' he asks.

'Haven't you found it yet? It wasn't *that* well hidden.'

'I haven't really been in your room since you left.'

'In the last twelve years?'

'I never want to go in there again. Do I have to spell it out for you?'

I realise what he's getting at and feel foolish for not understanding sooner.

'Oh, right.' I say. 'Forget I asked.'

He stares forlornly at his cola and spins the ring on his finger.

'Do you want a drink, Dad? I mean, do you want a *real* drink?'

He seems tempted by my offer but steels himself against it.

He says: 'Tell me more about your writing. I never knew you were a writer.'

'I'm not a *writer*, exactly. Well, not any more. I try to be but I can't write the way I used to. It was a lot easier when I was younger. Do you remember when I toured Italy? I wrote a lot during that trip. I was convinced I wanted to be a travel writer one day.'

'But you became an English teacher. There's nothing wrong with that. It's a proper job, at least. Unlike anything I've ever done.'

I smile solemnly and think: *yeah, people* assume *it's a proper job, but have they ever tried it? Look at the burns on poor Liu's hands – that'd change your mind. That's real work, that is. I wouldn't know real work if it pissed in my fucking eye.*

'Are you sure everything's all right? I mean, moving yet again …'

'I'm fine,' I lie. 'I promise. This is what I want. It could be worse, you know. All my friends are waiting for me on the other end and we're having a massive party when I get there,' I lie again. 'I seriously can't wait to leave.'

'I wish you'd settle down and get comfortable,' he says. 'I wish you'd meet a nice girl.'

I have, but she belongs to someone else.

'What's the rush?' I ask. 'I'm young, free, and single. I couldn't be happier.'

It's so exhausting talking in this way. I expend so much energy persuading people I'm not a lost cause.

'OK, if you're absolutely sure,' he says, and I think: *believe me, Dad – I'm not absolutely sure about anything any more.*

Once we've made it back to the flat, it takes a mere ten minutes to move my few possessions to the boot of Dad's car.

'Have a great time,' he says, 'and I'll keep an eye out for the shoebox you mentioned.'

I tell him not to worry about it. I'm not even sure why I'd want to see it again.

He drives away and I wave to him when he sounds his horn, then go upstairs to my room and get into bed to nurse my hangover.

I hear Jack scrambling home with someone at around midnight.

I picture Le Marais and Notre Dame and the Panthéon and, splayed out over all of them, Jess and Jess and Jess.

Part Two

PARIS

1

As I'm watching clouds pass by below us, the girl I've been talking with excuses herself and goes to the toilet. I unscrew another miniature and savour its burn, collecting a little platoon of empty bottles on my tray table.

I remove the scrap of paper from my pocket and go over the address written on it for the fiftieth time. I close my eyes and picture the circulatory system of the Métro and the lines I'll have to take to get to where Rick lives. I imagine how fine my first glass of wine will taste and how excellently it will complement my first plate of escargot.

After the girl has slipped back into her seat I ask what she's going to be doing in Paris. She tells me her boyfriend lives in an apartment in the Latin Quarter and that he's been planning some sort of big surprise for her birthday. I tell her he's a lucky man to have someone so pretty to make plans for and her smile dips like the wings of the plane.

She thanks me and gets back to her *Grazia* so now I'm left alone with my liquor and I think of how much I'd like to lick her, lick her all over.

I unscrew the next bottle. I've always hated gin but this one goes down without much incident, used as it is to obscure thoughts of where I am and what I'm doing – burning a trail away from the city I've always thought of as home and from the girl I've always thought of as *everything*.

This morning I told Jack I was leaving and he acted as if he was bothered in a way that wasn't just logistically. It occurred to me then that he was a far better actor than I'd ever given him credit for. We tried to leave on amicable terms but the Dom I'd brought into the house remained, so the extent to which he could forgive me was limited.

I didn't tell Jess of my intentions to travel and this is gnawing on me now, although I don't know why. I doubt she'd even care.

A new beginning, I think to myself. *Either that or another dead end.*

In a strange way, I don't want us to land. I want us to drift through the sky like this for ever.

After arriving at the airport, I find my way onto a shuttle bus to Opera. I let the landscape of France distract me by running my eyes across the edges of buildings passing by the window. I focus on the discussion of a nearby couple and attempt to translate as much of it as I can into English.

I step from the bus, striding confidently in front of an Opera house now sopping with rain. I watch a girl in black boots as she lunges over a puddle, laughing and flinging out French to a friend on her arm.

I approach an elderly man standing beneath an umbrella at the window of a brasserie. I vaguely remember the construction of the phrase *ooo ey le statione sill voo play* – I offer it to him and he points across the road to a Métro sign that stretches over the heads of its passengers like the blade of a scythe. I bid the man *merci* and a *bon soir* but he doesn't respond.

I enter the station and approach the *billet* machine. I buy myself a single ticket, hold it up in front of me, and let its smudged ink take me back to a time and place I'd assumed I was done with.

Before I turn away from the screen a gorgeous blonde in tight khaki shorts asks me in an American accent how to get a ticket to Châtelet.

'New in town?' I ask.

'Sure am. I gotta get to my friend outside Les Halles. She's found a hostel there we can crash at.'

I show her which buttons to press for future reference and pay for her ticket out of my own collection of currency. I give it to her and she thanks me and shows me teeth.

I watch her walking towards the turnstile and before she passes through it she takes the straw hat tied to her bag and pulls it onto her head.

I move amongst the tourists and the locals and the beggars, aiming myself towards Métro line 9.

I stop breathing when I notice my passport's missing.

I haul my bag through the crowd and find a space against the wall. I'm numb as I upend it and spill my clothes and underwear all over the disgusting floor of the station. I spread my cotton and denim around and empty each of my pockets as coins roll into the pistons of a hundred pairs of legs.

I go through every compartment of the bag but the passport is nowhere to be found.

I force myself through the horde of shuffling people, heading back to the ticket machines, desperately scanning the floor.

I can't see the fragment of my identity anywhere.

The assistant looks at me blankly when I say, 'Pardon ... monsieur, je voudrais mon passport, je cherche mon passport monsier ... c'est ... c'est vanish? Mon passport ... je suis ici ... mon passport, c'est kaput? Le stationne, ces't tres, tres nul ...? Tu est comprends pas?'

He runs a nail across the line of his sideburn, offering nothing.

I picture the pert khaki buttocks of the American girl I helped and *did she confirm she was new in town?* I can't quite remember.

I leave the station and sadness comes on like a fast-acting poison. I collapse into myself like the spent leather creases of an overplayed accordion. I take out my phone to call Jess but present her only with utterances; no words come, and she says *what's wrong, sweetie, what's wrong?* but I know she doesn't mean it.

I let the phone drop to my side.

I watch traffic tear around me from the island the entrance to the station sits on and just like that I find myself in Paris and a long way from home, alone, desperate, scared, despicable.

2

I hug Rick tightly to draw as much comfort as I can from him.

'I need a drink,' I say, to which he replies, 'I'm sure that can be arranged.'

We walk adjacent to the Pompidou centre. We dodge puddles of shimmering rain and turn down a narrow side street.

'You live here?' I ask.

'Yep. Pretty sweet, eh?'

He buzzes Alice who answers with a 'oui?' and Rick says 'ah, oui, oui, bonsoir, je m'appelle Rick, je suis –' but she buzzes him up before he can finish roleplaying.

He walks us through a small courtyard and into an unlit passageway. I use my hands to navigate the wall and swear that this is the only kind of darkness I'll surrender myself to for the rest of the night.

We climb stairs and enter the apartment. Alice embraces Rick and plants a brief kiss on his cheek.

Rick turns to me and asks: 'Are you hungry?'

I felt ravenous earlier but all that's been knocked out of me now.

'Just for wine.'

'Eh bien,' he says. 'Coming right up.'

I ask Alice if I can use the toilet while Rick busies himself and she tells me it's an ensuite reached by going through the bedroom. I fumble my way through their private domain and I can smell their kinship, I can feel the love they've made in here, and their discarded clothes meeting in the centre of the floor fill me with an odd sense of dread.

Rick and I find ourselves in a bar on the corner of two quiet roads. Rick orders a platter of cheese and meat for the table, although my stomach's still too constricted from the trauma of the call I made to Jess to digest any of it.

I finish my beer, go to the bar, and say, 'Bonsoir, je voudrais une carafe d'rouge, sil vous plait, avec deux bier, merci.'

The barman looks amused as he pours red liquid into a jug and I wish I could feel something resembling the wine; anything playful, anything sweet.

'Come on then, out with it,' Rick says when I sit down again. He picks up a chunk of bread and smears it with chutney. 'Why are you here? Why are you back?'

'I couldn't stand London any more, to be honest, mate. Too many ... I don't know. Too much rot.'

'I hear you. That city's a proper shithole. I don't understand why anyone would want to live there, especially with Paris being, like, an hour away.' He stuffs more bread into his chomping maw and says from behind it: 'Life's good here.'

'I hope you're right. The last time I was here went by so quickly, I hardly remember any of it.'

'Don't worry, there'll be plenty of time for you and Paris to get reacquainted,' he says, washing down the stodge with a shot of wine. 'What's gonna be your first move?'

'Funny you should ask, actually. I don't suppose you know where the British Embassy is?'

He pauses.

'No, I don't. Why?'

'My passport was stolen.'

'What? When?'

'About half an hour ago, in Opera station. A girl distracted me while I was using the ticket machine and I think someone took it from my pocket.'

'So ... you're saying you were pickpocketed right before you came here?'

'Yeah.'

'You were pickpocketed in Opera station?

'Yes.'

'Wait a second; let me be clear about this. You got off the

airport shuttle, walked into the station … then had your passport stolen?'

'Yes, Rick. Yes, that's exactly what happened.'

He takes me by surprise when he charges the air around him with a laugh that builds quickly, a laugh that makes the barman flick his head up in surprise. Glasses balanced on a tray by a fit young waitress rattle and clink together. He looks at me and laughs and laughs and sprays breadcrumbs across the tablecloth, and I'm astonished when I feel the corners of my own lips start to bend upwards. Despite myself, despite all things, I laugh along with him, making an honest attempt to betray the desperation clawing at my core.

'That settles it then,' he says, waving over the waitress and ordering yet another jug of Christ blood.

We leave the bar at around midnight. I trace each pipe of the Pompidou centre with my yolky drunken eyes.

Rick almost falls into the road and I steady him without knowing how.

I check my phone: *nothing*.

'Thanks for letting me stay,' I tell him.

'No need to thank me, mate. It'll be great having you around, stay as long as like. And don't let Ali get to you, by the way. She's just a bit … French.'

'What do you mean by that?'

'Well, she didn't make much of an effort to welcome you earlier, did she? Sometimes she can be a proper *BITCH*!'

He shouts the last word and it echoes around the street he lives on. I'm concerned that Alice might have heard it from their apartment.

'Don't say that. You have a good one there. I think she's great,' I lie.

'Oh, don't be such a pussy. It doesn't suit you.'

He takes out a key and presses its sensor against the lock of the gate. I don't want to say anything more before bed but the alcohol inside my head is pushing words out and I have no choice but to let them all drop out of my mouth: 'Rick, I love this girl but she doesn't love me back and it's an absolute nightmare and I think it might be killing me.'

He looks at me as if he's going to say something deep and meaningful, something that will turn the tide of my emotions, but instead he vomits wine and cheese and beer all over my jeans, sleeves residue from his chin, and says, 'Pardon, monsieur. Je suis très désolé.'

3

I wake with a post-it note stuck to my cheek. It reads: *So hungover. Thanks mate. Help yourself to food/drink. B.Embsy = nr Concorde (line 1). Bonne chance!*

I lift my head still weighted with sleep and look around the room. I press the balls of my hands into my eyes and pull myself together as much as I can. I already miss Jess so much that it's making my whole body hurt – it's the reality of us being separated by the Channel that's digging into me now, as is the idea that without a passport this situation can't be remedied whenever I feel like it. I'm rendered sick by the thought of her. I don't want her to be wearing one of those dresses she has, the ones that cling to her, and I don't want her to be smiling, and I don't want her to be thinking of anything or anyone other than me and of what the two of us have.

I already know coming here was the wrong thing to do.

My thoughts turn to Catherine and the time I spent with her in Italy. We lived without caring, moving on whenever we felt the need for change, and neither the Vatican nor the Duomo of Milan could hold our attention for long. Perhaps coming here was my attempt to recreate that state of mind, but I'm not the same man I was back then and changing cities no longer seems to reinvigorate me.

After all, this is not Milan or Rome, and I am not free.

This is Paris and I'm trapped.

I get to the Métro station and make my way to Concorde. I remember being here before, but distantly. I just about recognise the glittering sliver of the Champs Élysées, crowned by the Arc de Triomph which from here looks like a child's toy. I check the map I took from Rick and Alice's breakfast bar and walk to where my new passport is going to be. I'm ashamed it's my first day here and I want nothing more than the rectangular indentation of it be lining the inside of my jacket pocket; the link back home and to the girl I long for re-established.

I arrive at the Embassy and step to the window. I say 'my passport's been stolen' and without a moment's hesitation the clerk hands me a form and says: 'Fill this out.'

I get as far as my name and the address I had when I lived here last before noticing the form requires a crime reference number. I take it back to the clerk and he says, 'Of *course* you need a crime reference number, haven't you been to the police station yet?'

I consider saying *I don't know where I am or what's going on* but instead I say 'no, where is it?'

He gives me a new map with its location pre-circled. It seems this kind of thing happens a lot, but this thought alone does little to console me.

I walk towards the Métro line that would funnel me towards the police station. At the very last moment I decide I'd rather walk along the Seine instead, my mind enslaved by a parasitic hangover, my every action ordained by the alcohol still in my veins.

I reach the Eiffel Tower – the rusty nail holding this entire city together. Men and women scale its height and look out at the view and at each other. I remind myself that the bond they have is finite – they'll either break each other's hearts or watch each other die. There is no other alternative.

If Jess were here, I'd take her to the Tower's highest platform. I'd ease my tongue into her throat, gently, softly, and nothing else would matter but the two of us up there in the sky. I send mental arrows of hate to every couple I see while at the same time imagining how sweet it'd be to have Jess by my side.

I'm nothing more than a hypocrite. I wish, like the Tower itself, I had a little consistency.

I count the steps leading to its peak in an attempt to calm myself down.

Just for a moment, I consider scaling its height and

throwing myself off it.

I walk the streets of Paris aimlessly and by the time I reach Rick and Alice's apartment, night has engulfed the city.

I press the button marked *Deschamps* and Alice answer with a 'oui?' I say *hello* and she buzzes me up without another word.

Rick is lounging on the sofa bed, reading a battered copy of *A Clockwork Orange* and listening to a song on the radio I can't quite place.

He says: 'Hey man, good day?'

'Yeah, not bad. Cheers for leaving me with that address. And sorry for not putting the bed away.'

He closes the novel and rests it on his legs.

'No problemo. Did you get everything sorted?'

'Kind of,' I say. 'The wheels are in motion, at least. How're things with you?'

He tilts his hand in a *so-so* gesture.

'I've had a raging headache all day long because of you,' he says.

'Because of me? I didn't force the wine down you, did I?'

'No, I suppose you didn't. *Touché.* Sorry about your jeans, by the way.'

'It's fine, forget it,' I say, refraining from telling him I rinsed them clean in the kitchen sink after he'd gone to bed.

'Here's something to make it up to you,' he says. 'I spoke with my boss and he says he can meet you for an interview in Bastille tomorrow.'

My stomach tightens and I think about how much I want to be in London.

'I think you'd dig it,' he tells me when I don't respond. 'It's teaching general English, about six hours a day, to a class of about twenty. It's pretty easy – a lot less complicated than all that business bullshit we were doing the last time you were here, anyway. Sound good?'

It sounds like my own personal hell with what I've been going through recently but I have to try to move on. I need to start something new, something not Jess, but oh God do I miss her, oh so much; Paris holds nothing next to her.

'Yeah, mate,' I say, 'it sounds great. Thanks a lot for sorting that out.'

'My pleasure, *mon ami*. If you need help with anything else, just ask.'

I need help with lots of things, with almost everything I have going on in my life, but before I can explain myself Alice walks in carrying two plates that she lays on the dining table.

She says something to Rick in French that I don't understand.

They open a bottle of wine and pour out two glasses, pick up their cutlery, and start eating, and without either of them noticing I leave the apartment and go to McDonalds.

4

The café where my interview is taking place is difficult to find – its awning is so understated that I walk past it twice before realising this is where I'm meant to be. The place is full. The air is filled with thick French and the sound of coffee beans being pulverised by a colossal bronze grinder. A waiter balances two plates, a jug of water, and a couple of cups on a tray. I expect him to ask where I want to be seated but instead he delivers the order and returns to the kitchen.

I choose a table at random, sit down, and focus on the task in hand.

I have to *get a grip*, exactly as Jess said I should.

I go over a few things in my head. What a noun is. What a verb is. I answer stock questions under my breath*: I want to work for you because I'm passionate about teaching and I very much enjoy watching students develop their English language skills and I don't have a choice, there are no other viable options. In five years I see myself working for you but higher up, maybe something similar to the role you have now. Who knows, maybe I'll be interviewing potential teachers for your fine school in the near future, ha ha ha ... Yes, I can start straight away. No, I don't have a reference from my last job because I did something inappropriate with one of my students but let's not dwell on the negatives, my good man: what do you think of my outfit?*

As I'm dithering over the best way to sit I see a man who I think might be New Director entering the café. He carries a leather briefcase similar to the one Rick told me to look out for.

He stops near the door to exchange French pleasantries with a waiter and they take time to laugh at each other's jokes. I wave him over. He offers his hand and I take it and shake it without feeling worthy of it. He introduces himself, tucks his legs under the table, and pulls a few papers out of his briefcase.

He says, 'Right, something nice and basic to get the ball rolling: can you tell me what the difference is between *either or* and *neither nor*, and how you'd explain it to a class of thirty pre-intermediate students?'

He stares at me with a trace of something in his eye – possibly sadism.

He orders two lattes while in my head I'm manipulating neither either or and nor, forming examples and definitions that don't seem to make any sort of sense. I'm confused by the question. All I can really focus on is how ridiculous I must look; sitting here in a hostile café in a country I'll never fully understand and wearing a violent red tie that is clashing with the red my cheeks are now turning.

He won't stop staring so I say, 'Well, neither is used with two things, when they're both negative, and either is used for two positive things, like, I will have either the ... no, wait ... sorry, I mean neither is used when you don't want something, and either is used when you want one of what is being offered, and you don't care which one, and ... and or is used with either, and neither, and nor is used with ... both ... of them ...?'

He rests his chin on a bunched-up fist and nods as if I'm being in any way coherent.

The waiter returns with our drinks. I'll bet he's witnessed many a prospective young teacher being mauled by this behemoth. Maybe it's some sort of club the two of them are members of.

'All right,' New Director says, and writes something down. He may as well be drawing a caricature of me, of me and my stupid fucking tie because we're one question in, one minute in, and I've failed the interview already.

'Imagine you had a class of thirteen advanced students who all worked in a bank. What would you prepare for the second lesson that they had together, aware that they were good friends who knew and worked with each other previously but now had different positions in the company?'

I lift the coffee cup to take a boiling sip and scorch my tongue and loathe everything deeply and intensely, conceding to the prospect that I'm going nowhere and that Jess will haunt me for ever. I clear my throat with the intention of forming another miserable, meandering answer but the waiter sets off the coffee grinder so my words are lost.

New Director comes closer to listen to my agony and never takes the look of utter disappointment from his face.

He watches and waits.

I say: 'I want to work for you because I'm passionate about teaching and I very much enjoy watching students develop their English language skills.'

He asks a few more questions that I struggle through but it's painfully obvious he has no intention of offering me any sort of employment, any sort of salvation, any sort of buoyancy aid to stop me from drowning in the choices I've made, and when he finishes his coffee he says it's been nice to meet me and that he'll let me know. He shakes my hand again and as he's leaving (and I'm pretty certain this isn't just me being paranoid) he and the waiter share a knowing glance.

I am brought the bill for both our drinks and I pay and leave a tip because I don't want to have to wait for the change. I exit the café and walk the streets for hours with nothing better to do than to dwell on the fact that I'm lost and in love and neither here nor there.

For a second my inebriation takes me back to a dance floor in Camden – I'm moving to the music and looking for a hole to fill and it all seems so sweet, but when the barman puts down the glass he's been wiping dry and asks if I want another drink I'm returned to this dive bar in Bastille. I go over and over and over that which can't be altered. I keep imagining New Director's smug dough face with piss-hole eyes and I'm twisting it and stretching it until it all comes apart.

Tomorrow: the police station and paperwork and the first step towards a new passport and home and Jess ...

I tense up at flashbacks of the last telephone call I had

with the girl I love.

I go to the toilet to void my stomach and it looks like blood from the red of the wine.

I decide to take the Métro towards Rick's apartment, knowing I'll have to change a few trains to get there. As I'm nearing the platform at Tuileries a booming voice announces something in French that I don't have the ability to translate, and after the first twenty minutes of waiting for my final connection a man in a bright orange vest approaches me and gestures towards the exit. As I reach the stairwell I see a rat the size of a cat spring out from a gap in the wall and cross my path and in my confusion I think to myself: *isn't that supposed to be lucky?*

I follow a girl along an empty avenue from twenty feet behind, watching the oscillation of her hips and listening to the clicking of the heels of her boots. Streetlights stretch her shadow back and I tread on her outline. I pass my silhouette over hers to connect with her in any way I can. She looks over her shoulder. She starts walking quicker once she's confirmed I'm the same man I was ten minutes ago, still pursuing her *(I don't know why)*. I match her pace and call out to her with awkward French, losing her when she disappears into a bar that's elegant enough to refuse my patronage.

The cold air does nothing to sober me up. I walk for an hour taking turnings randomly and when I end up in the same place I started I cave and flag down a taxi, telling the driver the Métro stop next to which I think I'm staying.

On arrival I'm told how much the fare is but don't quite follow so I offer all the money I have stuffed in my trouser pocket. I fall out into the street and the taxi drives away, leaving me in the place where I no doubt belong – in the gutter.

It takes another quarter of an hour to locate the button labeled *Deschamps* and when I do I dimple it with a trembling finger as the sun begins its climb into the sky. Rick comes down to the gate in a pair of striped pyjama bottoms and a rugby shirt, looking at me like I'm an adversary of his. He pulls me into the courtyard when I start spilling out all the agony I've collected since this morning.

We get to the apartment and I find the sofa bed isn't laid out so I start kicking it and prodding it as Rick eases the door closed behind us. He whips me around and whisper-shouts *SHUTTHEFUCKUP!* and in him I see a terrible blend of anger and disgust.

I fall onto the sofa, exhausted from everything, and as I'm drifting into sweet oblivion I hear what I think is the low vibration of Rick and Alice arguing, swearing – wishing me dead.

5

In the dream, I stand in front of a whiteboard in a classroom I don't know. My class consists of fifteen replicas of the same person: New Director.

Tell them what you told me, Elizabeth whispers into my ear. *Tell them it's not possible to love a man like you.*

'Elizabeth …'

Call them sluts. Throw them out.

'… I'm sorry.'

A version of New Director raises a hand to ask a question and I have no choice but to give him the satisfaction of asking: *what's it like to be so alone?*

Another hand, another question: *what's it like to be an alcoholic?*

How does it feel to love someone who doesn't love you back?

What's the difference between neither nor and either or?

Why did you come back to Paris?

Are you happy with the way things are going?

Have you ever considered ending it all?

What's the difference between Catherine, Elizabeth, Sophie, and Jess?

How would you describe the past continuous tense to an elementary student?

Do you know what you're doing?

Do you know who you are? then all together, in a chorus that builds to a painful crescendo: *WHO ARE YOU WHO ARE YOU WHO ARE YOU WHO ARE YOU WHO ARE –*

The impact of rolling onto the floor jolts all of my bones. Pain explodes in my skull, ignited like a cigarette to tug at through the course of what will surely be another horrible day.

I knead light-bulb-with-blown-fuse eyes as I crawl through Rick and Alice's bedroom. I get nauseous when I

137

notice their tumbled-in quilt. If Jess and I had this apartment in the centre of Paris, we'd be set for life. She could indulge herself in all of her more artistically inclined hobbies; I'm unsure of what I could do but at least I'd be doing whatever it was with her by my side.

I swill my face with water and as I lower my head towards the basin the headache shacked up with my brain gives each of my retinas a tug. I'm sure to keep the shower scorching hot as I rinse my aching body and watch as my veins creep to the surface of my skin. I stand like this for twenty minutes or so, feeling better as each minute passes, but when I step out and towel myself dry the pain sneaks back and infects every inch of me.

The desk sergeant seems less than impressed, but why would he be? I'm taking up space in the streets of the city he's been sworn-in to protect, speaking terrible French and dousing him with alcohol breath. Following a dreary passage of not being understood, I quit and ask 'parlay voo Anglay?' He ambles backstage and I'm left willing the pain in my head to subside for a single moment, knowing that it won't.

A short blonde female officer takes his place and says 'hello, how can I help you?' with a syrupy French flavour that prods thoughts of Sophie Angier into my tumbling brain.

'I've had my passport ...' *(present perfect too difficult for her from the look on her face)* '... my passport was stolen.'

She produces a document from somewhere near her waist and offers it to me. I walk to a podium near the window that must've been set up specifically for morbid occasions such as this.

I complete as much of the form as I can and take it back to the front desk, where the first desk sergeant sits and waits for me to return. He scans it briefly before clomping on it with a rubber stamp dipped into crimson ink.

Once I've left I realise I still have the pen I used to fill out the form with. It amuses me that I've just stolen from a police station but this amusement is all too short-lived because the red wine in my system refuses to lie down and die until, it seems, I lie down and die.

It's the same clerk sitting at the counter of the Embassy and waiting for me to re-cap who I am and what I'm doing here. I repeat my predicament and offer him the paperwork I've brought across from the police station. He takes it and examines it, attaches it to a clipboard and asks, 'Do you have form A2A/5BB?'

I answer by saying, 'Of *course* I have form A2A/5BB.'

I give him the sheet I filled out when I was here last. He looks it over and compares the crime reference number I've scribbled on it with the one on the crime report.

He says, 'OK, so what we'll do is get you an emergency passport prepared. That way you can get to England and sort yourself out a proper one at the post office. It'd be much quicker and easier than getting a permanent passport here. When are you leaving Paris?'

Jess parts the reeds of my illness for a moment and beckons me onwards with a curling index finger ...

I say, 'As soon as possible.'

'We'll need to know an exact date, so come back when you've made the necessary arrangements. It should take us around five working days to get everything ready. Will you be all right in Paris until then?'

Not really, I think, *because waiting that long to go home to her will seem like an eternity, like a sentence of some sort.*

'I'm staying with a friend so I guess I'll be fine for a while.'

'Good to hear. These things happen, unfortunately,' he says.

I think of the first thing I'll say to Jess when I see her again. *I missed you* would be too soft. Perhaps something like: *every moment I spent away from you was torture?* I'm unsure at the moment, but I have five long days (not accounting for weekends) to figure all that out.

'Isn't there any way I could get this sorted out any

139

quicker?'

'We're in France,' is all he thinks he needs to say about that.

He leafs through my papers again, asks 'where are your passport photos?' and I feel so stupid when I have to say, 'Oh, yeah, I forgot about those.' He points to a door at the far end of the room and says 'there's a photo booth in there. It takes francs so you'll have to give me ten euros in exchange.'

We swap currencies and I go to the room he indicated. It's windowless and contains the photo booth and a water cooler with no drum attached. I drop the forgotten coins into the guts of the booth and prop myself on the stool. I clench my jaw so it looks angled and refined and rub my cheeks to get the blood flowing into my face again.

Two flashes follow and as each of them sparks I see a translucent vision of Jess appear then disappear.

The machine buzzes and whirs and almost dies as it forces the strip of photographs out of itself. I pick them up to examine them and my confidence level drops. In the pictures, I look drunk and old. I lean against the wall, my nose in the crook of my elbow and my photographic entrails dangling from my other hand.

After a few moments taken to compose myself I return to the counter. I surrender the photographs to the Embassy worker and attempt to divert my mind from recollections of the way I appeared in them.

That wasn't me.

It *couldn't* be.

(*WHO ARE YOU???*)

6

I'm ushered up to Rick and Alice's apartment and when I enter I notice my clutter has been arranged on top of my bag and my bag has been left in front of where I've been sleeping. Rick sits at the dining table as Alice vacuums the floor of their bedroom.

'Hey,' I say. 'What a day. What a hangover. Excuse me for last night. I got a bit carried away, I think.'

'Yeah, we need to talk about that.'

He looks pained. I already know what's coming. My bag and my things, piled up the way they are, say it all.

'Mate, this place is a bit too small for the three of us, so we were wondering if –'

A surge of anger rattles through me and I counter immediately with, 'Oh yeah, Rick, I'll go. I know you don't really want me here, after all.'

'Wait a minute, would you? Let me explain before you go off on one. It's not what you think. Ali has a friend who's going travelling for a few months and he wants to rent out his apartment.'

'Yeah, Rick, I'm sure isolation is *exactly* what I need at the moment.'

'Having an apartment to yourself in Paris would be awesome though, surely?'

I stare at him.

'Look, I'm really sorry, but it's … it's not strictly my decision, if you know what I mean …'

As if on cue, Alice prods the other side of the door to their room with the head of the vacuum cleaner.

'It's nothing against you or anything,' he tells me, but I still don't believe him.

I search for more words but I've been deflated by my host's animosity (no matter how subdued) and see no point in speaking further. Besides, I don't have much of a case I could put forward.

I've been insufferable to be around, that much is true.

Rick drinks from his glass as I attempt to think about the next logical step I could take. I can't help feeling upset that they could only stand three night's worth of my company.

I think to myself: *This is what it's like to be alone.*

I meet Marcel outside his building and he shows me up to his apartment, the door to which creaks as if in agony when I shove it open in the way he demonstrates.

Marcel says, 'Oui, zis is how we enter it,' and follows close behind as I walk into the flat. He has a thick beard and dreads and is wearing a Sonic Youth T-shirt emblazoned with a pox of cigarette and joint burns. He's clothed in Bermuda shorts and sandals, seemingly unaware of how cold it is in here – the place he refers to as 'ze living room.' A coffee table covered in tobacco flakes and mug rings stands before an ancient sofa draped in a torn blanket. There's a portable television on the floor next to the table that's not plugged in to anything.

'An zen we av ze kitchen in ere.'

He opens a curtain masking a doorway in the corner of the room, revealing a stove spotted with dried sauce, a sink, a microwave, and a box of assorted cutlery. A strange smell permeates the air. The frosted window pane lets in next to no light so he pulls on a cord and an uncovered bulb above our heads comes slowly to life.

'You av to be careful,' he says when he shows me how the hobs work; on, off. He indicates the nearest hob to us on the left, slashes at his throat, and says 'not zis one, c'est kaput.'

We clamber over a bag of empty wine bottles, slip through the curtain, and back into the living room. We walk to the front door. To our left is another curtain, behind which is 'ze chambre.' Marcel manipulates the moth-eaten cloth and I stoop under it and find myself in a cramped space with a sagging mattress resting in the middle of the floor.

An ensuite bathroom houses a shower and a toilet – both battered ceramic relics engrained with immovable grime. As I'm staring at the Beatles poster on the wall, the toilet chokes absurdly on its own sloshing discharge. I look at Marcel and he says 'oui, it does zis sometimes.'

I roll my head around to take in more of this disastrous hole than I really need to.

I thread this thought through my head like I'm lacing up a shoe, and I double-knot it twice, tie it up real tight: *Five working days then home to Jess.*

'Did Alice say you the price for ze rent?' he asks.

'No, she didn't mention anything about that ...'

When she came to sit with us last night she let Rick do all the talking. He explained that Marcel had been Alice's good friend long enough for us to be able to trust him. He told me where the flat was but I'd never heard of its location *(Val de Fontenay)* and when Rick assured me it was a trendy up-and-coming area I could've sworn I saw Alice biting her bottom lip. I wondered whether or not Rick had been embarrassed by the actions of his girlfriend but decided in the end that it wasn't really worth thinking about.

I wait for Marcel to give me the good news. He takes me back to the living room and motions for me to sit on the sofa.

He starts writing out figures seemingly at random.

'D'accort, so we av ze rent, an ze building charge, and zen ze money for ze elek-trisity en ze gas so, OK, it is about zis much.'

He writes the number *112* on the pad and circles it.

'Zis is for une semaine, one week. It iz good?'

One hundred and twelve euros is a lot cheaper than a hotel, maybe cheaper than most hostels, and worth paying to avoid staying another night in a place where I'm no longer welcome or ever *was* welcome to begin with.

'Oui, that's OK, Marcel. Merci.'

He smiles.

'OK, pour une ... month ... I will say ... four-five-zero. It iz good?'

I'm anxious about annoying him as I'm sure he was no doubt looking for a more long-term tenant

(five working days)

and I'm certainly not that. I extend my facial features to break the language barrier – communicating worry, communicating guilt.

'Marcel, I think I just want it for a few days. Maybe cinque jours, maybe one week? Une semaine, and finish? C'est bonne?'

He expresses what I assume is a gesture of regret in choosing me to take his flat but discover it's only one of confusion when he picks up the pen, draws a looping question mark, and laughs. He doesn't understand what I'm saying. I take the pen from him and write *1 semaine, et finis? OK ...? Oui/Non.*

He reads what I've written out loud then says, 'Of course! It iz no problem. Please you give me one week now,' he indicates the number he previously wrote, 'and you want more time, you leave more money on ze table. I collect après mes vacances. After, after, oui?'

I shake his hand in agreement, wiping my brow in an overelaborate gesture to show how relieved I am. I count out euros and he collects the money, balls it up, and puts it into his pocket. He reaches into his other pocket and pulls out a bag of weed and a packet of rolling papers. He turns the marijuana in a circular grinder with a skull and crossbones stuck to its lid before retrieving a remote from behind a sofa cushion and hitting *play*, causing a stereo on the windowsill to start leaking *In Utero* into the air.

'You smoke?' he asks, putting two fingers to his lips – the international gesture.

I slap him on the back and say 'Marcel, for you? Anything.'

We sit smoking and conversing in broken French and broken English and as the album spins around we get more and more stoned. We sit and listen and bask in our clotted senses.

'So, where are you going? Off on a thrilling adventure?' I ask, but he doesn't understand. I point at the door and at Marcel and say 'where you go?' and he smiles and blows out smoke and says 'ah, oui. Azzia. Thailand. I like … erm … surf? Yes? Surf?' he mimics a surfer catching a wave and I say 'yeah, Marcel – surfing is cool. I wish I could surf. It must make you feel so free,' but again, he can't keep up with my English.

He changes topic by asking 'you like French girls?' and miming a pair of tits with his hands, the joint held between his lips. Despite my indifference I say 'yeah, French girls are sexy. All English men like French girls, I think. Do you like English girls?'

He burns a generous helping of the joint and holds the smoke in his lungs for a few seconds. At the end of a prolonged exhalation he says 'I like English girls, I like French girls, I like *all* girls.'

We struggle through a few more subjects and smoke a few more joints. Halfway through the second rotation of the album Marcel goes into the bedroom and reappears soon after with a bag strapped to him.

'OK, enjoy your stay, my friend. Ze keys are zere, and I will arrange with Alice when to collect zem after ma vacances.'

'What, you mean you're leaving *now*?' I ask. He nods and lights a cigarette. I laugh at him and at Kurt Cobain and at the hovel I'm surrounded by and the laughter soon transforms into a harsh grating cough I cover with my hand. I stand to see him off and am compelled to embrace him before he goes. I want to wish him a *bon voyage* but by the time I've regained the capacity to speak he has taken leave of me, trapping me in his home like a forgotten ghost.

As I'm unpacking my things a folded piece of paper flaps to the ground.

I pick it up and read it: *So sorry about all of this, mate. If you ever need anything, give me a call. Rick. P.S. Pour*

Vous ...

This is followed by a French phone number labeled: *Louise*. The digits alone are enough to bring her to life. For a moment Jess takes a few baby steps backwards and lets Louise come to the front of my rack of thoughts. I remember the way she tipped ice over Elizabeth in Spitalfields and find myself sniggering into the haze of my intoxication.

I get hard enough to masturbate over recollections of her breasts and unintentionally ejaculate onto some of the clothes I've laid out on the mattress.

7

I wander around the supermarket swinging an empty basket at my knees, overwhelmed by all of the options. I leave with a baguette and two packets of brie and six bottles of cheap wine.

I battle through an ice-wall of rain to Marcel's and can't remember the code to the front gate. I take my phone out of my pocket to retrieve it but stop when I see I have two text messages waiting to be read.

I drop the shopping at my feet and the wine bottles clang together. I don't care whether or not they've broken.

Jess?

No, not Jess. I have two texts from Louise. The first reads: *HELLO, YOU!! OMG! Bonjour! Welcome back to Paris!! I'd love to get a drink tonight kind sir, where shall we meet? Anvers at 8? Lou XXXX.* The second reads: *PS. U need to work on your French if u wanna live ici ;-) lololol xxx*

I stand getting wetter and wetter, considering what she might mean. I check my outbox and realise I must've texted her at some point last night.

I'm yet more horrified when I discover I texted Jess, too.

I read the message I sent to Jess first. It could be worse. It just says *miss u, Bunny.* No kisses or anything. The only disconcerting thing is she hasn't responded yet. The message I sent to Louise was actually wordier: *LOUisE, JE SUIS ICI EN pARIS! JE VOUDRAIS UNE RENDEZ-VOUS AVEC TU EN AJORD OUI TOMORROW!! TU ES TRES BIEN!! CEST POSSIBLE? KISS KISS!!*

I let myself into the building and walk slowly up to the apartment. I turn the key and hurl myself against the door until it reluctantly opens. I sit and listen to Nirvana and bite my nails, my poor mind suffering from the punishment I subjected it to last night.

I manage to send Louise a text agreeing to meet at Anvers

after a couple of minutes spent staring at my phone.

I head to the bedroom for a nap. I rest my head on one of Marcel's paper-thin pillows, thinking over and over: *four working days.*

I slip into sleep and what I dream of is the tobacco-stained sludge-grey weave of Marcel's mattress adrift in the middle of the room. Its springs dip where Jess's pink frame is pressing into it. I lie next to her and examine all the slight edges of her face and creep through her hair and it all feels so real when her curls catch in my fingers. I deliberate over certain words but words are so meaningless. I pull her towards me and for a moment she becomes a part of who I am, we are the same being as we shimmer and twist inside each other. I beg her with my body to know I love her more than time, more than words would ever allow me to inscribe.

The ecstasy becomes too much and I am woken by the sound of the toilet backfiring.

I pick up my phone to check the time.

I lose myself in memories of the dream I had, picking through the specifics of something that never actually happened.

8

I arrive at Anvers and spend twenty minutes shivering and smoking and watching a street performer dancing with a cane and a bunch of fake flowers. He finishes a rep every three minutes or so and goes back to the start of his routine. He is on an endless loop, much like I am. The key difference is that he doesn't seem to mind.

Louise grips my shoulder. She's wearing a black fur-lined coat that ends around her knees, skinny blue jeans, and high black boots.

She wraps her arms around me and says, 'It's so good to see you!'

'You too,' I say into her hair.

'Please excuse my lateness.'

'Nothing's changed, has it?'

She laughs and brushes my chest and I feel myself warming up in increments.

We walk through groups of tourists and clusters of tireless street vendors selling French flags and berets and Eiffel Towers and snow globes and tea towels daubed with effigies of various monuments. We arrive at the base of the slope and see Sacré-Cœur towering over us, holding its shape against a night sky dotted with silver stones. We stop walking for a moment to look up at it, disturbed only by the whirring and jangling of a rotating carousel ahead of us.

Louise takes me to the steps and before we even start to climb, I am winded.

We talk about why I'm in Paris again and I lie and say it's because I missed this place so much. I confess to her she's partly to blame; the way she spoke about this city during her visit to The Water Poet was *inspirational.*

She loves that she's had this effect on me, enough to show me all of her teeth.

We're halfway to the summit. I afford myself a short

glance back to see the city being birthed from the stone canal of the street we just came from. The higher we get, the more of it is shown to us – it's pecked at by street lamps and shaken softly by the lovers and friends gathered in its cavities.

When we get to Sacré-Cœur itself, we sit on a step beneath it. Louise takes a bottle of merlot and two plastic cups out of her bag. She pours a generous helping of wine into each cup, picks up hers, and taps it against mine, saying, 'Welcome back.'

I watch her studiously as she sips.

'How's your second Parisian adventure going so far?' she asks.

'Well, let me see. I had my passport stolen the first day I got here. I screwed up an interview for a job I've been doing for the last five years. Oh, and I'm living in an apartment in Val de Fontenay that kind of resembles a crack den. How about you, Lou? How are things with you?'

'Are you serious?' she asks without a hint of a smile, despite the lightness of touch I applied to my predicaments.

'Yeah, Paris has really gone out of its way to welcome me back. I'm so grateful. Thank you, Paris!'

I shout the last three words out to the horizon, willing them to rebound from the grotesque chocolate biscuit that is the Tour Montparnasse and to ricochet around Gare du Nord for a while before circling the Panthéon once or twice.

She pours us another few measures of red.

'That's terrible! Are you OK?'

'Yeah, yeah, I'm fine,' I lie. 'It's my own stupid fault, all of it. I had my passport in my back pocket in Opera station. And I didn't prepare at all for the interview. And I didn't arrange for anywhere to stay in Paris before I left London,' I lie again, 'so the crack den is all I could get at short notice. At least I'm here, though. That's got to be a good thing.'

'Couldn't you have stayed with Rick?'

'I didn't want to impose,' I say.

'You could have stayed with me if you'd asked.'

150

'See above.'

'What, you think you'd be imposing? Don't be ridiculous. I'm renting this massive space from an awesome artist. There's enough room going spare; a rare thing in Paris, I know. It's so cool. There are photographs all over the walls of her with famous people; there's even one of her with Serge Gainsbourg, if you can believe that. I'm sure she would've been fine with an extra person staying. She's an amazing woman, super laidback.'

'Aren't you living with your boyfriend, though? The guy I met in Spitalfields?'

She tenses her shoulders when she says: 'Ben and I have become estranged. By which I mean he's a lying, cheating bastard.'

'Ah shit, sorry Lou,' I say, trying desperately not to show how pleased I am that Ben wasn't as perfect as I'd feared.

'It's fine. I'm better off without him anyway,' she says with her head lowered. 'At least that's what I've been told …'

To cheer her up I point to a puppet show that's started on the balcony below us. An old man crouches behind a couple of stacked crates, waving around two woolen dolls and pinching at his vocal chords. He's drawn a crowd together that lean into each other for warmth as Louise and I sit with our legs touching.

I have no doubt this is the most content I've been since I landed.

We pick up our empties and stand by using each other's elbows to steady ourselves. We descend a thousand steps. Louise navigates us through alleyways and along dark rows of closed boutiques until we appear outside Pigalle Métro station. We stand in front of the whirling blades of the Moulin Rouge – roaring neon ugliness with promises of stockings and heels and tits. We walk along a row of shops and stare into windows filled with dicks and faux-leather whips and skin-tight fetish outfits.

She points out a gimp mask studded with bronze circles, whispers, 'Christ, look at *that!*' and grips my forearm.

We decline the advances of women enticing us into their sex shows, having to be quite insistent with someone who assures us that if we declined her offer, we'd be missing out on the *hottest night of our lives.*

I explain to Louise that the last time I walked down this street I was propositioned by a prostitute who thought I was looking for a blowjob.

'What a beautiful story. Tell it again,' she says, and I laugh.

We reach a three-story monolith with the word *SEX* flashing on its front. I figure I must be drunk from the wine or drunk on her or possibly drunk on all the huge rubber cocks because when she angles me towards *SEX* I don't protest. On entering we are immediately surrounded by offshoots of a deranged imagination – furry handcuffs hang next to inflatable sheep and French maid costumes. Louise picks up a tub of chocolate penises and holds it out to me as if she's offering me one and I struggle to hide my amusement from the man standing at the till.

She takes my hand and leads me to a curtain, next to which is a sign she translates as: *Warning – Hardcore.*

'Well, it looks as if we don't have much of a choice. We simply *have* to go in here,' she says. 'I honestly see no other alternative.'

She slides us underneath its stale striped fabric and even I'm shocked by what we find. Televisions strobe with images of women locked up tight by a man at each end. Rows and rows of DVDs rest in racks and are flicked forwards on their hinges by shifty-looking men. There are shelves on the walls holding mystical trophies: rubber fists and fleshlights and leather paddles and cuffs and chains and choke collars.

I look to Louise and she isn't smiling any more. I think about telling her that for a moment this was my life but instead I just let this thought rest on my brain like an abscess. *Lollipop86* and Sophie and Elizabeth and all the others are haunting me and this is their Indian burial ground. I see Jess walking into my room in her raincoat all that time ago, for ever ago, and letting it drop, showing me her lingerie and her curves and the coiled-up curls in all her hair dotted wet.

'Let's go,' I say, suddenly desperate to be anywhere other than here.

I walk her (or she walks me, I can't quite tell) to the Métro.

'Lou, it was so awesome to see you.' I say.

'You too. What are you up to for the next few days?'

'I'm waiting for my passport to be ready. Then I'm heading back to London, I think.'

She opens up her mouth in surprise, shows me her tongue and her teeth and her throat.

'You're not, are you? Already?'

'I have to. I've got things I need to be getting on with.'

'But you only just got here! Why leave now?'

I wring my hands with anxiety, not wanting to talk about it.

What can I say?

'I was gonna tell you there are jobs going at GBL,' she says. 'I mentioned you were in Paris and they said they'd be happy to have you working there again.'

'Really? God, they must be desperate or something.'

She nudges my shoulder and smiles.

'Do you want to know what I think?' she says. 'What *I* think is that you should stay in Paris, get your old job back, move out of the crack den, and into somewhere a bit more chic. Reinvigorate yourself! Who needs London when you've got the Sacré-Cœur and *SEX*?'

I stare at her as she considers what she's said and goes the claret of the wine we've each had too much of.

'That came out wrong but you know what I mean.'

'Yeah, I hear you,' I say. 'I'll think about it.'

She kisses my cheek and descends into the belly of the station, turning to blow me another kiss before walking through the barrier.

I have no idea of how I'm supposed to get to Val de Fontenay and to the ragged pit I'm living in.

I give it a minute then head into the station myself. I scan the Métro map on the wall and feel like grabbing my brain and wringing it out when all I can focus on with any sort of clarity is *a few more days, a few more days, just a few more days then you-know-who.*

9

I shoulder myself in front of a desperate-looking English family and when the clerk at the counter sees me he rolls his eyes as if to say: *you again?* He tells me my passport will be ready when it's ready and they still need to know the date of my departure. I tell him it's difficult for me to buy a ticket as I'm not even permitted to enter an internet café without proper identification.

I leave with nothing resolved. I walk out in a daze and find an empty bench near the Seine, where I can check my phone in peace. I have a text from Rick asking how I am and a text from Louise saying she had a great time last night and a text from Dad asking if I'm alive but nothing from Jess, nothing at all from her.

I pick up lunch from a small bakery on the left bank, offer a ten, and get two back. I don't want to know how much money is left on the overdraft of my account.

I bounce around points of interest like a moth at a light bulb. None of it sinks in – not the Arc, nor Notre Dame, nor the Louvre, nor the obelisk of Concorde. It all seems so superfluous, and I? I am aimless.

I wish Marcel had left behind some weed or anything else to wrap my brain up with. The only thing I have that I can use to kill time with is my laptop. I open it and click on the .doc file called *Jess#1*. I write about everything that's happened since arriving in Paris and it takes about an hour but when I read it back it doesn't sit right. I'm not happy with any of it.

I delete everything except *I dream of you each night ... fuck* and close the lid of my computer.

I lie on the mattress and listen to the toilet groaning under its own weight. I inspect the pictures Marcel has stuck to the walls of him with a multitude of girls and in each shot he looks genuinely happy, as if he is exploding with it.

His pillowcase stinks of marijuana and beer and smoke and I pull it over my face and cry but for barely a minute, so I'm making good progress with that.

Night comes slowly and with sickness. There's nothing for me to do. I wish I had my guitar here but then wonder why because I'm no good at playing it. I find an old bongo drum in the living room covered in beads and with a thick brown skin and I tap on it a few times but get bored quickly.

I look in cupboards and shelves for more CDs I can spin. I find a battered wallet filled with CD-Rs behind one of the speakers. I choose a disc to play at random as I don't understand the way Marcel has marked them. I'm caught off guard by the sound of a woman's voice speaking in rapid French and the two words I can place are *Marcel* and *J'adore*. She starts strumming a ukulele and singing in her native language and I have never in my life heard anything as beautiful or as real as this.

I let the song play as I walk into the bedroom to take another look at Marcel's photographs. I want to put a face to the voice. In one shot Marcel sits on a picnic blanket with a girl under each arm. To his right a friend of his is holding a guitar and I bet the way he plays is exquisite – I can tell by the shape of the chord he has wrapped around its neck that he knows what he's doing, more so than I ever will.

In another of the pictures, Marcel's standing with a girl in a bikini upon an expanse of pristine white sand. With this image, I'm deposited from the solitary constraints of the apartment and onto the Sicilian coastline, where water from the ocean runs across the ridges of my toes and dampens the ends of the hair of the girl I carry. I let waves bloom around my legs and run my free hand through their flesh. I find a spot behind an abandoned wind breaker where I can spread her out and explore her. Her skirt is short and her legs are warm from the sun. I lock my arms and bend at the elbows to enter her, a hundred push-ups not an issue for someone so young and strong, and we swell with orgasms in the same way that a wave is birthed on the horizon to later crash against the sand and rocks of the shore. We inspect constellations and trace them with our fingers as distant salsa music moves the air of a nearby clubhouse. A shooting star pierces the sky and when she tells me to make a wish I say *Catherine, I wish my life could be like this for ever ...*

The music of the ukulele stirs the air of the flat in Val de Fontenay. I take my time choosing a girl that matches the timbre of the voice of its player, eventually settling on a pretty brunette who looks the least like Jess or Louise or anyone else I know.

Ukulele Girl laughs through a final verse. She brings the song to a close with the rapid strumming of the ukulele's thin strings before saying goodbye with a flurry of air kisses. She leaves me behind on the sofa, my heart in small pieces.

I play the song a dozen more times and imagine my name is *Marcel.*

10

I decide on waking to contact Louise and GBL to ask for my old job back. I don't need to tell the school I'm planning on leaving Paris within a week or so. Working would go some way towards paying for my new passport and might also cover the cost of a ticket home. Anything to take my mind off things would be a blessing, too; anything to stop me from sinking into the sticky tar that the mattress on the floor of Marcel's bedroom seems to be coated with.

Louise answers her phone and I tell her I've caved and I'll come and work for GBL again. 'That's wonderful news!' she says. 'What made you change your mind?'

'You did, Lou. You really can be quite persuasive when you want to be.'

'Interesting. You should consider that filed away for future reference.'

I smile and sense her doing the same.

'I'm at school now,' she says, 'so I'll put Michelle on and she can tell you what she needs from you. Speak soon!'

Before I have a chance to reply I hear the fumbling of the phone as it's passed from one hand to another, then Michelle the Director saying, 'Hello, we have classes for you if you want them. Do you want them? Could you start tomorrow morning?'

'I –'

'We're not enough teachers at the moment so if you want work we need get you in a class as soon as possible. We've got classes lined up but no one to teach them, if you see what I mean, so could you start teach tomorrow morning ooorrrrrrrr …?'

'Michelle, I –'

'Bien great great great so do you want to pop in later on and pick up the files for the class? It'll be en La Défense and it iz intermediate and yes would that be OK at one o'clock today?'

'Well I suppose it would, but –'

'Great one o'clock I see you later merci merci au revoir I see you later.'

She hangs up and I hold the phone against my ear. I let its dial tone buzz my confused mind for a moment.

I can't believe I'm a fucking *teacher* again.

I leave the flat to go to the supermarket but instead find myself standing at the bar in a dump called *L'Absinthe.* It's a place populated by men with terrible posture standing and sipping toxic green water from filthy glasses. The walls are covered in murals of naked women with huge breasts and leather boots and caricatures of devils and beasts with monstrous dicks and pitchforks. Discordant metal music is coughed up by speakers housed in varnished pine and suspended in each corner of the room.

I pick up a menu that has at least thirty different types of absinthe listed next to gradually increasing prices. I choose a drink from the middle of the list – I don't have money to burn but at the same time I doubt there are many things worse than a cheap glass of absinthe. I mangle the name of my drink of choice and a barmaid with a nose stud and lip ring retrieves a medieval device from behind the counter. She hooks it up and sticks a cube of sugar on it and lets the absinthe pour through it and into a chalice below.

As a double bass drum prescription rains down from the speakers above my head I swallow the drink and gag on the sting in its tail. I ask for another but one grows into two three four more and what can I say other than I'm having fun at last? A few more of those and things get confusing. The pictures on the wall start rippling – painted flames flicker and the mouths of screaming women stretch out into oblongs.

'Jess would fucking *love* the place,' I tell a decrepit biker thumbing the paddles of a pinball machine. I wave the barmaid over with the intention of ordering another glass but the absinthe already in my belly and my head tells me I should leave this hell behind. I raise two hands shaped as metal horns to the people in the bar before I go.

I get the distinct impression I'm the coolest patron this place has ever seen.

I let myself into the flat and stagger to the mattress. I check my phone. I have a message from Jess that reads: *Where are you?* I go over these three words again and again. Their digital lines ripple on the waves of my alcoholism.

I reply saying *I'm in Paris but I miss you baby I'm coming home as soon as possible xxx.*

Paris??? Why? she asks.

I dunno I needed to clear my head but it's been a total clusterfuck so far.

This time she doesn't respond. I rest the phone on the pillow so that if it buzzes with a text from her in the middle of the night, it'll wake me up. I close my eyes to see her clearer. I paint pictures of her in my head – the birthmark on her foot, the freckles on her cheeks, the length of her hair and the depth of her bellybutton.

I imagine her curved rump pressing up against my cock as I drop into an absinthe coma.

11

I get off the Métro at Opera station and feel slightly nauseous when I near the place my passport was taken. I clear out of there as quickly as I can and walk towards Poisonniers and the offices of GBL, the blood in my veins thin from my latest binge.

Juliet buzzes me in and I wait for her to welcome me back to Paris but instead she just says 'hello' and asks how she can help me. I say 'Juliet, it's me. Don't you remember me?' and she says 'Michelle is expecting you. You can go straight in.'

Michelle the Director sits next to the window to catch enough light, as the building the school operates from is old and murky. The highly strung planning department (a young Canadian called Maurice and American Amy) are positioned in front of her, both speaking *en Français* and scribbling onto the already well-inked surfaces of various documents laid out in front of them. They each notice me entering but acknowledge my second-coming in the way Juliet did – with total and utter indifference.

Michelle the Director waves me over and I'm left cradling my acute absinthe hangover for a couple of minutes as she brings her most recent telephone conversation to an end.

After she hangs up the phone I say 'Michelle. How're you?' She ignores the question and says 'D'accord, here is ze documentation for your first class. It is for Société Générale in La Défense and intermediate level, as I say you. It is OK?'

I take the papers from her. She watches as I rifle through each page without knowing what I'm looking for. I notice the records of work the last teacher left start off neatly bullet pointed, underscored, and printed but descend into disorder as the weeks go by. The latest entry, dated a few days ago, is nothing more than a wicked scrawl that reminds me of the time I worked here last. There never was enough time to get things done. There never was enough time to think. Most of the administration I had to complete was done on my lap on the way to school or dotted with marmalade during a hastily eaten breakfast.

I slip the papers back into their plastic folder and say, 'Yes, that all looks fine.'

'Bien, well I suggest you go and get a plan together. You remember where the textbooks are, don't you? We're still using *Blue Sky Business,* they're in the same place as when you left us before, and the CDs are all there also, in the cupboard next to the computers. C'est bien?' she asks as she lifts the phone to her ear and starts dialling.

'Oui,' I say. 'Merci, Michelle.'

I get up to leave. On the way out I nod at both planners but they're either too busy to notice my gesture or they just couldn't care less.

I take a minute to compose myself before entering the staffroom. The one person in here I know is Louise. She says 'hello, you' as she presses an open book to her chest and lifts the lid of the photocopier until it sticks.

'Hi.'

'Welcome back!'

'Thanks,' I say. 'You know, you're the only person who's said that so far.'

She closes the lid of the photocopier, takes her papers, and strides over to the textbooks to desperately scan each of their titles. I consider saying hello to the other teachers but they all seem so engrossed in what they're doing that I'd feel like an idiot for disturbing them.

Louise wishes me luck and says she'll see me soon. I go to the balcony to watch her jogging towards the station before taking my place at the table to wait for a spark of inspiration I know won't be forthcoming. *Blue Sky Business* falls open on a double-page spread that describes in detail how to address one's superiors and inferiors – a hierarchy this course seems to endorse. There are numbers and figures and telephone role-plays and case studies and lots of graphs too, too many to count. On the Y axis is the love I have for *J* and on the X axis

164

is time. I can't help but wonder why the line is rising up and up and up when there are so many variables that should be pulling it down. Will Louise ever be a factor? Inwardly I sketch a new line (*L*) but which would be the line of best fit?

Information overload causes my absinthe-soaked brain to throb. I close the book and instead study the text I got from Jess last night.

She's thinking about me. That's all I need to know.

I find a bar nearby where I can darken my lips and teeth with red wine, *Blue Sky Business* at my feet, and my first lesson planned in the only way my short attention span will permit.

As I people-watch I notice a girl with blonde hair conversing with a friend outside a café on the other side of the road. I concentrate on all of their movements to the extent of watching their chests swelling with each inhalation. I run to where they're sitting. I whip the map they've been studying from their table and it brings cups and plates with it that collide with the pavement and break.

They look at me with terror stretching their lips apart.

'Having a nice fucking stay?' I ask.

They're too shocked to speak so I help them along.

'Don't you remember me?' I say to the blonde. 'I'm the one you distracted at Opera station so your friend could rob me. Does that sound familiar?'

She puts a hand to her breast and twirls the charm of the necklace wrapped around her throat.

'How many people have you played that game with? How many holidays have you destroyed?'

'Je ne … je ne comprends pas …'

'Where's my passport?' I ask, and she shakes her head.

I'm pulled away from them by a waiter. He says something to me in French and shoves me hard until I almost fall into the path of an oncoming car.

I look at the girl again, realising my mistake.

I escape across the road. I retrieve the textbooks from where I was sitting and buy another bottle of wine to be consumed on the way home. I'm humiliated enough to drink a quarter of it in a single swig.

I recall a line from the dream I had the other night: *Another hand, another question: 'what's it like to be an alcoholic?'*

After that, I could've ended up in any part of Paris but chose to ride the Métro to Père Lachaise cemetery. I'm upset but don't know whether it's because I miss Jess or because I'm trapped in France or because I just threatened an innocent girl when provoked by too much wine. I'm swinging between maudlin and morose and want to surround myself with death but also peace and tranquility – at least on holy land I'll be given sanctuary from the carnage I've been creating over the past few days.

As soon as I step into the grounds of the graveyard I'm reminded of Highgate and the conversation I had there with Jess. I lower my head and walk blindly. London, Paris – it's all the same. What good is getting on with things without the person who completes you? There was no point coming here. I wanted change but all I got was a mirror image of the place I left behind. I thought fleeing to a foreign country would save me but it's made me more monstrous, if anything. I can't help replaying the scene from the café in my mind; I must've terrified those poor girls by charging at them the way I did. I feel as if my very existence is something I should feel guilty about and alcohol lends me the tools to dig a little deeper. I reflect on all the time I spent destroying the misplaced hopes of *LovedUp* girls in London. I cringe at thoughts of Sophie's tight orifice and am almost brought to my knees by how young she looked when wearing my oversized T-shirt. I tear up at thoughts of how badly I treated Jack by letting a stranger take Liu's bed and how I almost drove a wedge between Rick and Alice. All of this is bad enough without even considering how badly I've wronged Marcus by sleeping with the girl he'll no doubt go on to marry. *I deserve all I get,* I whisper to myself, dabbing at my eyes with the collar of my shirt. The constant pain in my heart and in my head is my penance for being such a terrible person and everyone would be far better off if I put myself into the ground at the foot of one of these headstones.

I'd be naïve to ignore that this is the second suicidal thought I've entertained in the past week.

I make my way to Jim Morrison's grave and retrieve what I set out to get – three unopened bottles of Jack Daniel's whiskey, left behind as a tribute by mourners who didn't for one second consider how insensitive they were being.

I lean against a nearby tree and unscrew one of the bottles.

In the silence of the graveyard my mind turns to Catherine. I go over the journey we took together, spanning the length of Italy and the northern coast of the island that sits beneath it. We moved at every opportunity. We never stopped because to stay in one place for too long was to stagnate. If I hadn't abandoned Catherine in Sicily then perhaps we could've travelled together for the rest of our lives. Maybe I would've become the travel writer I'd always dreamed of being. It saddens me I'll never know how different things could've been if I hadn't left Catherine behind – a decision that meant I would one day be in London for the party at which I met Jess, and of course meeting Jess changed things for ever.

Every action has a consequence, I think as I gaze around the cemetery. *Birth begets death. Love begets heartache. Alcohol begets hangovers.*

Everything begat Jess.

I wonder if Catherine looks at the poem I wrote for her whenever she gets lonely. The words of the poem are more relevant now than they've ever been before – I just didn't think at the time they'd ever be associated to any girl other than her. They describe how we'd always be on the same journey and that our shared experiences would bond us together for ever.

Despite the distance I've put between us, I remain in the same place in terms of Jess that I have inhabited for almost nine months; a period of gestation that's only seen my love for her grow stronger.

I wonder whether or not coming to Paris will alter our relationship, for better or for worse.

Paris begets ... what?

I drink some of the whiskey. I take in a breath to sing the first line of a Doors song then realise I don't know any of the words.

I put all three bottles in my bag with *Blue Sky Business* and leave Jim Morrison and the graveyard behind.

For a confusing moment I wish Louise was here, under my arm, holding me up as I walk.

In the safety of Marcel's apartment I fill my stomach with pasta and try to pull myself together. I use the glow of my mobile to locate my laptop. I open a new document to write a letter of apology to the waiter and the proprietor of the place I defiled before heading to the cemetery. Contemplating cause and effect has made it clear that what I did could've hurt their business and I'm so tired of always being the bringer of grief. I want to make amends for the destruction I've caused and for whatever consequences I have set in motion for the café.

I watch the cursor flicker on the white of the page for what must be an hour.

I pour a fresh glass of whiskey when I become convinced it's the only thing that could send me to sleep. I recline on my back with my hands on my heart in the way that corpses in Père Lachaise and Highgate are laid to rest.

12

I don't belong here.

They read their broadsheet newspapers and type into their BlackBerrys as I sit and watch the tunnels of the RER rolling by.

I'm an impostor.

I open up the plastic membrane at my feet, remove *Blue Sky Business*, and start going through it. I don't really know what it is I'm supposed to be doing.

We get to La Défense much sooner than I'd anticipated and the congregation within this tin vessel stands and waits for the doors slide open. They file out and bunch up at the bottom of the platform steps and I wait for them to move on and for my path to become clear.

I stride past anaemic cafés and fast food restaurants and a six-piece string band busking for coins. I join the desperate queue of suits and almost fall onto the escalator with an invisible palm of the woman behind me urging me on. They want me to hurry but there's nowhere I can go. I'm almost on the heels of the suited man in front of me and still they want me to inch further forwards, more to the side, more out of the way.

We climb to the tableau of the business park and the escalator regurgitates our chewed up carcasses out onto the quad. The Grande Arche appears as a colossal monolith that casts its shadow over all of us. We march towards the office block of Société Générale in tight formation and as we pass the arch's dead white stone it feels as if we should each salute it.

After entering the building I approach the receptionist and say 'bonjour, jai rendez-vous avec six estudients a neuf heure, je suis son prof d'anglais' and he's holding up a hand to stop me before I've even reached the end of my monologue. He could tell I was the English teacher by the way I carried myself across the room, by the purple pillows I have stored under each eye.

He picks up the phone and after a short conversation he ushers me into a lift. I start climbing to my class, up to my trial.

I see them through the frosted glass of the training room wall – all six of my students, ready and waiting. I can make out their suit jackets and side-partings and tightly wound buns from here. I'm not quite ready to face them. I rest against the door, pushing it open only when it seems as if the distorted outline of one of them notices me through the window.

'Hello, hello, how are you, *ça va*?' I say.

I immediately get the sense I'm out of my depth. They could eat me for breakfast. They could smear me all over their croissants and devour me as they scanned their Financial Times for the FTSE100; the pounds stacked against the euros stacked against the dollar signs in their restless pupils.

I press my soaking hand into each of theirs and theirs are all chalk-dry.

I'm like something *le chat* has dragged in.

I swallow hard. I sit down and take out my papers.

I say 'It's cold today, isn't it?' and a student replies with a *oui* then a *yes* then a *very cold, oui*.

Blue Sky Business mocks me when I open it, as do the meaningless notes I made at GBL yesterday.

'First, to introduce myself: I'm from London, in England. I like music and reading and French food and French wine –

(a*nd Jess and absinthe and drugs and vacant, soulless fucking*)

I'm twenty-eight and I've never been married.'

I show them my ring finger as proof.

'I live in Val de Fontenay at the moment but soon I want to move somewhere like Place Monge or Oberkampf or Parmentier. I've been an English teacher for five years.'

They look less than impressed.

'Could you introduce yourselves to me, please?' I ask.

The man next to me is clean-shaven and has parted hair and reeks of a pungent cologne. He coughs into a manicured fist and says, 'Sure. I am Peter. I have worked here since three years. I am data analyst. I like read economy article and I have a wife and three childs.'

'It's nice to meet you, Peter,' I say, and he nods solemnly.

The woman adjacent to Peter is older and greyer. She says, 'Hello, I am Marie. I have worked here since twenty-four years. I am data analyst. I like play golf. I am married and I have four children and one grandchildren and two dogs.'

The others laugh out of politeness and I fail in determining which part of that was supposed to be funny.

It goes on like this. Man, woman, man: data analyst. I want them to talk as much as they can about their jobs and their lives and interests because after this I don't have a lot more planned. Jean-Pierre wraps up by telling me he's a data analyst living in Trocadéro with X number of kids and Y number of wives and then I'm left floundering.

'Great. It's nice to meet you all,' I lie. 'So, let's begin. Please turn to page thirty-two.'

They flip to where I told them to flip and their pictures and fonts are nothing like the ones spread out in front of me. I notice then that their copies of *Blue Sky Business* have different coloured covers to mine.

I've been working from the wrong material.

'Actually … actually first, close your books and we'll do some listening.'

Books are closed with confusion.

'Sorry, I read my plan wrong.'

There is no plan!!!

'We're going to hear two people talking about the importance of good customer service,' I say with a trembling voice. I get up and walk around the room looking for the CD player I was assured would be here. 'In pairs,' I make a peace sign and indicate groups of two, 'talk about what sort of things you think might be mentioned.'

I hear them mumbling to each other in French as I manage to locate a relic of a stereo that's been stuffed behind a cabinet. I blow dust from it and plug it in. I put in the CD, press play then pause.

'What do you think will be mentioned?' I ask.

Obviously: silence.

'Anyone?'

Nothing but eyes.

'Well, I'll play the conversation now,' I tell them. 'Make notes, please, and we'll have a discussion about it afterwards.'

I press play and the CD spins quickly, peaks then slows. It stops spinning altogether. The digital display where the track number should be simply reads: *NO.*

I hit play again but nothing happens.

One of my students clears his throat. They each point pens at pads and wait.

I make the peace sign again and say, 'OK, scratch that. In pairs: talk about your favourite...*thing.*'

After six months have passed, it's the end of the lesson. I walk to the gents dripping with sweat, look at myself in the mirror, and half-laugh half-cry. I never want to put myself or anyone else through that again.

I hear the students walking past the bathroom and summoning the lift. It's not necessary to share their first language to make a good guess at what they're talking about.

I have nowhere else to go and nothing else to do so I meander around a nearby shopping centre. I go to the cinema and pay for a ticket for the next film that's playing and can't be blamed that this is a French flick about attractive young lesbians finding themselves (with both hands).

I sit alone in the dark and fail to comprehend a single word of it. I illuminate my face with the glow of my mobile phone and consider sending Jess another message.

13

I arrive at the park gates early. Louise and I arranged to meet here when I took my admin back to GBL – I dropped it into the pigeonhole and ran downstairs before Michelle the Director or American Amy or anyone else could catch ahold of me. I found Louise outside fumbling with an armful of books. She laughed at her own juggling act and I took the books from her as she rearranged herself.

We spoke about my first lesson. I told her it went as well as could be expected and she said my students were most likely in love with me already. 'If you want to celebrate getting through it,' she said, 'I'm going to Vincennes tomorrow with a few of the girls. We're gonna hire a couple of rowboats and take them out onto the lake. You're more than welcome to come if you want to join us.'

I told her I'd think about it as if there was ever any doubt I'd be here now, standing at the entrance of the park in Vincennes with my hands in my pockets and my mind on her body.

I watch her approach from a hundred metres away, flanked by a girl on each side. I pull my scarf over my chin. I'm awkward as I watch them getting nearer. I make a point of checking my phone, of fiddling with the button on my suit jacket, of buffing the front of my shoes on the backs of my legs.

She closes in and wraps her arms around me and today she smells of talcum powder and cherry lip balm.

'I'm so glad you came!' she says.

She introduces the other girls as Emily and Kate. Emily looks down at leaves on the ground in front of her and tugs at the sleeves of her coat.

Kate looks straight through me and says 'hello.'

'Hello, ladies,' I say, then feel ridiculous for saying it.

We start walking into the park and along its channels, its

sprawling dirt paths lined with bare trees. As we're walking two abreast, I make sure I'm next to Louise.

We step ahead of Emily and Kate and find our own rhythm.

'So, how are things? All good?' she asks.

'Yeah, not too bad, thanks. Although it feels like I'm still sort of finding my feet.'

'I reckon that's normal. It'd take anyone a few days to get their bearings back in Paris. It has its own … intricacies.'

'Intricacies? You mean like *SEX*?'

I worry this memory will embarrass her but instead we just smile at each other as we walk beneath skeletal trees, stretching away from the two girls following us.

'Have you heard any news about your passport?' she asks.

'I went to the Embassy the other day and they told me to keep waiting. I need to get a ticket back to London too. I haven't even done that yet. It's all a nightmare, basically.'

'On the bright side, though, it means we get to keep you here for a bit longer.'

Her face is flushed from the frost in the air and it makes different parts of me ache.

She looks behind us at the two intruders and says 'Those girls are so *slow*! God, is there anything more annoying than a slow walker?'

We stop to let them catch up; something that I do quite reluctantly.

As we wait, I take the pack of cigarettes out of my inside pocket and slide one of them out. I ease a matchstick from its box and all the while I'm staring at Louise. I light the cigarette and inhale and she watches me pucker up around its filter. I blow out the smoke and it brushes against her as it exits my body.

I notice a tree trunk over her shoulder. One part of me wants to press her against it but another part wants to just sit amongst all its dead leaves and pull her head against my shoulder. We could sit like that for hours and I could play with her hair.

She blinks away whatever she was thinking about when Kate and Emily reach us and Kate says, 'Slow down, you two, what's the rush?'

There might be something to hurry towards, Kate, but I'm not yet sure of what it is.

We carry on walking, this time clustered together in a group. Kate asks Louise something about an English class she taught the other day. The two of them start talking about phrasal verbs and halfway through listening to them, I get lost.

Emily walks at my side.

'How do you and Louise know each other?' I ask.

'We used to work together.'

'At GBL?'

She nods.

'I'm teaching for them at the moment,' I tell her. 'I had a class in La Défense the other day and it went horribly.'

She doesn't say anything in response.

'What do you do now?' I ask.

'I'm a receptionist for an insurance company.'

'Oh,' I say, and I'm left thinking: *is there a finer way to kill a conversation than that?*

Louise hands over a heap of money and her bag and chooses two boats for us; one called *Mickey*, the other *Nemo*. I step ahead of the two strange girls and bundle myself in a boat with Louise.

'I'll row,' I say.

'You'll row *first*, you mean. I'll take over when we get to the island in the middle.'

The attendant kicks us off and I get us moving. It's more difficult than I imagined it would be and for a while I'm worried I might be taking us around in a circle. The water around us glows from the sunlight resting on it. I aim us towards the island at the centre of the lake and its pastel autumn shades. We're surrounded by beauty but it's all quite unnecessary. Louise's skirt has ridden up her legs. They're long and naked and perfect but I don't want to be between them. I want her to rest her feet on my lap so I can rub them. I want to lie behind her and put a hand on her hip and stroke it.

I want to leave behind all needling thoughts of Jess and lose myself in Louise's hair.

'A wild couple, they are,' I say, to distract my racing mind. 'Kate and Emily, I mean. I bet you three have had some *crazy* times together.'

'Don't be mean. They're lovely and sweet. And they *are* fun in their own way, thank you very much.'

I poke my tongue out at her and cross my eyes and she laughs before ordering me to *behave*.

'I found out a little bit about Emily on the walk here,' I say, 'but Kate remains an enigma. What's her story? Did she work at GBL too?'

'Nah, I met her at a language exchange in St Denis. We went separately to improve our French but ended up just speaking to each other. It felt like the only actual French people there were slimy men trying to pick up girls like us.'

'Girls like *you*, you mean.'

She says through a smile, 'Hey, didn't I tell you to behave?'

'You might've, but I didn't promise anything.'

I paddle us further along the water.

'Speaking of the girls, by the way, I think someone likes you,' she says.

'What? Who?'

'Emily. I think Emily's into you. Despite what presumptions you might have about her, she's a bit of a goer. She's never normally that quiet, believe me.'

'Right,' I say, and I keep on rowing.

We arrive in front of the island so it's time to switch places. I lock the oars into their rowlocks and read the swaying of the boat as I plant my hands onto the bench I was sitting on and move backwards towards Louise. She clambers to my side and the boat moves more vigorously.

She's laughing and screaming as our bodies touch.

She flails around with the oars and gets us nowhere. She gives up because she's laughing so hard and we sit and float for a few minutes, adrift from all the shit that awaits me back on land.

We dock and step from the vessel and greet Kate and Emily, who are waiting at the booth for us.

'What now?' Kate asks.

Louise answers by retrieving her bag and taking two bottles of wine out of it. 'Now, dear Kate,' she says, 'we drink.'

We walk to a clearing in the middle of a bunch of trees. Louise takes a blanket from her bag and splays it out. We sit on it and fortify ourselves the best we can against the chill in the air. She then produces a small plastic cup for each of us and we are poured a decent measure of wine as she announces to everyone: 'That was so fun!'

Kate and Emily seem unaffected but I say, 'Yeah, it was great.'

'Salut,' she says, and once again we tap our cups together.

Kate starts narrating a directionless story about something that happened to her on the Métro the other day and we all give her the impression that she has our attention. I can feel Emily checking me out. The alcohol is lending her elements of a confidence she didn't seem to have earlier. I start telling them about what happened at Opera station with my passport and about the place I'm staying in at Val de Fontenay. My account is long and I buff it up with lots of unnecessary detail and they flinch and laugh in all the right places. I touch upon the sadder parts of my tale and Emily looks concerned. She wants to lead me off somewhere and take care of me. *I don't want you,* I feel like telling her. *There is no room for you in any of this.*

The branches of the trees surrounding us move on a subtle breeze but by the time we've finished the third bottle of wine, we're cold no longer. Louise surprises us all when she produces yet another wine bottle and I start to wonder how

177

deep her bag might be.

Kate says, 'No more, no more,' but doesn't hesitate in sipping from the cup when a fresh one is given to her.

We're halfway through that bottle when Emily sidles up and rests against me. I look to Louise and she raises her eyebrows and gives me a look that I fail to make sense of. Emily rests her bob on my shoulder and I turn my nose to her and sniff but I can't pick up anything other than the scent of the mildew and the wildlife surrounding us.

The peace we have foraged for ourselves is broken by Louise's phone ringing. She takes it from her pocket to see who's calling and her whole body drops. She answers the call as she gets to her feet and makes a move towards a large tree a few metres away from our clearing. Kate says she needs the toilet and also disappears, leaving me behind with Emily.

We sit without speaking. I hear the song of a bird somewhere above us and I fantasise about flying away with it.

Inevitably, Emily takes a hold of my cheek. She turns my face towards hers and touches her lips against mine. They are soft and sweet but at the same time bitter because I don't want this. I don't know why I'm letting this happen. I sense her heart beating quicker as mine starts shutting down. She takes my hand and presses it into her chest and I cup one of her breasts but don't know why.

It feels so good but I am so full of *hate*.

We part mouths and I see Louise standing ahead of us with eyeliner meandering across her cheeks. I want so much to get up and go to her. I would take her in my arms and comfort her and we'd stand in this clearing as if we were a part of its nature.

'Sorry,' she says. 'I'll leave you two alone.'

I want to tell her not to be so ridiculous and to come and sit with us but the words won't come. She walks away as Emily moves towards me again, folds up my lips in hers, and what choice do I have but to kiss her back?

I kiss her back but I don't know why.

I don't know why I do this to myself.

We separate at Châtelet to take our respective Métro trains home and I surmise Emily wants to be a part of my destruction when she links my arm and I can't shake her off.

I'd like to say something insightful to Louise before she leaves about the unimportance of love and the damage it does but I can't get anything out. I can't tell her how I'd like to go home with her. It's impossible for me to vocalise how much I want to put her to bed, to stroke her hair until she falls asleep.

Kate walks off drunk without a word of farewell.

'Is she OK?' I ask Louise, who smiles sadly at me and says 'Yeah, Kate always does that when she's had a few.'

We linger on each other for a moment. I think she would've wanted me to follow her back to her place but there's nothing we can do about that now.

I watch her go and I'm burning up for her.

I take Emily onto a train and we find a seat and hold each other. I pull her against me but only because I'm thinking of Louise.

We reach Val de Fontenay. I walk her to Marcel's building and let her into his apartment. I take her to the mattress and we undress each other slowly. We stretch out and hold each other and kiss each other and it feels delicate and tender but only because she's no longer Emily; she's Louise, then Jess. I kiss her with longing. I give her some of the love I have stored up inside my chest; I unburden myself of it as if it's pus that I'm squeezing out of a spot.

I want to use Emily to absorb some of my pain.

I kiss her and lick her and pet her and she's Jess then Louise then Jess again and when I push myself inside her she's both girls combined.

14

Emily rests fingertips on her tender morning-after belly and looks at me as if she can't believe what she's done.

'Good morning,' I say.

It's happened again.

'Hi,' she whispers, her alcoholic confidence replaced by an unforgiving hangover.

I take a towel from the floor and head into the bathroom to hide for a couple of minutes. I run both taps and count to five hundred. I return to her only when I've plucked up enough courage, finding her fully dressed and sitting on the mattress.

'Where am I?' she asks.

'Val de Fontenay.'

'Val de Fontenay?'

'Yeah.'

'Where's that?'

'It's on the RER A line,' I say. 'I'll walk you to the station. Let me get dressed, I'll be with you in a minute.'

She looks away when I drop my towel, even though last night she had what I was hiding in her mouth.

I put on jeans and a clean T-shirt and usher her out of the flat. We walk towards the station with a strip of daylight between us. I take her to her platform and before the train arrives she asks 'can I have your number?' I say 'sure' and give it to her. I'm glad she doesn't call me straight away to give me hers because I've swapped around the last two digits.

I wait for the next train, which takes me to the centre of the city. I would like more than anything to go to the Embassy to see if my passport's ready, but as its Saturday the office is closed. I've had enough of not knowing when all this will end. I could invent a departure date for use on their stupid fucking forms and play the hapless tourist if questioned at passport control *(sorry, sir, I thought I could travel whenever I wanted seeing as I've paid good money for this so called "temporary" passport. Do I not have rights? Am I not a man? If you cut me, do I not bleed!?)*

I travel to the Louvre in the hope that all the beauty within it will settle me but when I get there the queue to enter stretches from its glass pyramid to the outskirts of the courtyard. I walk to Notre Dame and have a similar issue but at least I can appreciate the ornateness of its exterior.

I can't stop thinking about the look Louise gave me before she left to catch her train home last night.

What did that look mean?

The faces carved into the great cathedral offer no answers so I descend into the Métro station, nudging aside tourists pressing bags into their hips. I nuzzle against an Italian father to follow him through the gate and travel for free on his ticket.

I smear myself against a cluster of people on the train. The heat of the carriage irritates my hangover. The jostling of the train makes me think I might lose my stomach onto the bare legs of a girl in a short skirt swaying in front of me.

I alight at Auber and resurface from the station to find myself lost amongst yet another hoard, caught in a crowd of people who twist and writhe to avoid one another. I dodge the advances of a homeless man and am carried without any sort of say in the matter into Printemps, a department store already decorated in extravagant lengths of tinsel in anticipation of Christmas.

I'm squeezed through throngs of faceless shoppers as if being passed through a tight colon, deposited near the lifts where I am at last placated by thoughts of the rooftop bar that by this time should be open.

The barman pours lager into a chalice then uses fingers to indicate eight euros. My own fingers still carry Emily's scent; I rub them with the coins that make up my change in the hope that the metal will shift it. The first sip of beer is sickly but the second helps a little more. I carry it out to the roof terrace, one of only a few people to do so as it's freezing out here. I take in the view but briefly, more occupied by the drink that reawakens the wine already in my system.

As with my heart, the emptier the glass gets, the less solid everything seems.

As with girls, the more I consume, the sicker I feel.

I get the barman to refill the glass twice more before running out of money. I tuck the drained glass under my arm and hide it behind my coat, determined not to leave it behind.

The lift takes an age to arrive and even longer to descend. I spill out and stumble through the masses as they dote on afghan blankets and leather gloves and diamond earrings none of them can afford. My face feels tight from the overwhelming certainty I'll get caught smuggling out my trophy. To punctuate my concern a hand locks onto my shoulder; I shrug my captor off and run towards the exit, almost forcing some of the people browsing to topple over from the vigour of my desperate fleeing.

The French language covers me in its goo as I struggle towards the street and when I break into the winter air I drop the glass and it shatters and scatters all over the pavement. I dash to the end of the road and strafe to the left, darting down an alleyway and narrowly avoiding an overturned dustbin.

I double-back on myself to confuse anyone who may be pursuing me and end up propped against the outer wall of an art gallery, my lungs burning from the effort of escaping. I decide there's nowhere else to go now but to Marcel's – back to the stink of the sex I had but didn't want.

Before I get into the station and lose signal, I get a message from Louise: *Have a good night last night? I feel like death (slight red wine headache) Wanna meet?*

I reply without hesitation: *Absolutely, xxx.*

She meets me on the corner of her street, takes me to a café, and orders on my behalf.

'Sorry about yesterday,' she says. 'Ben called and I lost it.'

'Are you all right now?'

'Yeah, but I just wish he'd leave me alone. When the trust's gone there's no real point in carrying on, is there?'

I agree by sipping at my latte.

She says, 'But enough about all that – I'm dying to know what happened between you and Emily. Give me all the juicy details, and don't hold back. I'll know if you're holding back.'

'I don't want to talk about it,' I say.

'Don't be like that! Spill it. I'm happy for her. You're a great guy.'

'Well, it's not like we're together now or anything. We were just really drunk, that's all.'

She brings her cup up to her lips and for a second I am its porcelain.

'I'm pretty sure that's not what she thinks about it,' she says.

'Jesus, I'm such a bastard.'

'No, you're not!'

'I am. I shouldn't have done that. I don't want to hurt anyone,' I say. She rubs my calf with her toes.

'Alcohol does strange things to us,' she says. 'I mean, look at me. I get a call from Ben after a few glasses of wine and it causes me to break down like that? It's pathetic. I feel like such an idiot. I feel like I ruined a perfect day.'

'Come on, Lou, of course you didn't. In fact, yesterday was only special because you were a part of it.'

Something passes between us then as we watch each other drink.

'On the other hand, you're fucking *awful* at rowing,' I say, and she laughs and touches my arm.

She invites me up to her apartment and I sit at her fold-out table as she prepares something for us to eat. She reemerges from the kitchen moments later carrying a wooden platter of cheese.

'I figured we'd have a break from wine after what

184

happened in the park,' she says as she takes a seat opposite mine. She picks up a piece of bread and a knife and drops them again when her phone starts ringing. She looks at it and cancels the call, picks up the knife.

It rings again and the blade clatters against her plate.

'Shit, what does he want *now*?' she says. 'Sorry about this.'

She leaves me with the food and goes to her bedroom. I take this chance to inspect the view from the window. I look over the frost-kissed roofs of buildings which are centuries old. The dome of the Panthéon breaks cover and reaches into the sky.

Louise re-enters the room, takes a seat, and starts slicing a piece of brie into thin triangles. She stops when she looks at me and we balance on this moment long enough for tears to spring from her eyes. I'm pulled towards her by an unnamed force. I close her up in my arms and let her move against my chest. She spills out some of her sadness and I catch all its droplets and absorb them into the cotton of my shirt.

I carry on holding her until she goes to the kitchen for a glass of water. When she returns she says, 'Sorry. I'm such a wreck.'

I tell her not to be so hard on herself.

'I know I should hate him for what he did,' she says. 'And I do, in a way, but there's still a part of me that's totally under his control. I don't know why, but I can't get past it. I can't let it go.'

I resist the urge to ask what Ben did as I don't want to upset her further. 'It'll get better over time,' I lie. This is a common misconception. 'Trust me.'

She puts her hand on mine and says: 'You're such a sweetheart.'

'I don't think I am.'

'You are, though. You're a better man than you think you are.'

I swallow hard. I lift my fingers so they interlock with hers and we flex them closer together.

'I think you're amazing,' she says, and for a moment our emotions bend and twist in unison.

'Why did you really come back to Paris?' she asks, and I think *because of a broken heart.*

'I can't tell you.'

'Why not?'

'Because if I got into all that now I'd feel stupid and weak and I don't want to be like that in front of you.'

I close my eyes to make her vanish but when I open them again she's there and we are still attached. She looks at me and I use the sagging of my shoulders to beg her not to ask me again.

She takes a deep breath.

'A few weeks ago,' she says, 'I went into our flat in Angel, took off my coat and my shoes, shook my umbrella dry outside, closed the door, and locked it. Then I heard them. I heard the springs of our bed. He was in there with her and they were both naked. They were listening to my Nick Drake CD and burning a few of my candles. I knew the girl he was with. It was Elizabeth.'

I think about Elizabeth's confessions of love for me as she ran her tongue over my body. I visualise throwing her out with her clothes not even on yet and collapsing into a pile on my bedroom floor.

'Elizabeth?'

'I know. I couldn't believe it. I just stood there and watched them. She saw I was there and she screamed and wrapped a blanket around herself. Ben came up to me and tried to hug me …' She sniffs and sobs as I cradle her hand. 'I didn't know what to do so I just ran. I left my umbrella in the hall and got soaking wet. I stood on the corner of our street, too shocked to cry, too shocked to do anything. The next day I contacted GBL to get my job back, the day after that I went to the apartment with Mum and moved all my stuff out, saw my friends one last time in Hoxton, and three days afterwards I was on the Eurostar on my way to Gare du Nord. It all happened so quickly.'

'That's unbelievable,' I say.

'The worst thing is he calls me four or five times a day and each time he does it's like he's running this between my ribs.' She picks up the cheese knife and looks at it for a few moments. When she puts it down again she shakes her head rapidly, as if shaking away remnants of the memories that cling to her.

She turns to me and says, 'So, that's my story. Now it's your turn. What happened to make you want to leave London? What was your tipping point?'

The prospect of emptying all my grief out onto Louise's living room floor causes anxiety to bleed through my body. I don't want her to see me in this light.

I already feel my breath getting quicker and I'm adamant the last thing I want to do is confess. It takes another empathetic hold from her for me to reconsider. It takes her foot brushing against my shin for me to appreciate the emotional scarring tying us together.

'Her name's Jess,' I watch myself say. 'We met at a warehouse party in Dalston and I haven't been the same since.'

She closes up my hand by using both of hers. I stare at this strange pink clam for a few minutes before I carry on speaking.

'She has curly blonde hair; it's like nothing you've ever seen before. She has piercings and a great taste in music and she dresses really well.'

'She sounds nice.'

'She is,' I say. 'She's like … it's like she's from a different planet or something.'

'Were you two together before you left?'

'I don't want to get into it,' I say. 'There's nothing really to get into, to be honest.'

'There is, though. There's definitely something. I can see the pain in you, so clearly,' she says. 'I could see it in London. I could see it at Sacré-Cœur and in the park and I can see it now. It's coming from you in waves.'

There's a lead weight resting on my heart.

'Lou, please. I can't do this.'

'You can. Of course you can. Open up. I'm here for you. I want to help you.'

Louise vaporises and is replaced by Jess, and every fragment of her that I'm projecting onto the seat opposite mine is impeccably recreated; every kink of her hair is correct, every eyelash is accounted for.

The weight starts to climb through my body.

'There's …'

'What? There's what?' Louise asks.

The weight almost ruptures my throat when I let it go and unleash a portion of my infinite sadness into her breast.

I say through the pain of it all: 'She loves someone else.'

We sit on the balcony without feeling the cold because of the amount of wine we've put into ourselves. We've moved our chairs closer together and are bundled up under a blanket and looking out at the stars.

There's no need to speak, not any more. We let the night unfold in front of us.

It starts getting late. Louise gets changed in the bedroom into a T-shirt and a small pair of lace pyjama shorts before I'm let back in. She crawls under the duvet while I roll out the sleeping bag and zip myself into its nylon womb.

After ten minutes she asks me to get in next to her and I shuffle up against her and curl around her waist and sniff her hair, once, twice, before we both drift off to sleep.

15

I walk beside the river, passing men selling books bound in ripped sleeves. I dodge tourists bunched around the entrance of Musée d'Orsay and push onwards past elegant ladies drinking espresso and smoking cigarettes. I walk to the river and follow its length until I reach the Grand Palais. I step along the Champs Élysées and up to the Arc de Triomphe.

I stand on its island and let the afternoon traffic circle me.

I pick a direction at random and arrive once more at the feet of the Eiffel Tower. I tussle with a thousand bodies until I'm sitting on the marble steps of the Trocadéro.

I cross the road to the Métro, board a train, and alight at Poissonniers, where I head to the offices of GBL, sink into *Blue Sky Business* and start planning something for the lesson I'm giving later today.

Louise greets me with a brief 'hello' before half-running out of the building, towards the Métro line that will take her away from me and to her class in Marie de Clichy.

I enter the classroom and the same six students wait in the same six seats, all at perfect right-angles. They immediately open their notebooks to the exercise I asked them to finish for homework before I tell them to shut them again.

'No, no, today we're doing something different. First of all, who can tell me what this is?'

I uncap a red marker and draw a crude representation of an office phone onto the board.

Jean-Pierre announces to the room that 'zis iz uuurrggghh telefon.'

'Well done, Jean-Pierre,' I say. 'It's a telephone. Something we use every day, yes? Now, why is it difficult to speak in English on the telephone? Why is this so difficult? Anybody?'

Nobody.

189

'Maybe because *peopletalkveryquicklyonthetelephone*?'

There's a moment of quiet confusion as they decipher what it was that I said. Then they get the joke and smile triumphantly at each other.

I dot a bullet point on the board and write it down. I do the same for other suggestions I elicit from the students themselves: distorted voices, a lack of body language, strange English expressions such as 'hang up' and 'put through' (which I draw an arrow to in green and tag as *phrasal verbs*.) With the board sufficiently inked, I give out a worksheet I made copies of at GBL earlier. I ask them to complete it in pairs and they do so with enthusiasm.

It occurs to me that this job used to be so much more than *professional time-waster*. As there's more room in my head now following the mental irrigation of the other night, it's easier to remember things like that.

The ninety-minute lesson is over before I've even made it through half of my lesson plan. As the students leave they humble me with their words of thanks. I grab a macchiato from the machine before heading down the lift and towards the RER station.

I sense the rumbling of coins in my pocket. A message from Louise: *Lesson = nightmare, day = nightmare, meet you in VDFontenay in 1hr? Ill be at exit station – le girl who is seriously windswept xx ps got a surprise for u!! x.*

She lets the flakes of a croissant catch on the threads of her scarf. I call her name and she starts stroking the front of herself.

'Sorry, I missed lunch. How did you get here so quickly?'

'I made it straight onto a train at La Défense. I'd have made you a sandwich or something if you'd waited.'

She drops the empty wrapper into a litter bin and brushes away more crumbs.

'Maybe next time,' she says, and in a strange way it excites me.

When we reach Marcel's apartment, I slide in the key and

open the door by using the method I've now become accustomed to; shoving into it with my shoulder, just to the right of the lock. I hear Louise sniggering behind me as I fall into the living room.

'It's not too bad. You're all talk, man,' she says as she enters. She wrinkles her nose and looks around for somewhere to sit, settling for the arm of Marcel's sofa.

'Drink?' I ask.

'No thanks.'

'It's horrible in here, isn't it?'

'It's fine! I've seen worse places than this in Paris, believe me.'

'You might think that now, but … well, tell you what: let me give you *le grande tour*.'

I walk her across the infested carpet to the kitchen. I cast an arm over the wretched room behind the curtain as if I were a game show host and say, 'Voila. Le cuisine. C'est magnifique, non?' Rust and dust assault the two of us, standing at the threshold and leaning in. She's putting on a brave face. Her apartment is immaculate, pine-scented, and germfree, whereas this is nothing more than a breeding ground for all kinds of bacteria and mold and airborne plague.

I steer her away from its filth.

'And through 'ere, ah, oui mademoiselle: zis iz where ze magic 'appens.'

I walk her into the bedroom. The floor is covered in bundled-up clothes, rolling tobacco, corks, and spent bottle tops. 'I wasn't expecting company,' I say, but it sounds like a sorry excuse even to my own ears.

'It's charming, in its own way,' she says, and as if meticulously timed the toilet roars with one of its heinous watery discharges. She snaps her head towards what constitutes the *bathroom.*

'I forgot to mention – the toilet is haunted,' I say with a straight face. We hold each other's gaze for a moment before she starts laughing and soon we are holding each other and shaking up and down.

'This place is bloody *awful*.'

'I told you it was but you didn't believe me!'

'It's a good thing I'm such an awesome friend then, isn't it?' She pats the bag on her hip and says, 'Ready for your surprise?'

I'm ushered towards the mattress. I scoop up everything on it and move it all to one side. I sit with my back against the wall and Louise follows suit and sits as close to me as she can get. She removes a few sheets of paper from her bag and arranges them in front of us.

'I think this might be your future,' she says. Each page details a different room in varying parts of Paris, all in decent districts. She's written a name and a time above each address. 'This city is where you belong, as far as I can tell. I'm here to help you move on. It's time you had a fresh start.'

I look at her and smile.

'You really are something else. Do you know that?'

'Of course I do,' she says. 'Truly, I am the greatest.'

We kiss briefly as another hideous death-rattle is thrown up by the toilet.

16

We make our way to the tall stone fountain of Place Monge and walk across jaded cobblestones trodden on by a hundred thousand feet this week alone. The air around us pulsates with life; just what I need after time served in Val de Fontenay.

We slip into a grid of restaurants and bars and regard the place in front of us with growing disbelief, double then triple-checking we have the correct address. It seems too good to be true. Louise thumbs the buzzer marked *Conti* and converses in flawless French with the tinny whisper coming from its grille.

We're summoned through a red door pressed like a rose between the two restaurants that bookend it. We climb a flight of stairs and are grabbed by a woman in a nightdress, who motions for us to enter her home.

We tread through an uneven terrain of newspapers and food cartons and used-up tissues and empty cigarette boxes. Dishes, plates and bowls balance as a precarious tower that reaches from the kitchen sink. Beside the stove is a toilet cubicle, where dead flies stick to spider web nets.

We're escorted to the lounge, where a teenager rests chest-down on the floor and prods at the buttons of a gamepad.

The woman who owns this little piece of purgatory says, 'You teach Antoine English, you pay half.'

The bedroom is about the size of the one I had in Camden but is almost entirely filled with assorted clutter. I take Louise's hand. I tap an *SOS* against her skin. She says something to Mrs Conti in French and turns me towards the exit.

I struggle to hide my relief when we make it back outside and onto the street.

The second and third rooms we visit also don't quite

match up to our expectations. One has no window and large tears in its carpet, exposing stained floorboards and bent nails. The other would have me sharing a room with a Spanish student; two single beds and drawn-out nights of discomfort and indignity and the musk of a strange man invading my nostrils. In each of these places I give Louise a fervent scratch on her hand, telling her without words that I think we should be leaving.

We arrive at the gates of the fourth and final flat at around five o'clock and daylight has already bled away.

'Think positive,' she says.

We're standing outside an ancient four-story building in République. We could see the canal from here if it wasn't so dark.

We get called up to the apartment and are greeted by a handsome man in a striped jumper. He says, 'Hello, my friends! Welcome, I am Guillaume,' as he lets us into his home. He takes us into each room and presents each space with enthusiasm and pride. The bedroom is huge; the bed a gaping landscape of possibility. Guillaume asks me questions about what music I'm into and what job I do and where I like to drink and each of my answers seem to please him.

Louise apologises before answering an incoming call. After hanging up she becomes pensive and quiet. I ask her if she's OK and she responds with, 'What do you think of this place? Pretty nice, isn't it?'

'It's totally cool,' I say.

I walk her back to Guillaume in the living room. I ask him when the room would be available and he says by next week. I also ask if he'd need a deposit to hold it and he says 'No, man, your word would be enough for now,' so I say 'I'll definitely think about it. Can I let you know for sure in the next few days?'

He starts writing down his mobile number as I cup Louise's waist and pull her against me. She tenses up at my touch, almost as if she can tell I'm not being completely sincere.

She's quiet when we leave, perhaps as nervous as I am that we seem to be on our way to Val de Fontenay. The train starts and stops every few seconds, never having a chance to stretch out; much like the thoughts I sometimes have of starting something new.

In the middle of the night Louise stirs against the arm she has commandeered; her head snug in my elbow's bend. The ceiling drops towards me and I recoil away from it. It's nothing more than an illusion carried over from my seeping state but still it makes my muscles cramp. I start to think I might be going mad. To lessen my anxiety I roll onto my side and burrow into Louise's back.

I close myself up around her and implore her with my lips on her skin: *keep me safe*.

17

The next morning, we split a croissant and a pot of coffee and sit facing the street.

'What's your favourite thing about this city?' Louise asks.

'Good question. I've never really given it much thought. Probably the Eiffel Tower, though, if I had to choose.'

'Really? You surprise me,' she says. 'That's quite a cliché. That's not what I was expecting at all. Why'd you choose that?'

'I'm not really sure. I suppose it's because of what it represents. You hear Paris, you think Eiffel Tower. It's the beating heart of the city, isn't it? Or maybe the backbone. Yeah, that'd be more apt. It looks more like a backbone than a heart, doesn't it?'

She says, 'I guess it does. But that's what I mean. *You hear Paris, you think Eiffel Tower*? That automatically makes your choice a bit of a cliché, no?'

'It is what it is,' I say, and take a bite of my half of breakfast. For some reason she laughs and squeezes my fingers. 'Go on then, *Mademoiselle* – put me right. What's *your* favourite thing about Paris?'

'At the moment,' she says, 'it's this café.'

After we've settled the bill I'm taken to a vintage shop in Montmartre where Louise can look at all the pretty dresses and skirts and trinkets, fur, glass, scuffed black leather, and brown suede. I drape each garment she gives me to carry over extended arms and take in the contours of a broken record player as she spools through metres of threaded beads and chain bracelets and lengths of cotton and silk. 'You would look amazing in this!' she says as she dangles a green silk tie out in front of me. It has a rotary sign imprinted onto it in mustard yellow. 'It's very fetching, it's very you, oh yes, oh definitely.'

'I suppose.'

'Believe me; you'd look like a true English gentleman in this. It'd bring out your eyes, too.'

'If you say so,' I say, and she says 'Yes, I *do* say so. It's *gorgeous*. It feels so soft, too. Feel it.' She puts it in my hand, careful not to disturb the things I already have bunched up in my arms.

I watch her getting out of her flats and into a pair of heels. She clip-clops over to another rack of clothes and plucks fresh finds from it. She holds one dress against her front and then another, inspecting her reflection in a full-length mirror with a chipped gold-painted frame.

'What do you think?' she asks.

'I think you should try them both on. Then I think we should go and grab a coffee or something.'

She looks amused. 'Not one for shopping, are we?'

I wearily lift the plethora of vintage up to my chest and say, 'Don't get me wrong, I love clothes. I just hate the process of buying them and getting them home.'

She smiles and rolls her eyes in a way that shows I'm amusing her. She asks the bored-looking assistant something in French and is pointed elsewhere. 'Come,' Louise says, so I follow her to the fitting room, letting the things we've foraged so far drop onto a rocking chair edged in tinsel.

I can't help but listen to her slipping out of her jeans and shirt. I see a suggestion of her through a gap between the curtain and the wall.

'Can you help me with this?' she asks.

'Help you with what?'

She slides the curtain open so I can see the landscape of her back picked at by occasional freckles, a white strap and clasp and strands of auburn hair.

'Zip me up, stud.'

I raise a hand until it hovers a few centimetres away from her. I pinch the zip and the cloth and start to scale her spine as she lifts her hair away from her neck.

She turns around and says, 'What do you think?'

198

The dress grips her and lets her go in all the right places.

'You look …'

'What?' she asks.

I take in air to form new words but no words come. We stand and stare at each other in silence – a grungy fool in stylishly torn jeans and Pavement tee and suit jacket; a twenties starlet in a polka-dot dress whose beauty has robbed me of my ability to speak.

We find an arty wine-bar populated by writers rattling on laptop keys and students sketching nearby trees in pencil. Louise orders a carafe of red with two glasses. She places the bag containing her new dress between our legs. I slide our chairs closer together and hold her against me and stroke her arm as we wait for our drinks to arrive.

'What next?'

'I don't know,' I say. 'What do you want to do?'

'Maybe we could stay here for a while, then you could come to mine and I could cook you something?'

'Sounds great, yeah. What kind of thing were you thinking?'

'Picky are we?' she asks.

'No, not at all. Hook me up with anything as long as there's a nice merlot to go with it.'

'We could talk a bit more about the flat in République, too. I really think it'd be good for you, you know?'

I smile and say nothing. When the waiter delivers our wine I fill my glass to the brim and drain it twice.

Paris hums in front of us; the music of its birds, the syrup of its language. My phone rings and catches us both off-guard. We untangle ourselves from each other so I can retrieve it from the pocket of my jeans.

Jess's name appearing onscreen carbonates my blood.

'Excuse me a second,' I watch myself say as I clamber out of the chair, almost topple over the table and what's left of the wine, and disappear around the nearest corner.

Jess's voice shifts pitch when she says, 'I need you, where

are you, when are you getting to London?'

'Are you OK?'

'*No, I'm not fucking OK!* Why aren't you here, sweetie? I need you, sweetie, babe …'

I lean against the café Louise and I were attending before this intrusion.

'I really, really miss you,' she says.

I collapse into a sitting position and use my feet to grind myself against the wall.

'I miss you too, Jess, but you can't just call me up like this whenever you want to. You can't start laying these things on me. It seemed pretty clear to me before I came here that your choices had been made.'

'But I love you,' she says.

'What?'

'I love you, I *love* you!'

'No, you don't. We've been through this. You love Marcus, you don't love me. Maybe you love the *idea* of me, the escapism or the thrill or something, but no, Jess, you don't love me. You don't *love* love me, not in the same way that I –'

'Marcus has gone,' she says. 'I've kicked him out. I've dumped him. I accept now how wrong I was to choose him over you. It's worked, all right? Your nasty trick has worked. It's time you came home. Please, come home to me. We can work this out, sweetie, I promise.'

Aside from the sound of her voice leaking through the receiver of the phone from hundreds of miles away there is empty French chatter and the rattling of glasses and plates. Nearby there is a twenties starlet looking through bagged vintage trophies and patiently awaiting my return.

'I love you,' Jess says. 'Let me know when you're getting here, OK?'

I tell her I will and the line goes dead to compliment the stopping of my heart.

Louise welcomes me back to our spot with her hand held out but I don't take it. I tell her I'm not feeling well, which isn't a complete lie. She looks concerned when I tell her I need to go home and get some rest.

I kiss her on the cheek and leave her behind with the artists, pretending not to hear her when she starts calling out my name.

I travel to the embassy and walk into the waiting room, fully aware I'm being manipulated. Independence has been made impossible by the puppeteer pulling at my strings. I distantly hear the objections of a young, good-looking Asian couple when I shoulder myself in front of them and if it was possible to speak I would tell them I have no choice. I have no say in anything I'm doing. I would tell them I'm being played but my lips have been glued shut by the girl that operates them.

I sit opposite the clerk and before I can speak he slides me an envelope, saying, 'We still need to know the day of your departure.' I give him a random date and he picks up the envelope, retrieves a piece of paper from, it and scribbles on it with fresh ink. He rubber-stamps the paper and replaces it, seals the envelope, and gives it back to me.

As soon as I've left the embassy, I take out my passport. I turn to the photograph and I look as awful in it as I remember. I'd started to sense a certain distance between my former self and the person I've recently started to become, but this new form of identification confirms I'm the same man now that I ever was and ever will be

(WHO ARE YOU?)

and there'd be no use in telling myself otherwise.

I check my made-up departure date and realise it's in three days' time. Despite the vapid plan I had to board whichever plane or train came first, this is the only date the passport will be valid on. With this, as with everything else in my life, there seems to be no alternative. All of this is inevitable. All roads lead to London and to her.

I'm coming for you, Jess ...

I'm coming because I have to.

I leave the RER train at Val de Fontenay and pick up a couple of bottles from the supermarket on the way home. I get a text from Louise *(are you OK love xxxx)* that I choose to ignore for fear of complicating things further. I enter the flat and drop onto the sofa. I go for the bag of tobacco in my jacket pocket but instead take out a length of green silk and a receipt for twelve euros. She has written on the back of the receipt: *put this on NOW, English Gent! Love Lou xxx.*

I hold the tie in one hand and the receipt in the other and I sit like this for a very long time.

18

I cancel the alarm clock's grating call to arms, ignoring the fact I'm due in La Défense to give an English lesson in an hour. When I wake again I check the time on my phone and find I have six missed calls from GBL and two missed calls from Louise, along with a text: *where are you? What's happening? I'm worried xxxxxxxxx.*

I've heard nothing from Jess since yesterday. I compose a message of my own telling her I'm returning to London in two days.

I roll over and go back to sleep, riled awake a few hours later by frantic knocking – it's Louise, flustered in her white blouse and black skirt and tights and coat marked with dead drops of rain.

'What the hell's going on?' she asks before I have a chance to greet her.

'Not much. I'm ill.'

'That doesn't give you an excuse to ignore me.'

She shoves past me and into the flat and today her smell is orange peel and figs.

'Do you want a drink or something to eat?' I ask.

'You do know you had a class today, right? I volunteered to cover for you but do that again and you're out of a job, and that's coming straight from Michelle. You can't skip lessons whenever you want to. Why didn't you call the office and tell them you were sick?'

She notices the empty bottles and a glass quarter-filled with sticky, clotted red wine.

'You don't look very ill to me,' she says.

I tell her to sit down. I touch her tail bone and she tenses up slightly.

'I can't believe you left me in the bar yesterday. Harsh.'

'I couldn't be sorrier about that,' I say. 'In fact, I'm sorry about a lot of things. I'm sorry about everything. I'm sorry

I've dragged you into all of this.'

'Dragged me into all of what?

'Lou, this isn't who I'm supposed to be.'

WHOAREYOUWHOAREYOUWH–

'I don't understand what you're saying.'

'I'm not supposed to be here.'

She grips my knee and says: 'You need to be a bit clearer.'

'I'm going back.'

This is the moment everything shifts.

'What?' she asks.

I don't know.

'I'm going back to London. I'm going home.'

'When?'

'In a couple of days.'

She eases herself away from me.

'I don't understand.'

'Me neither,' I say. 'Not really. I just know London's the place I need to be.'

'But if you left now, you'd throw away everything. I don't think you've thought this through properly. What about your job? What about the apartment we looked at? You told me you were interested.'

'I was. I *am*, I think. But I've got no choice. All this has been predetermined.'

'That's bullshit!' she says. 'What does that even mean?'

'It is what it is.'

'You're not leaving because of *her,* are you?' she asks.

I'm mute, which speaks volumes. I go to hold her again in any way I can but she's made herself impossible to get at.

'You are so much better than all of that and it's so frustrating how clueless you are.'

I'm unsure of how to respond. She pivots her body towards mine and grabs for my hand with both of hers and starts stroking it.

'You don't need to go backwards,' she tells me. 'You have everything you need here. I wish you could see that. The

204

past is done. We all need to move on; otherwise we'll be trapped in the same place for ever.'

I'm numb.

She says, 'There's more here for you than just a teaching job and an apartment.'

Our eyes meet and I notice then how wide her pupils are, how the gentle green circling them is the same shade as the tie snaking around the bottles and glasses on the table.

'You might think you're doing the right thing, returning to whatever it is you think left behind, but you're not,' she whispers. 'I swear to you, you're not.'

Whichever way I fall my ending will be bloody and empty and lacking any closure but Louise is so real, sitting here beside me and giving me everything she has to offer. She's a beautiful and enchanting get-out clause, a safety net of good intentions, and I could let her catch me if I really wanted her to.

'I think you should leave,' I watch myself say. 'I'm going back to London, and that's pretty much all there is to it.'

19

I place Marcel's keys on the table in the living room with an extra fifty euros of goodwill and a note that says *Merci*. I slam the door closed as if to punctuate my exit and haul my bag though the hallway and down the steps.

I get to the station and use the last of my Métro tickets to hitch a ride to Gard du Nord.

Once it's been fleetingly inspected I slot my emergency passport into the side of my bag and take a seat in the departure lounge, giving my mind a chance to yank its own starter cord and to set itself in motion.

I attempt to halt it with the *STOP* sign but it doesn't work.

I thought I was past all this.

Zero working days ...

The gate leading down to the Eurostar opens and we're ushered through it. I look to the entrance of the station and bid this city a final farewell for the second time.

I see what I think is the shape of Louise carved into a crowd of imminent passengers.

I find my place on the train and before long I'm under the ground and under the sea.

Part Three

NOWHERE

1

She finds me with my bag at my feet and my clothes dripping with rain. She throws herself at me and lets herself get wet. I flare my nostrils into gaping holes to fill them with the smell of her hair. I burn for her. I kiss her with hunger, I kiss her with purpose. She tastes of vodka but that doesn't matter; she's drunk, but who isn't? I'm intoxicated and can't stand up straight. I'm stoned on the weight of her stacked against my body.

I'm overwhelmed by being here at last.

'I missed you so much,' I say as she starts unbuckling my belt.

In the middle of the night I slide over to her and spoon her waist and submerge my face in her hair. I want to stay awake like this until the morning. I want to savour every second I have with her, now she's mine to keep.

It makes no sense but for a second I imagine Louise coming home and catching the two of us in bed together, and for no reason at all I think that for her it'd be like finding Ben in bed with Elizabeth all over again.

2

I make light work of soaping myself down with a bottle of blue gel I assume must've been Marcus'. It feels good to use it to clean her come off with; sort of like a mini-victory.

I take a towel from the airing cupboard, wrap it round my waist, and go to the living room, where I find Jess reading a fashion magazine.

'Morning, Bun,' I say. It seems appropriate to use her pet name now we're living together.

She takes the time to look at me, which is something I'm unashamedly grateful for.

'Where did you get that towel from?' she asks.

'From the special towel place.'

'Oh,' is the only word I need to learn she's mildly annoyed.

'Is there a problem?'

'No. No, there's no problem. I put a towel out specifically for you to use, but it doesn't matter. Sorry to be so fussy. It's just a bit strange having you here, I suppose. It'll take some getting used to.'

'You do want me here though, don't you, Jess?'

At that she gets out of her seat and moves to me.

'Of course I do,' she says. 'It's strange, but in a good way. I don't mean to be bitchy. Give me a bit of time to get my head around things.'

We embrace and I let the towel drop. I feel her smiling as she places her hands on my body. I tell her I love her but she doesn't return the favor. I'm rushing her, I think. Her life is being put through so many changes.

I have to be patient.

She bends over the table and I fuck her so hard that her coffee cup tips over, spilling hot liquid onto carpet.

She abandons me for the office in a tight black skirt and

213

white shirt and she looks incredible. I tell her so but she doesn't seem to hear me.

I take this chance to stake out my new habitat, starting with the kitchen. I look through the window at the hedgerow on the other side of the road and think about all the times I hid behind it, watching Marcus and Jess act out the theatre of their lives in the room I'm now standing naked in. I touch the taps and the sink and the marble worktop and the drawers and cupboards and still can't quite convince myself that I'm actually here, and that this is actually happening.

I unzip my bag and empty it out onto her *(our)* living room floor to start sorting through it. A folded Métro ticket imprinted with ink from the first trip I took from Opera to Rick and Alice's house falls to the carpet.

This is the solitary proof I have that that place even exists at all. Reality seems to have had no part in all that happened in Paris.

Most of my clothes reek of Marcel's flat. In amongst them is something I don't recognise. I pull it through the soiled cotton and stale denim and it emerges like a dead snake from a pile of leaves; the tie that Louise bought from the vintage shop in Montmartre.

I stow it away in the outer pocket of my bag.

I take laundered tea towels from the guts of the washing machine and replace them with my clothes in the hope that on this day I'll get to wash the city away for good.

I waste time in front of the television, absorbing imbecilic daytime fodder. I flick through a few of Jess's magazines and learn the best way to please a man in six steps. I kick around the kitchen and make a pot of tea and roll a smoke of pot and smoke it leaning out the window. The joint tastes bitter and I burn only half of it; the other half I preserve as a gift for my Bunny for when she gets home.

I unscrew a bottle of vodka and shoot a few and when I start buzzing I find myself thinking of glasses of green absinthe necked in a bar in Val de Fontenay and cheap red wine consumed on a balcony overlooking the Panthéon.

I try not to think of the girl I drank so much with in Paris but this is proving difficult.

I pass time by turning on my laptop and opening the *Jess #1* document with the intention of adding to what I've written so far (*I dream of you each night ... fuck*). After an hour spent redrafting I've only managed to transform the full-stop into an exclamation mark.

I'm unsure whether it's from all the alcohol or from the shock to the system of being shunted from one place to another in the name of love but something is off, something doesn't feel quite right. I'm tired and confused and discombobulated.

Before making lunch I take the tie out of my bag and hang it up on my side of the wardrobe.

3

I deliberate over how I should break the news to him. I already have an idea of what his reaction will be. I'm sure he'll give me the same sort of talking to as when I barely passed my English degree and decided to travel Italy for the summer. I'm certain that, from his point of view, my seemingly directionless life path is something to be concerned about, possibly even something to be pitied.

He doesn't know my path in life has taken me to where I've always wanted to be – into the arms of the girl I love.

He answers the call and I hesitate briefly before saying: 'Hi, Dad.'

'Hey, son! How are you? How's Paris?'

I'm much too tired to fabricate anything.

'I'm not in Paris, actually. I'm in London.'

There's a moment of silence, then: 'London?'

'Yeah, it didn't work out over there. But everything's fine now. I'm living in a great house with a great girl, and –'

'What girl?' he asks.

'Just some girl I know.'

'*Just some girl you know?* You can't keep messing about like this. You want to get some roots down. How old are you now, thirty?'

'Twenty-eight.'

'Yeah, well, almost thirty then. Jesus Christ, when will you *grow up*? Where's your secure job, your wife? Where are my grandkids? Flittering around the way you've been doing is for the young and you're not that young any more, are you?'

'Yeah, I know, but –'

'I suppose you want me to bring all your boxes out of the basement? I told you I had a bad back. Getting them down there in the first place was difficult enough.'

'Sorry, but at least I'm happy now. This is what I really

want –'

'Oh, and Paris wasn't? That's not what you told me when I came over. You told me you couldn't wait to get there. You said you had everything sorted out for when you arrived. Was that a lie?'

'It wasn't a lie, not exactly. I honestly thought I could've had a better life in Paris. I was wrong, I admit it. I made a mistake. But at least I did something. At least it was an adventure,' I tell him. 'What have you done with your life up to now to match that?'

'Wait, who do you think you are, exactly?' he says, his voice getting louder.

WHOAREYOUWHOAREYOUWHO –

'Who are you to take the high ground with me? All *you've* ever done is fuck things up,' he says. 'You're a complete waste of space, son. You're a total disappointment.'

I hold the phone tighter, concerned I'm about to cry. I wish he'd show his support, just once. I wish he would've been there to consult during all the more difficult periods of my life, but he's never been there for me – no one ever has. His one concern has only ever been where the next drink's coming from. The first time I saw him drunk was when I was only six years old. I'll never forget it. He called me over to sit on his lap and watch television with him. He gripped me too forcefully and when I turned to him to say he was hurting, his alcohol breath stopped the words from leaving my lips. Since then I've never really trusted him. I always knew there were two sides to his personality – one side vicious, the other barely tolerable, and I've always been afraid of which one I'd get whenever I've spoken to him.

I tell him after a period of reflection, 'The mistakes I've made in life have led me to some truly wonderful things. Not just to the bottom of the bottle, I mean. I'm so glad I'm not you. You're the one who should be ashamed, not me.'

'*What* did you say, you little prick?' he shouts, and I have to hold the phone away from my ear.

'You heard,' I reply, but meekly.

218

'That's it – I've had enough of this, enough of you,' he says. 'I'm not listening to this shit any more.'

I steady my nerve by looking at the clock and picturing Jess walking through the door in a couple of hours.

'Things are coming together for me now,' I tell him. 'I think I'll be OK from now on. And I'll be fine without you, if that's how you want things to be.'

I hear him exhaling on the other end of the line. If I concentrate I can smell the alcohol on his breath, even from this distance.

'Son?' he says. 'Don't call me again until you've sorted your life out.'

He puts the phone down and the click the receiver makes is the last thing I'll hear from him for the next six months.

4

I walk to Stables Market then instantly regret it as its lanes are blocked by chatty tourists and drug dealers and I'm not in the mood for either. I escape into a café and peer through the bobbing heads of Spanish holidaymakers to catch a glimpse of the canal as I sip at my latte.

London's an ex-girlfriend I need to make friends with.

Cup down, bill paid, I leave the café and walk the canal and under its bridges. I come across the Camden reggae busker plucking the strings of his guitar and informing the world that *no woman, no cry,* and I drop a pound coin into his hat because I have to agree with the sentiment.

I start climbing Primrose Hill. I get to the top and hurt all over from alcohol and cigarettes and all other atrocities I've been putting my body through in the name of love. I stand with my back to the city before rotating slowly to take it all in and from here I can pick out St. Paul's and Canary Wharf and the London Eye and, for my sins, the Shard.

I want to get the impression I'm being welcomed back by all the concrete and glass.

I watch a jogger skimming the outskirts of the green field below and find myself not wanting to check out the curve of her buttocks or the schizophrenic vibrations of her breasts in motion, for now I have Jess. I can think of no finer definition of love than that.

I scramble down the hill's cheek and head to my former flat to check in with Jack. A stranger lets me into the building and at the front door I go for the key in my jacket pocket but there is no key, so I knock three times and wait.

Dom answers in a pair of shiny red shorts and a shirt which I think might be a replica of a Spanish football team's. The first thing he says is: 'I don't believe it! What's going on? Why are you here?'

'It's a long story, mate. Is Jack home?'

'He's in the kitchen,' he says, opening the door to let me past.

The first thing I notice is how neat the hallway is. All our old shoes have been moved. All the pictures on the walls have been taken down.

I find my former housemate standing at the stove wearing nothing but his underwear and cooking what looks like a Spanish omelette (to compliment the clothes that Dom's wearing, perhaps, because Jack always was one for coordinating things.) Relentless thumping techno escapes from a stereo balanced precariously on the windowsill. The smell of ingredients and the blaring din of the terrible electronic music make the air in here seem dense.

'*JACK!*'

He turns around with the spatula in his hand.

'Holy shit, it's you!' he says. He wipes his hand clean and embraces me, forcing all the air out of my lungs.

'What gives?' he asks.

'I'm back.'

'Yeah, I can see your back, but why? What happened to Paris?'

'It didn't work out.'

'*It didn't work out?* You were only gone for a couple of weeks!'

'Yeah, but believe me: lots happened in those few weeks. I had my passport stolen, for one thing. And I ended up living in this complete shithole in the armpit of nowhere.'

'God, misery just kind of follows you around, doesn't it?' he says, and I shrug resignedly. 'How did you get back to London without a passport?'

'With great difficulty,' I say. 'I had to apply for a temporary one. They tore the fucker up in front of me at King's Cross. It wasn't cheap, either. I've spent a fortune in the last month or so.'

'That's a shame,' he says. 'Ever-so-slightly funny, but a shame nonetheless.'

He resumes stirring the peppers and onions and mushrooms.

'It's not all bad,' I tell him. 'I finally got together with Jess. I'm actually living with her now.'

'Jess? Who's she?'

'You know; the one I was so fucked up about, remember? Around the time that …'

I was about to say *around the time that Liu dumped you* but it's a period I doubt either of us would like to reflect on.

'You can say it. There's no problem. She's the one you told me about after Liu left. Yeah, I remember her now. I'm glad things are working out for you. Pity about Paris, though.'

'Yeah, well, everything happens for a reason I suppose.'

At that moment, Dom walks into the kitchen and kisses Jack on the lips.

'You know what, mate?' Jack says, 'I'm gonna have to agree with you there.'

We each balance plates and pick at the omelette Jack made. He eats with Dom's naked feet held in his lap.

'So, this Jess girl – what is it that makes this one so very special?' Jack asks.

'I dunno,' I say. 'I love her?'

They look at one another then burst out laughing.

'You are so *gay*!' Dom says.

I shovel more of the omelette into my mouth; an action now made difficult by the smile I'm wearing.

'Still screaming in the middle of the night, Dom?' I ask.

'Only when I make him,' Jack says, and nudges his lover.

'This is so weird. As if you two are an item. What happened?'

'*Love*,' they say together, and now we're all laughing, and life is good (I think).

I ask to get into my old room, just in case I left behind anything I can now move across to Jess's place.

223

I'm surprised by all the boxes in here – magazines and records and clothes. Jack says, 'I forgot to mention – one of Dom's friends is moving in on Tuesday. That's all his stuff.'

I'm wounded I could be so easily replaced.

'That was fast,' I say.

'Hey, you know what Ahmed's like: one in, one out. We reckoned it'd be better if it was someone we knew moving in. I'd hate to get home one day and find a stranger living here, that'd be *terrible*.'

Dom enters and wraps an arm around Jack's shoulders.

'Why're my ears burning?' Dom asks.

'I dunno,' Jack says, 'too much gel?'

'Oh, *fuck off*. What do you call that fucking style of yours?'

Jack runs a hand through his hair and says, 'Hey, don't pretend you don't like what I've got going on up here. This is years of hard work, my friend.'

'Yeah,' Dom replies, 'and it's hard work having to look at it all day, too.'

Jack smiles tightly.

Dom says, 'Ah, I'm only joking, mate. Your hair's pretty hot. Actually, it might be your best feature.

Jack says, 'Piss off, gel-head,' rests a hand on Dom's and shows him teeth. When they look at me again they're both grinning. I want to say something but can't find the words. I feel awkward. They're in exclusive company now; a private society I'm not a member of.

'We'll leave you to it then,' Jack says. 'Let us know if you turn up any bodies.'

They walk down the hall and into the kitchen. Before they close the door and restart the techno music I hear Jack saying: 'Seriously, Dom – you do like my hair like this, don't you?'

I make a languid effort to dig through the boxes but give up after a few minutes. I know there's nothing in this room that belongs to me. I just wanted to see it again.

Jack comes back into the room holding an envelope.

'By the way, someone left this for you,' he says. I take it from him and he returns to Dom.

I move some of the boxes from the bed and sit down. The envelope has my name printed onto it. There's no address to compliment it, meaning it was delivered in person.

I open the envelope and slide out a torn-out sheet of notepad paper.

This is what it says:

To my everything,

Firstly, I want you to know I'm sorry. If I came on too strongly or if I did anything to anger you, I apologise.

Secondly, I want you to know I love you. It's true. I've loved you for a long, long time. I love everything about you. The desire I have for you to be happy far outweighs any sort of significance I'd ever place on my own wellbeing. I would do anything for you. I would do anything to give you happiness.

This love is like a slow death. It hurts so much that I want my life to end, simply to put a stop to the pain I have to endure every single day, every single moment. It's not your fault, not really, but what you're doing to me is the very worst thing one person can do to another. That is, to reject the love of someone you mean the world to. You are locked inside my heart. I'm resigned to this fact, which is the reason why I want you to be with Louise. This may seem confusing, but let me explain. I know how much you love her. When we sat together in The Water Poet, the love you had for her was all over your face. Who am I to stand in the way of that? Maybe that's why you reacted the way you did when I came back to your flat. Maybe that's why you threw me out. I ask myself: was this drastic response due to disappointment, heartache, confusion? I don't need to know the answer. It's not important. What is important is this: you'll always be my everything. In time, I hope you can allow yourself to appreciate this simple truth.

I wish you infinite amounts of happiness with Louise. Go to her. Tell her how you feel. I hope she can give you not only what you want, but also what you need; just as I would. Make the most of what the two of you share.

God bless and good luck. I'll help you in any way I can. All my love and heart and soul,

Elizabeth xxx

P.S. If you ever change your mind, I'll be waiting.

I read and re-read and re-read the letter and consider how I acted when I threw her out of here like she was nothing. I think about Louise telling me how she found Elizabeth and Ben in bed together.

I would do anything for you. I would do anything to give you happiness ...

My mind convulses at thoughts of what Elizabeth must've done to convince Ben to sleep with her. I can only assume a lot of alcohol was involved.

I'll help you in any way I can ...

I feel sick. I drop the letter into the wastepaper bin. I curse Elizabeth's name because I know that, for a while at least, I'm going to be haunted by the words she wrote. I truly am a monster. I have to wonder where it is my capacity to be decent may have gone. What have I achieved by being so abhorrent to Elizabeth, to Emily, to all the others I've wronged since abandoning Catherine in Sicily?

I glance around the room and follow the poltergeists of girls gone by; seventeen lovers bedded, and to what avail?

Elizabeth, what were you thinking?

I go to the kitchen, then to the living room, but Jack and Dom are nowhere to be found. I hear them talking in their bedroom and decide I should show my gratitude for lunch by doing the honourable thing of leaving them to each other.

I start making my way home.

Home!

That word feels so good when I say it out loud.

I've been inspired by Jack and Dom to take out a wok and chop a few vegetables and by the time Jess gets home I'm halfway done with making her an omelette.

'Hey Bunny, how are you? Did you have a good day?'

She doesn't say anything. She just steps into the bathroom.

I slop the mess onto two plates, place them on the coffee table, and wait for her to join me on the sofa. She enters shortly afterwards dressed in a fluffy pink bathrobe.

'I've made you a delicious meal,' I say. 'Voila.'

She sits on the floor in front of her plate. One of her breasts falls out of her gown and I watch it like a predator before she notices and tucks it back in. I slide from the sofa to sit next to her and she shuffles away to give the two of us more room.

'Where's the cutlery?' she asks.

'Shit, yeah, sorry. Let me –'

She sighs heavily before standing up and going to the kitchen. I look at her dish and at the steam rising from it and think about what it is I must've done to upset her.

She returns with a handful of metal and says: 'If you're going to use the wok that way, can you *please* fill it with hot water afterwards? Otherwise the egg and the vegetables will all get stuck to it and it'll get ruined.'

She starts digging through the food with her fork.

'What've you been up to today?' she asks.

'Lots of things, Bun. I've unpacked. I've gone for a walk. I've been to see Jack. I've made you this incredible meal. I've done lots.'

'Have you started looking for a job yet? Because I can't pay the rent on my own.'

'Really? I thought your parents owned this place …'

'They do,' she says. 'I still have to pay them, though. I'm not a charity case. It works out as six hundred a month each.

227

Quite cheap for where we are.'

'Six hundred a month ...' I say, with anxiety clogging up my throat. 'That should be fine.'

She's stirring the food. She hasn't eaten any of it yet.

'It's one of the reasons I wanted you to move in straight away.'

'Of course,' I say, chewing but not tasting.

We finish the meal without speaking further. She leaves the living room and walks into our bedroom.

I go to her an hour later (once I've scrubbed all the dishes and the wok thoroughly) and find her reading her e-mails in bed. I get under the covers with her. I prod her with my erection and she stirs uneasily against it.

She takes me in her hand and rubs me quickly, up and down, until I ejaculate all over myself. She wipes herself clean with a couple of tissues, passes me the box, turns away, brings her knees up to her chest, and closes her eyes

5

I have an appointment with a recruitment agency in East London at 3 p.m. but before that I decide to go to the Barbican to take in a spot of culture. There's something called a *Rain Room* installed in one of the galleries. I head to where the guide dictates and find myself at the end of a long queue.

The people in front are all chatting in French and it starts to annoy me so I put on my headphones to listen to some Hooded Fang.

The leaflet I picked up in the lobby explains that rain falls in the *Rain Room* but it's impossible to get wet because of sensors in the ceiling. I'm a wretch when I think it'll be the first time in a long time that rain hasn't fallen on me.

The queue dissolves until at last I'm at the front of it. The guide says, 'When you're ready, head through. You won't get wet.' I watch the French group walking slack-jawed through the cavern of falling water. They remain dry even when they wave their arms around. 'Off you go,' the guide says, as if I'm holding everybody else up.

I take a step into the room and flinch when I feel ice-cold water falling onto my hair.

'Wait,' the guide says. 'Come back.' She looks confused. 'Try again,' so I do, I take a large stride into the *Rain Room* but jump back out when I get covered by water.

The guide wrinkles her nose. She tries it out for herself and gets four, five, six, seven, ten feet into the room without getting wet.

'One more time,' she says. I decide to move faster, thinking my pace must be the problem. I run to where she's standing and get drenched by freezing water. I rush straight out again.

The guide looks at me as if I'm some sort of scientific anomaly.

'That's strange,' she says. I stand shivering and staring at her. 'That's über weird.'

She joins me at the entrance. I stay with her for a few minutes. She radios for help and a hipster moustache with a nametag dangling from his belt walks straight to us from the other side of the Rain Room without an issue.

'Doug, check this out,' the guide says. 'Sir, could you go one more time?'

I walk in and get a lot wetter. Doug tightens up his face in confusion. He sweeps an arm through the air and it remains dry. I do the same and mine gets soaked.

I decide to give up on the Rain Room. It's agitated me to the point that I feel like lashing out at Hipster Nametag. I ask the guide where the toilets are to dry off with a few paper towels.

I leave the Barbican and walk in the direction of the recruitment agency, my teeth rattling together like a snare drum roll.

At the agency, I'm shown to a computer and given fifteen minutes to wrestle with dummy spreadsheets. I can't concentrate. Not so long ago, I was teaching higher-ups in a French bank all about these strange diagrams of numbers and lines.

The woman in charge of my sorry bones waddles over and relieves me of my headphones and clipboard. I'm shown to an area of brown and grey and beige and seats with their stuffing spilling out. I wait here in this God-forsaken space for what feels like for ever before she calls me over and sits me at her desk.

She scrolls through information on her monitor, saying, 'There's a pretty cushy position here working for British Utilities … very   nice   site,   that … very   nice…data entry … customer service … working as a team …'

'Yep, yeah, sounds great.'

Sounds terrible, but the rent's six hundred pounds a month. Do it for love, do it for Jess.

'When can I start?' I ask.

'How does tomorrow sound?'

Sounds terrible, but the rent's six hundred pounds a month. Do it for love. Do it for Jess.

'Sounds great,' I say, and I'm given an address.

'They'll be expecting you at eight-thirty tomorrow morning, so –'

'– So don't be late?'

She nods.

'No problem.'

I give her my bank account details and sign something I don't bother reading.

All parts of me spasm in the lift on the way down to the lobby.

I walk into the kitchen with the intention of toasting a few slices of bread for lunch and find a message stuck to the fridge. It reads: *Sorry sweetie, sleeping at a friend's place tonight – she's having man-trouble and needs cheering up (muchos drama). Popped home earlier to pick up some stuff but you weren't here. Hope you got a cool job! See you xoxoxox*

I peel off the note and study it. It seems affectionate enough but I'm bothered by it somehow. *Relax*, I tell myself. *She's chosen you. You are the one she wants.*

I unscrew the bottle of rum I bought on the way home and tip a few measures of it into a glass.

Late afternoon limps into early evening. My brain has a mind of its own. It conjures thoughts of Jess in the arms of anonymous shadows that are all-tongue or all-cock. They're smearing themselves over her naked skin. I see her writhing around and shuddering with orgasm after orgasm after orgasm, each stronger and more potent than the last, and there is no man trouble, oh no, not where she's gone. I decide it's the lack of details in the note that's most alarming – things like her exact location and the name of who she's staying with.

Our bed is covered in the clothes she discarded before deciding on the outfit that would take her to wherever she was going. I pick them up and press them against my face before letting them drop to my feet.

I climb under the duvet, thinking: *Where are you, Bunny Rabbit?*

Je ne comprends pas.

I wake in the middle of the night, distraught she hasn't come home early.

I open the lid of my laptop and my eyes sting from the screen's glare. I double-click on the *Jess #1* document. I slide a blade across the sack of shit that's started to accumulate in my head since reading the note she left

(GET A GRIP!)

and it all spills out of me and onto the white chasm of the page: the doubt, the confusion, the want. I write questions I'd never vocalise, questions like *where are you* and *what are you   doing*   and   *who   am   I (WHOAREYOUWHOAREYOUWHOAREYOU) in all of this?*

I let my fingers spell out all my grief, making no alterations to typos or spelling mistakes. I save over the old version of the file after deleting the first line (*I dream of you each night*) because that statement isn't true, not any more. Recently, I only have terrible and violent nightmares in which my skull is caved in or I'm held under water to drown.

She's with a friend. The note says so. There's nothing wrong with that, is there?

I close the laptop and pour the last of the bottle of rum into my aching throat.

6

Having left a half-eaten bowl of cornflakes in the sink, I fall onto a bus that takes me towards the offices of British Utilities; towards what will be by all accounts *the new me*. There's nowhere to sit so I twist a death grip around one of the metal poles and sway with the motion of the morning rush.

I'm nauseous for a number of reasons.

After leaving the bus I'm swept away on an ocean of vacant husks, all trussed up in shirts and ties and all on the same voyage into plains of nothingness. A woman clicks her tongue and when I turn to her to ask what's wrong she barges past and jogs into the caféteria.

I'm reminded of Paris and La Défense. This may be a different city but the principals of killing time remain the same.

As we near the place we are obliged to inhabit for the next eight hours, we become surrounded by flat-packed offices and dead and rotted flowers. I doubt the architect who made the plans that these buildings were built from had much ambition. I can't help comparing the façade ahead of me with that of Notre Dame.

I wonder to myself whether or not anyone actually wants to be here as we bottleneck at the entrance of a red-bricked tomb and inch into the anus of another working day.

I give my name to the receptionist and she offers me a laminated badge that says *TEMP* on it (which I hope is a promise). She indicates a room at the end of the corridor and tells me my line-manager should be waiting for me there.

I walk through the double doors and encounter only rows of ugly drones tapping onto keyboards and speaking into telephone receivers. Several drops of urine roll down my leg as I'm too hungover to retain full control of my bladder. I leave the office behind to locate the gents, where I urinate and scream into balled-up tissues.

I wash my hands next to a balding man with a nametag clipped onto his breast pocket. I notice a ketchup stain on the front of his shirt but don't see why I should point it out to him. My own shirt still stinks of the body odour I expended during the ill-fated interview I had in Paris. I splash my armpits with hot water and smear them with hand soap in an attempt to shift this stench of failure.

I press a hand into the hand of my reflection and lock eyes with myself.

I whisper: *everything is going to be OK.*

I slap the side of my face and wait for the red handprint to dissolve before leaving the toilet.

I touch the phone in my pocket.

(Jess, who were you with last night?)

This time the line-manager is waiting for me when I walk back into the office. She greets me on full-beam and introduces herself as Kate Wordsworth. I follow her to the space she has cleared for me. A computer sits and waits to be fed. Kate Wordsworth logs me into it and opens a program from the desktop. She shows me how to transfer numbers onto the computer through the simple act of manipulating the mouse and striking appropriate keys.

It's a *revelation.*

After I've demonstrated I can recall each step she's walked me through, she retreats to the fishbowl office in the corner of the room. I look to my left and right and think about introducing myself to the bags of blood on either side but decide against it when I conclude we'd most likely have nothing in common anyway.

I start inputting numbers and three hours later I check my watch and only ten minutes have gone by.

Each keystroke makes this sound: *Jess, Jess, Jess-Jess, Jess-Jess-Jess, Jess, Jess, Jess.*

I let myself into the house and discover my girlfriend's not yet home. I stagger to the bed, sprawl over the humps of its bundled-up duvet and drop into a deep sleep in a matter of seconds.

I'm woken later by her tugging on my leg.

'*Helloooooo?*'

I pivot my head on a sore neck.

'Hey,' I say.

'Are you all right? What happened?'

'Work happened.'

'Ah yes,' she says. 'You're not used to real work are you, Mr TEFL teacher?'

She laughs and the sound of it clears away some of the dirt in my head. She seems happy and buoyant and relaxed and, God, maybe there really was no reason to feel so uneasy.

Maybe everything's fine after all.

'Take a shower,' she says. 'You smell.'

I crawl from the bed and walk to the bathroom to let hot water sock me awake. I towel myself dry and put on a pair of shorts and a Joy Division T-shirt.

I find Jess barefooted in the living room with her nose in a book. An empty plate rests on the coffee table. I kneel in front of her and cup her foot. I go to kiss her toes but she stops me and says, 'Hey, not while I'm reading.'

'Where were you last night?' I ask, the question falling out of me.

She looks at me and feigns surprise.

'I was at a friend's house. Didn't you get my message?'

'Which friend?'

Why am I pushing these buttons?

'Why's that important?'

'I'd just like to know.'

'You don't trust me?'

'No, no, it's not that, it's just –'

'Just what?'

She drops the book onto the floor without marking her place.

'It's nothing,' I say.

'No, there's obviously *something* bothering you, so what is it? Where do *you* think I went last night?'

'Jess, I –'

'Seriously, where?'

'Forget it. Sorry I asked.'

'I went to Kirstin's, if you must know. Her boyfriend's been cheating on her. She confronted him about it and he punched her in the stomach. I went to Clapham to stay with her, to help her get through it. Is that OK? Am I forgiven?'

'Jess, I'm so sorry. I didn't mean anything by it –'

She picks up her book to carry on reading, the conversation over as far as she's concerned. I try holding her feet again but she kicks me away. I tell her I love her but she says nothing back.

I go to bed alone and stay awake for hours until I feel her get in next to me. I roll over to face her.

I sniff her hair from afar and tonight it's tea tree shampoo and cigarette smoke.

7

I'm fully aware how unprofessional it is to throw a pencil across the room just so I can get out of my chair to retrieve it. I consume a gallon of coffee and several chocolate bars from the vending machines. I daydream about the point of the Eiffel Tower disappearing into a dense mist and the glass of the pyramid of the Louvre reflecting sunlight onto at all the tourists.

This job is a simple case of muscle memory. I'm starting to realise that teaching was far from the worst-case scenario. I never thought I'd miss the sensation of standing in front of a group of people and dictating their every move; perhaps this is the same sort of perverse enjoyment Jess gets from our relationship.

I finish allocates to my left and stack them on my right but the left-hand pile is frequently replenished. There's no motivation to work well, not here. At least with teaching there was the delusion of progress.

I almost break the fragile glass of the fire alarm when I go for my seventh toilet break of the morning. I manage to find some restraint by imagining how pissed off Jess would be if I lost this job and couldn't find the rent money to pay her with.

If I don't sharpen up soon then everything I've been through to get to this point will mean absolutely nothing.

In pairs, I think, *talk about all the reasons why I should stick this out.*

I play chicken with myself by pressing a stapler onto my thumb, up to the point that it nearly punctures my skin. I empty out a box of paperclips so I can count them out and put them back again.

I think to myself: *do it for love.*

Do it for JESS.

I'm so bored that I think I might be haemorrhaging important parts of my humanity, but I reckon it's better to be an empty drone and paired off than full of life and lonely.

I find Jess in the living room sitting with her laptop open. I walk into the bedroom to avoid breaking her concentration. It's chaotic in here. I haven't yet found a place for most of my things but I'm too exhausted to attempt that now.

I go to my girlfriend to see if I can tempt her from her work. I can't decide whether or not this is a selfish thing for me to be doing.

'Fancy a coffee?' I ask.

'Yeah, whatever,' she says, as if I've pissed her off. Then: 'Sorry, sweetie. Anthony's given me all this work to do for tomorrow and I'm really stressed.' She turns away from the screen of the laptop and looks at me for the first time today. 'A coffee would be great, thanks. There's instant in the cupboard and soya milk in the fridge.'

I think about saying *Who needs Anthony or deadlines or projects or applications or spreadsheets, baby, when we have each other?* but I fear doing so would anger her.

I prepare the drink, hold the cup in front of her, and wait for her to finish typing. When she's ready she slides a few papers away to make room for it.

I put the coffee down and some of it splashes onto one of her documents. She looks at it with wide eyes and says, 'Oh fuck, oh shit, you can't be fucking *serious!*'

She rushes to the kitchen for a wet sponge which she smears onto the stain, only making it worse.

She shuts the lid of her computer and holds stacks of papers against her breasts. She strides angrily to the bedroom and slams the door, leaving her coffee behind to get cold.

I switch on the television, muting it in an attempt to overhear the contents of a telephone call that Jess takes a few minutes later.

Perhaps she's confiding in her good friend Kirstin about how much of a liability I am, or perhaps she's speaking to someone she doesn't want me knowing about.

I'm certain going in to see her for an explanation would

be the wrong thing to do so instead I walk to the kitchen for a glass of vodka and stand at the sink, wondering what it is I'm doing here.

8

We sit and drink from glasses of black ale, conversation an element we can only dream of discovering. Every so often a member of the group straightens up as if they want to say something but instead they fill the void with beer or a pinch of crisps from the packet on the table.

When I can't take the tension any more I say, 'Have you all worked at British Utilities long?' and they look at each other panicked by the question, as if I'm interrogating them about a crime they've committed.

Madame Veiny Head (the leader of the group) speaks for them all when she says: 'Too long.'

We finish our drinks so I buy another round. It costs over thirty pounds but I don't care; it's the only way I can convince them all to stay.

Three of them are drunk already and the other two are halfway there.

I ease fresh glasses from the tray. I'm stared at reverently and with trepidation as I lift the first sambuca to my chin and tell my captivated audience to follow my lead. The shots are raised and swallowed once I've proclaimed an ironic toast to British Utilities.

I hand each of them their red wine chasers and explain that this was all I used to drink when I lived in Paris, expecting a reaction of some sort but getting nothing. I deliberate over whether I should also talk about my predicaments at home, about how I think Jess has started to turn on me, but if it isn't tales of billing enquiries or misread metres or faulty valves they don't seem to be interested.

I turn to Madame Veiny Head and say, 'Tell me something about yourself,' focusing on the yellowing patches of skin at her temples and the slender blue tubes beyond.

She slurs: 'What do you want to know?'

'Something. *Anything*. What do you like doing outside

work?'

She looks at me as if this is an alien concept.

'Do you read?' I ask. 'Do you watch films? Do you exercise? Do you knit? Do you write? Do you paint? Do you cook? Do you –'

'I like long walks, she says. 'Long, lovely walks … rambling and that.'

I swallow quickly.

'There you go! That's something! Tell me more. Where do you like to ramble?'

'Anywhere,' she says. 'I like the countryside, I suppose.'

'Yeah, the countryside's brilliant. Have you been rambling recently? What's you're all-time favourite rambling spot?'

She points her half-opened eyelids in my general direction and says, 'Why are you so interested in me? Why are you asking all these questions?'

'Because I want to learn more about you,' I say, but what I think is: *because I want to put off going back to Jess's place for as long as I possibly can.*

I stare into her eyes and in them I see confusion, distrust, and fatigue.

Once we've left this pub behind, I'll tell her how incredible I think she is and that she's being wasted working for British Utilities. I'll confide in her that the best thing the two of us could do would be to fall into her car, to drive into the evening stream of traffic, to steer into the current of steel and lose ourselves. I'll paint her pictures of new lives blossoming – marriage and children, a house in the countryside, land to work, soil to tend to, crops to grow, peel, and eat, with London and Paris and the rest of civilisation only existing as foggy, unfathomable memories. I'll talk her through our kinship, culminating in the two of us resting on the planes of a feather bed; flesh sag, decrepit skin, moles and warts and liver spots as dots to join with thumb nail blades, yellowing tongues, and the business ends of walking sticks.

I'll beg her to think things through as she buckles up her

seatbelt. I'll entreat her to see things my way. I'll breathe onto the glass of her windscreen and write *I HEART YOU* into the pool of my steam.

I'll ride the bus home and try not to hate every moment of my journey there.

So it goes.

I take a few deep breaths before sliding my key into door. Jess walks into the hallway holding a bottle of polish and a duster.

She says, 'Where've you been?'

'Out … out with the people from work … for a few … few Friday drinks …'

We're both caught off-guard by a tear that spills out of me.

'What's the matter?'

I shake my head and sniff a fraction of the sadness back into my head.

'Come here,' she says, and once she's put the cleaning products onto the ground, I go to her. I say into the side of her head: 'I love you, Bunny. I love you so much.'

'What's up? Did something happen at work?'

'No, work's fine. I'll have the rent for you by the end of the month.'

'Shush, don't worry about that for now. It's OK, babe, I'm here, Jess is here, aw come on sweetie, it's all right, it's all right …'

I tremble against her and wonder why everything has been so hard since I got back from Paris. She holds me out at arms-length and studies me. I must look a mess because her expression is one of almost awe, and not in a good way.

'Tell you what – let's have a party or something tomorrow. We should celebrate your homecoming. You did so well getting a job so quickly, too. Yeah, let's have a party. Let's cut loose! How does that sound?'

I'd like to tell her that all I want is for the rest of the world to be destroyed and for us to be its two remaining survivors.

What I manage is, 'Sounds good.'

Once I've calmed down, I decide to take this opportunity to get her into the bedroom. I grip the end of her T-shirt and lift it until it reaches her ribs. She carries on removing it as I unbutton my trousers and step out of them. I use the wall for balance as I slip off my socks and boxer shorts. I step towards her and find her lips with mine but hers feel locked together. I run my tongue over them and they're dry and tasteless. I fiddle with the clasp of her bra but I'm clumsy and drunk and reeling from the outpour I subjected her to in the hall. She reaches behind and removes it herself. Her breasts are pert and pink. Her nipples are indented discs of ribbed red silk that I pinch and stroke until swollen and erect. I ease her out of her knickers and poke around inside her with my finger. I lick her neck but she doesn't get wet. I slot the same hand into her mouth and smother it with sugary saliva. I return it to her sex, pass it through her pubic hair, and bury two fingers, causing her to moan into my chest. I face her away from me. I lift her leg and probe with my penis until it slides inside her.

I focus on the curve of her behind until I come.

She goes to the bathroom to clean herself off. I let myself drift and when I open my eyes again I find she's no longer lying next to me.

The sound of the television bleeds through the walls but I'm too ashamed to go and sit with her.

9

I'm hanging badly but the punch won't mix itself so in goes the gin and in goes the vodka. I don't want to dwell on where Jess might be so in goes the whiskey and in goes the rum. She said Kirstin needed her again so in goes the wine. She seemed so sharp with me when she told me where she was going, as if daring me to ask her anything about it, so in goes the tequila and a fistful of limes. I'm preparing the house by myself for a party being thrown in my honour but I'm sure everything's fine. It has to be.

In goes the worry and in goes the pain.

I was tempted to follow her to see where she was going but then who would make the punch?

Please God, please may it all be true; please may Kirstin be the victim of her half-crazed violent ex ...

Out comes a glassful that I knock straight back. It needs more of *everything.*

I leave the house and walk to the shops in Kentish Town as a distraction more than anything else. I find a vintage shop filled with battered blazers and loafers and shirts and broken umbrellas. I go straight for the suit jackets as mine's started to wear thin. I want to look as good as I can for the party tonight, for my sake as well as Jess's. It'll be the first time she's displayed me in public in front of her friends, so I'll need to look as good as (if not better than) Marcus ever looked.

The first jacket I test has sleeves that are frayed and the second is far too large and makes me look ill. The third I button up and inspect in the mirror and it hangs pretty well. It accentuates the width of my shoulders and the tapering of my waste in a way I think Jess will appreciate. I twist and open my arms and bend my elbows to see how it shifts and imagine the way I should be standing when Jess's friends arrive at the party.

A middle-aged woman with great legs emerges from behind the curtain of the changing room and I'm instantly returned to the shop in Montmartre and the moment Louise stepped out in the polka-dot dress.

I miss her more and more each day.

(In goes the longing and in goes the want.)

At nine o'clock I'm sitting in my finest jeans with my new jacket worn over a pristine shirt. Interpol fills the space around me. I'm surrounded by half-inflated balloons and the bowl of punch is now only two-thirds full. I've been waiting so long to hear from Jess that when my phone vibrates with a message from her I feel quite queasy. It says: *New plan pre-party drinks at Ol' Blue Last – Scott's bandz giggin2nite then back to ours for partyyyy!! see you here in mo x*

I'm immobile for a while but another cup of punch gets me on my feet.

On the tube to where Jess instructed I should be, I can't help staring at a girl dressed in leather. Her lips are painted black and her eyelids are silver. She has green braids of wool threaded into her hair.

The punch in my system causes me to ask: 'Excuse me, can I ask what you're reading?'

She glances over her Kindle and says, *'Catcher in the Rye.'*

'One of my favourite books,' I say, despite having never read it. She nods and looks back at the text.

'So, where are you going tonight? Got any cool plans?'

She doesn't respond to the question.

'Hey,' I say. 'Didn't you hear me? I asked where you were going. Wherever it is, can I come with you?'

She flicks her eyes at me before taking her phone from her bag. I'm convinced she's going to give me her number but instead she plugs a pair of headphones into it. I fail to get her attention again even when I bend at the waist to look into her face and kick her feet with the end of my shoe.

I alight at Old Street and when I look at the girl again through the window she lifts a middle finger and uses her full, succulent lips to form the words: *FUCK YOU.*

10

The Old Blue Last is filled to capacity with students and drunks and tourists thinking they're in some sort of cathedral. I make my way to the staircase leading upstairs to the gig. I walk a lap as an indie band in black drone and sway and move the heads and feet of everyone watching. I scan the crowd for the expansive mesh of Jess's blonde curls but can't spot them anywhere.

I turn towards the band and take in three songs and they each sound the same, though the name of the band imprinted on the bass drum is *Agony* and I have to kind of admire them for that.

As they're announcing the final song of their set, I hear Jess laughing and screaming from the doorway (I'd know those particular sounds of hers anywhere). A tall girl with a bow in her hair hooks a hand under Jess's armpit to steady her. I watch helplessly as they head to the bar with the rest of their entourage – it must be twenty people in number, all of them thin and cute and hip. I see a girl in pink leggings and green skirt and red jumper wearing a neckerchief covered in printed pictures of holly and berries. I see Monsieur Moustache in thin jeans and brown shoes with pointed toes and a tight black T-shirt with *Stay Loose* woven across it in spiky red thread.

They are the bourgeois.

I'm a mess in my vintage jacket and jeans. I'm a real disgrace.

I battle through the crowd and take hold of Jess. She looks at me without really seeing me then carries on her conversation with a man in horn-rimmed glasses. She's given what I assume is a double rum and coke as Belle and Sebastian starts coming through the speakers. She shrieks into the face of Monsieur Moustache and pulls him onto the dance floor. I watch her vanquishing her drink before tossing it over her shoulder and flailing her arms above her head, almost in time with the music. She looks so good that I feel reduced to the size of a cube of ice from the glass that she discarded. I'm worthless next to her.

Moustache twists and sways like a halfwit. I read Jess's arms like semaphore flags: *I'm having a good time and I don't care who knows it.*

I go to the bar to buy myself a large red wine and a shot of butterscotch-flavored vodka. I find myself wishing Jack or Dom or Madame Veiny Head were here. I invited them along but none of them got back to me.

Seeing Jess with all her friends reminds me I don't have many of my own.

I consider wandering onto the dance floor but what I have to offer in that regard would only shame me further. The way they're all moving is quite bewildering. They pivot their waists and shake their hair and they look ridiculous but at the same time achingly cool.

I squirm to a wall on the opposite side of the stage and end up standing beside a girl in a cherry-red leather jacket with pigtails in her hair. She gets my attention by shouting, 'So how do you know Jess?' into my ear.

'Jess?'

'Yeah, you two know each other, right?'

I watch my girlfriend dancing for a few seconds and think, I don't know: *do* we know each other?

'We met at a party a while ago and now we're going out.'

'Ah, that old tale,' she says, and takes a sip of beer. She seems amused by something she's not sharing.

Belle and Sebastian finish up but are followed by Le Tigre and Jess goes wild.

'How about you, how do you know her?' I ask, following the question with a hit of awful wine.

'We go way back. We met when we were kids. We haven't seen each other for a few months, though. I'm staying with a mutual friend in Brixton and I wanted to come along tonight to surprise her.'

'Awesome,' I tell her. 'She'll dig that, I'm sure.'

She listens to the music and moves for a while before leaning in once more to say, 'Sorry, where are my manners. What's your name?'

I give it to her and she offers me her hand.

'I'm Kirstin,' she says, 'nice to meet you,' and the bottom drops out of my soul.

I touch the base of the sink with my nose. I toss my head back and fling a stream of water onto the wall behind me, determined not to pass out. I stare at myself in the mirror

(who are you?)

and the moronic look on my face forces my arm up and out. I punch the glass and damage myself. Blood spatters across the silver surface and when I bring my fist to my mouth to nurse my knuckles bitter spots of crimson fall onto my shirt.

I rest my hand in the sink and let my blood blossom out into its water.

'Are you mental or something?' I'm asked by some drip. I don't answer. I just grit my teeth at his reflection until he gets the picture and leaves without pissing.

I hold my injured hand and suck my knuckles as I heave myself through the audience in waiting. It takes a lot of effort to spot Jess with such blurry vision. She's encased within a cocoon of the denim and leather of her friends. She's resting her head on the shoulder of Monsieur Moustache and listening to a fluorescently dressed girl talking about an art installation in Shoreditch.

I twist Jess's hand and tug her away from her familiars, easily done with her being so slack from alcohol. I drag her outside to pockets of huddled-over smokers cowering behind upturned collars and hoods and stamping their heels for warmth. I manipulate her until she's leaning against the wall and when she tries to get away I grab both her wrists and push her backwards.

She tells me to stop but I don't listen.

'Where were you today?'

She glares at me and says: 'It's none of your business.'

'Stop fucking with me, Jess, because I've had enough. I can't put up with this sort of shit any more. I know you weren't with that Kirstin girl because she just told me she hadn't seen you in months.'

Her cheeks suddenly expand and I think she's going to cover me in vomit. Her colouring is off and it's difficult for her to stand straight.

'Jess, have you taken something?'

'Oh, fuck *off!* Why can't you just leave me alone?' she says. 'You're always fucking *there*, aren't you? It's driving me *crazy.*'

I'm overcome by the surging need for violence that reminds of the way I ejected Elizabeth from my room and how I terrified the girls outside the café in Paris. I feel strong, I feel powerful, I feel full of hate and pain and nausea, and I would throw her to the ground and choke her if it wouldn't attract so much attention.

'Were you with him today? Were you with Marcus? You were, weren't you?'

She doesn't answer so I pull her towards me and shove her back. Her head collides with the wall and makes a sickening thudding sound.

'*Tell me where you were, Jess*!'

She's unresponsive so I take ahold of her shoulders and shake her. She swipes at my face but misses. She kicks at my shins but finds only air.

I gather a bunch of her curls in my hand and bring my other hand back to strike her. She closes her eyes as if awaiting impact.

Before doing something I'd really regret I'm able to let her go. I steady myself by thinking of the weight of her body held in my arms. I picture her swaying to the music of Pavement and smiling at me with all her teeth. I slow my racing pulse and subdue my rage by remembering this is the girl I'm supposed to be in love with.

I figure the best way of exacting any sort of revenge on her would be to leave her here like this – squatting in the gutter and crying into the hem of her dress. I fasten my jacket and walk off into the night, towards our house, and it takes but six steps for me to start bawling my eyes out.

Somehow, I get back to the house. I go straight to the bedroom. I pick up the duvet dotted with our mutual come stains and embrace it. Her clothes stink of her and I use them to wipe away tears, spit, blood, and snot. I grope for the wardrobe and inspect each of my ties under moonlight until I'm holding the one from Paris out in front of me.

I had the chance to start again and I refused to take it.

I wrap the tie around my neck and nose and constrict my head to try to stifle all negative thoughts and sever the link between my brain and my heart. I yank at my hair so hard that some of it comes out in clumps. I howl at the moon and at the passing traffic outside.

It's not easy finding my way to the living room in such opaque conditions and I almost fall over two or three of the balloons I inflated before leaving. I stamp on them and they explode in a way that's not quite satisfactory.

I clutch the bowl of punch under opposing sides and lift it up, up and over, and as it cascades onto my upturned face

(*down comes desperation, down comes self-loathing*)

I leave my mouth open to catch as much of it as I can. I throw the bowl against the wall and it drops to the floor unharmed.

I lurch around with my eyelids glued shut by the sticky syrup of the punch. I crash against the table and cry out in pain. I put the tie between my teeth and bite hard until it subsides.

Louise, standing next to me, whispers: *There's so much more here for you than just a teaching job and an apartment.*

I walk into Camden and don't care about how loud I'm being as I openly weep. Passers-by pivot their necks to look back at me when they walk past. I don't know where else to go so I let my legs take me the same way they have a thousand times before; back to the flat I once shared with the only friend I have.

I pound on the door until Jack appears.

'Fucking hell, what happened to you?' he asks.

I fall into him and stick us together with the tacky punch covering my shirt. Dom appears behind him to see what's going on.

'Mate, tell me what happened,' Jack says. 'You look like shit.'

I can't say anything. All I can do is let out a long wailing sound that sounds ever so slightly like *Jess ... Jess ... gone*, and now we're back to square one.

11

Jack and Dom have learnt to leave me alone. They sometimes ask how I'm doing but when they do I roll over on the sofa and hide in its cushions, which is all the information they need in regards to my wellbeing. My power of imagination builds with each drink I take, each drug I ingest. My discomfort is intensified by persistent bursts of ethereal visions of Jess and Marcus screwing each other senseless in front of me, right there on the living room floor, and their limbs intertwine as they grind against each other.

It's been a few days but it feels like for ever.

Sometimes I'm able to stumble to the kitchen, where I open the same cupboard and read the same labels of the same tins of food each day. I'm on a hunger strike. I refuse to eat until she admits she was wrong and welcomes me home. Yesterday morning for breakfast I had a cigarette and a tablet of ecstasy that Dom passed me in secret (it must have been Jack's) and I sucked on it until it dissolved. My synapsis rallied against its intrusion and fought in the name of my infinite despair but the drugs won out in the end (*don't they always*?) and for a few precious hours I felt something resembling acceptance, even contentment. I congratulated Marcus and sent him mental messages of inspiration, and what I inked onto them with the marker-pen of my delusion was: *take care of her, man. Keep her safe.*

Jack donated the last of his weed to my cause. I've smoked so much of it in the past forty-eight hours that the stash has almost run dry, so now I unwrap the plastic film and inspect the miniscule flakes of green that remain. I ball up the film and thrust it into my empty head and go over it with my tongue until I've extracted all I can from it.

With no drugs left, I'm forced to leave the flat and walk to the canal. I throw money at Dealer and to monopolise on his expertise in the field I point to my face, to the misery cut into it. He hands over three small sachets based on his recommendation – one filled with tablets, one with powder, one with hash. His friend gets up and comes at me when he sees me rubbing some of the powder into my gums, threatening me not to be so brash when there are police patrolling each end of this stretch of canal. I take a step towards him. I tell him to do his worst, to ram the hefty bone of his forehead into the bridge of my nose, to drive a fist into my face and loosen all my teeth as I no longer need them; not to smile, not to eat. I start pleading with him to hurt me, to tear my arms from their sockets, to bludgeon me with the smartphone he's holding, to drown me in the slime green waterway the two of them call their *base of operations*. They focus their attention on the ground beneath them, no doubt wary of police or passing tourists.

There is no comforting to be had here. I run home and roll a joint in the bathroom so I don't have to share it with my housemates. I light it with a match that I drop into the toilet bowl and puff on it with tears streaming down my cheeks. The female of every species is the one who has all the control. This has always been true, I reflect, as I fill my lungs with smoke.

I ruminate on the spider that mates once then eats its mate. Jess has enough venom dripping from her incisors to slay an entire army of men like me.

In the mirror, my eyes are the colour of double-decker buses, of pillar boxes, of all the tokens I left Paris to return to. What's worse is that my skin has erupted into craggy acne and I simply *have* to manipulate each spot until yellow pus slithers out.

I cradle a towel against my chest. I whip the sink with the towel before attempting to rip it into strips.

The futility of my efforts leaves me angrier.

I rake nails across the bumps of my face then fling open the medicine cabinet. I remove a bottle of antiseptic liquid and upend it. I smother my skin with it and it burns so much that I find a few tears to shed that I didn't know I had.

As I'm kneeling in front of the toilet and emptying my stomach my phone starts ringing. I'm rendered sicker when I see it isn't Jess that's calling.

'Hello?'

'Hi, mate, how are you?'

'Who's this?

'It's Phil. We worked together in Paris.'

'Hey, Phil,' I say, these six words so far being the most I've spoken to him since we met. We exchanged phone numbers on the day we started working at GBL, but only as a formality.

'Listen,' he says. 'I have something I need to tell you.'

'Really?'

'Yeah, and it's not going to be an easy thing to hear.'

I reach for the sink and lift myself until I'm balanced on the toilet seat.

'What's up?' I ask.

'Mate, it's about Elizabeth.' My tongue is stilled by the image of her weeping in my bedroom. 'Do you remember her? We worked with her in France. She was the girl who dropped ice onto Louise in the pub, if that helps.'

Nausea comes quickly and I tame it by pinching and twisting my naked thigh.

'Yeah, Phil, of course I remember Elizabeth. What's the problem? What's going on?'

'I'm sorry to have to tell you this, but she died last night. I thought you should know. I realise you weren't that close to her but she was a sweet girl, I'm sure you'd agree, and she loved you to bits.'

I say: 'I don't understand.'

Nothing for a few moments, then: 'Me neither. It's complicated. She was depressed, I suppose. I remember her telling me something about her heart being broken by some horrible bastard.'

I killed her. I'm responsible.

'Do you mean she … committed suicide?' I ask.

'I don't want to get into the details. I just thought it'd be

257

nice to give her a send-off. She was an important part of our lives. We did share that experience in Paris as a group, after all. And as I said, you were very special to her. I'm meeting Gary in The Water Poet at eight. I've spoken with Rick and Alice but they can't make it. I can't get through to Louise, so it'd be just the three of us, but it's better than nothing. We owe her that much, at least.'

I tear off a few sheets of toilet paper to dab my face with. I cast my mind back to the letter she wrote: *you'll always be my everything. In time, I hope you can allow yourself to appreciate that.*

'It'd be great to see you th –'

I hang up the phone before throwing myself to the floor. I lie in front of the toilet and bring my knees to my chest and whisper *no no no* as I wrap myself in my arms. It might be arrogant to think I'm the sole reason behind what she's done, but I can't help it. The look she had on her face when I forced her out of my room will always be with me. I go through all the ways she could've done it. I hope it was quick and painless. I hope she didn't slit her wrists or drink a cup of bleach or throw herself into traffic. I hope I wasn't the last thing she thought of before she slipped away because I'm not worth it. I'm not worth the love or affection of anyone. I'm nothing but poison.

Every action has a consequence.

Everything I come into contact with is left worse off by my influence.

I go to the living room with an open bottle of cough medicine and take a deep swig of it, thinking: *what exactly is this thing called love, and why is it so fucking terrible?*

I can't concentrate on the television because Elizabeth is sitting at the foot of the sofa. She's staring at me with adoration.

She isn't breathing.

I open one of the packets of drugs and put its contents into my face.

As the room darkens around me, I get another phone call

from Phil. He says, 'How does it feel to have your emotions fucked around with?'

'I'm sorry,' I whisper. 'I'm so sorry …'

'She might not be dead, but you soon will be,' he says, and then hangs up.

Afterwards, I have this deranged drug-fuelled fantasy in which I'm sitting on Jess's sofa upon a homogeny of Primrose Hill and Montmartre. Girls in hooded robes approach me and smear my face with menstrual blood; Sophie Angier saying *Blood of the Innocent,* Elizabeth saying *Blood of the Tormented,* Lollipop86 saying *Blood of the Neglected.* It might be the result of a cocaine nosebleed that has dried and caked onto my skin but I swear I can actually feel their markings afterwards, as if they weren't just a part of my delusion.

Before I lose consciousness I watch the mirage of two figures approaching, cloaked in black and white robes and drawing blades from straps on their legs. I breathe shallowly from the trauma of one of the blades sinking into my chest, the other swung back with the intention of removing my head from my shoulders.

12

The sight of all my things piled up in front of the house twists my insides. I stretch over my bags to knock and I'm crying already.

Get a GRIP!

She looks beautiful. I have an impulse so intense it's almost sickening to fall to her feet and kiss each of her toes.

'Hello,' she says.

'Jess, I –'

'Wait. Come into the living room.'

She sits on the end of the sofa as if she's about to chair a meeting. Her posture is perfect. It's clear to see she means business.

I sit well away from her and say: 'Let's get this over with.'

I'm dwelling on where she's gone; the girl who came to mine in a taxi wearing nothing but a raincoat and stockings.

This is going to hurt, but what's new?

'It's not working out.'

'I know,' I say.

'Whatever I felt for you, I don't feel it any more. What I mean is I don't love you. I doubt I ever did love you, to be honest, and I have to be honest because to not be wouldn't benefit either of us.'

I pass my hands over my face and aim my watery eyes at her.

You are evil. You are pure evil. You are a twisted, attention-seeking, selfish, sick, deluded bitch who gets off on hauling men through the thorns of your own self-loathing. You are a sadist. You are manipulative. You crave the love and attention of those around you because it makes you feel as if you are in some way significant. When you were a young girl you'd remove the legs from insects just to watch them squirm. I know you. I know who you are now. I can see you

261

clearly. You destroy things. You have no personality. You have no class. You have looks, but no grace. I don't know what I'm doing here. I should be in Paris. You are the infection that's killed my sense of worth and self-esteem and the ability I once had to be happy. I don't deserve this. I don't deserve you, no one does. You should be trapped under a glass and studied.

I wish I'd never met you and I hope you die alone.

'Please don't do this, Jess. Give me another chance,' I say, but she remains indifferent.

'I've said all I needed to. I'd like you to leave now. And don't forget the cheque.'

I give her my contribution to the rent for the brief time I was here. She compares the amount I wrote on the cheque with what she believes she's owed.

She walks me out and I watch her as she closes the door, I watch more and more of her getting cut off behind it, and when she's disappeared I pick up all my stupid possessions and walk to the tube feeling nothing and everything at once.

13

I open the laptop to check my *LovedUp* profile. My subscription has expired so I can't read any of the messages, although apparently I have over thirty of them and an even greater number of profile views and wolf-whistles. I click my way to a porn website instead to watch a big-breasted French maid being drilled with three dicks and it makes me feel so sad.

Jack comes into the living room and takes in the chaos I've surrounded myself with. There are bottles and cans and rolling-paper packets and the ends of joints and shreds of tobacco and empty drug wrappers everywhere. My blanket is covered with stains and I haven't washed in days.

'You can't go on like this,' he says. 'You're starting to freak Tim out.'

I crumble a lump of hash into a cigarillo skin.

'Who's Tim?'

'Don't fuck around, you *know* who Tim is. Tim's the guy who's taken your old room, remember? Jesus, he thinks you're the next Howard Hughes or some shit.'

I laugh as I light the joint.

'Fuck him,' I say, and Jack gets angry.

'No, no, not fuck *him*. Fuck *you*!' he says, his voice getting louder. 'Fuck *you,* you self-righteous prick!'

I take smoke into my chest then cover him with it.

'You're a fucking disgrace.'

'I don't want to hear it,' I say, because even through my pharmaceutical haze, things still have a way of stinging.

'It's time you found your own place. You're really fucking things up. Dom's pissed, the landlord's getting suspicious. Tim's starting to hate living here already, and –'

'Tim? Who's Tim?'

'The *new* guy! Tim is the *new* guy! Listen to what I'm saying for one bloody second!'

I absorb some of the joint and my head starts spinning.

'So Tim's the new guy. Wonderful. I'll meet him properly next time he's here.'

'Don't bother. We all want you to move out. This is getting ridiculous.'

I kick out my feet and a few of the empty bottles tip over and roll away.

'I fucking *knew* it!' I say. 'I knew you'd turn on me eventually. The same thing happened in Paris, the same thing happened with Jess. Am I fucking repulsive or something?'

He fixes me with an unflinching stare and says: 'Right, no bullshitting now. I'm just gonna come out and say it. In all honesty, and with no exaggeration, I have never in my life encountered such a pathetic human being. It's just a girl, for fuck's sake! We've all been dumped at some point.'

'Jack, you don't understand what this is like. I love her. My heart's broken. I'm going through hell.'

'Wait, how can you say I don't understand? Are you forgetting about Liu? Do you need reminding of what I went through when he left? That was *real* love, mate. That was the fucking *epitome* of real love. It was a long way from what you thought you had with the fucking slut that did nothing but ruin your life. Liu and I had intimacy. We were best friends as well as lovers. That Jess girl; I mean, did you even *like* her? Think about it: what was it about her that you actually *liked*?'

'Liu meant nothing to you, Jack,' I tell him. 'How can you call that love? You were fucking other men before his pillow had even gone cold.'

He stands over me and pulls my shirt until our noses are touching, until the elastic of the neckline makes a ripping sound and stretches out. I drop the joint onto the floor when I reach for his hands to fight him off.

'I want you out of this flat as soon as fucking possible,' he yells, and I reply: 'It wasn't so long ago that you said the same about Dom, don't forget!'

He drops me back onto the sofa and I pass my fingers

over the carpet, looking for the remnants of the spliff.

'You are a horrible human being. Why do you want to hurt me so bad?'

'You're the one hurting *me,* not the other way around!'

'Get out of here,' he says with tears in his eyes. 'Get out of here and don't come back.'

'Oh I will,' I say. 'As soon as I find somewhere to go, I'm gone. You can count on that.'

'Perfect, I can't wait. None of us can.'

He leaves me to my hovel and returns to his boyfriend. I roll a fresh smoke and open a beer.

Fuck him, I think to myself. *Who needs friends?*

I bring the tie up to my nose to sniff it.

14

I don't want sex – I just want pain. I want to be chastised for all the things I've done. Sexual desire is a tumour I need removed. Sexual attractiveness is something I need peeled away from my flesh like the skin on a rotting piece of fruit.

I arrive at a phone box covered in cards. I settle on Ruby first – not because of her big lips or fishnet stockings but because of the leather and chains and whips she's surrounded herself with in her photograph. She answers the phone sounding old and ill, her throat chaffed by years of getting men off orally but not in the traditional way. I tell her I'm scum and I need to be punished. She starts describing how soft her breasts are and how moist her vagina is getting and how much she wants me to fuck her with my big hard cock.

I drop the receiver into its cradle out of boredom and tip a line of cocaine out on the ledge where coins are kept. I ingest this through a rolled-up five-pound note and the burning in my nostril bleeds to the back of my throat.

I choose the card of a different woman. It's not the sight of her quaking sacks of fat reigned in with black stockings and undersized corset that interests me – it's the black leather cap and riding strap that makes me want to give her a call. Before she has a chance to say anything sexually alluring I tell her that all I want is to be tortured. I ask what sort of arrangement would have to be made to get the two of us together and she gives me the name of a hotel and walking directions from King's Cross station.

She tells me to bring money and contraceptives, with extra emphasis placed on *money*. I ask if she'll let me call her Jess and she says: *if you have the money, you can call me anything you like.*

I hang up the phone and drain all the cash I have left from the first machine I come across. I take a tube train to King's Cross and walk to where I've been directed. I find a doorway with a torn awning that reads: *The Royal Hotel*.

I enter and walk to Reception. I ring the bell and a man in a polyester suit appears from behind a curtain. He says, 'You here to see Candice?' and I nod sheepishly. 'Room 248. Knock like this ...' he taps an odd rhythm on the reception desk and each knock makes this noise: *Jess ... Jess-Jess*.

She lets me into the room and tells to wait while she finishes in the bathroom. I unbutton my raincoat. I sit on the bed and take off my shoes. I loosen my tie and hang it from the lampshade. The girl who gave it to me transcends time and space and whispers: *you're a better man than you think you are*.

Candice dries her hair and sits next to me in her dressing gown. The sudden impact of her weight on the spot of the mattress adjacent to mine propels me upwards.

'So, what do you want?'

'Make me hurt,' I say. 'Give me pain.'

I expected this answer would shock her but she just nods and says: 'I can do that. It's two-fifty up front.'

'Yeah, the money's over there.'

She walks across the room to inspect it; a task made difficult by how tight her leathers are. She licks a finger to examine each note.

I think: *Be worth it, Candice.*

She opens a drawer and removes a long black strap, a muzzle, a candle, and a lighter. 'This is my special drawer,' she tells me. 'The hotelier and I have a bit of an arrangement.'

I'm totally numb but won't be for long ...

'Bite down on this.'

I hold the rubber ball in my mouth and she ties it securely around my head.

'Get down on all fours,' she says, and I reply with *Nnn-kn. Dnn nn nnay nn cnn crr ynn jnnn?*

'What? Wait, I can't hear you like that.'

She loosens the gag and I say: 'You told me on the phone I could call you *Jess*. Is that still OK?'

'Well, yeah, if you like. I won't understand what you're saying with the muzzle on, though.'

'Not a problem,' I tell her. 'Now put the gag back on, please.'

After I'm in position she takes the strap to my back and buttocks and explains in detail how disgusting and pathetic and warped I am. I agree with everything she says. I say *hit me harder, Jess!* from behind the rubber ball. I picture the sadness Jess has filled my heart with leaving my body through opened pores and nicks in my skin.

She gets me onto my back and pinches my nipples. She lights the candle and drips wax onto my stomach. She takes my penis in her hand and I'm relieved when instead of massaging it she twists it and wrenches it and almost snaps it off.

For once, the tears on my face are not because of emotional pain.

Candice pounds my cock until it bleeds.

At the point of orgasm I mutter: *who am I?*

15

Next to the canal is a fleshy point that leaks hot piss onto my face while Lookout watches, hands in pockets; a silhouette marked by the burning tip of a cigarette. I roll myself into a ball and stay small, as small as I can get, sure I could melt into the pavement if I concentrated hard enough.

'Fuck with us again and we'll fucking *wreck* you,' Dealer says.

I'm placated by the thought that this was not caused by fate, this is not part of a conspiracy; I brought this on myself.

'*Do* it, then! *Kill me*, you fucking *cunts*!' I scream at them. Dealer dares me to repeat myself but instead I spit urine out onto his shoe, which I feel carries a similar sentiment.

The shoe gets buried into my stomach.

'Stay down,' Dealer says.

'I'm gonna take all your drugs and all your money to pay Candice,' I tell them. One of them asks who the fuck Candice is and I laugh and say: 'You don't want to know.'

Dealer says, 'Next time you try stealing from us, we'll put you into the fucking ground. You get me?'

'Promise?' I ask, holding my stomach.

Dealer goes to kick me again but Lookout pulls him away, saying, 'Come on, man, he ain't worth it.'

'I have to agree with you there,' I tell him.

They leave me to nurse my wounds and I rinse piss out of my suit jacket with water from the canal. I ask people outside the Blues Kitchen if I can have a cigarette but no one pays me much attention. To them I'm just another down-and-out looking for a freebie. They don't know the lives I've led, the places I've seen, or the people I've fucked. They don't know how I've ridden railway lines that stretch the length and breadth of Italy. They're unaware I've overseen the sighing

271

of the world's most romantic city from the peak of the slope of Montmartre.

I hold the hand of a girl and imagine her fingers are Jess's until her boyfriend pries me off her and tells me he'll call the police if I don't leave.

'Where am I supposed to go? Back to Paris?' I ask, and he looks at me blankly.

I go for one of the sachets of drugs in my pocket before remembering that there are no drugs.

I drink the last few drops of whiskey from my hipflask and drop it and kick it under a bus.

I take my phone out of my pocket and it turns on despite being sodden with urine.

'Candice,' I whisper. 'I need to see you again. Are you free sometime tomorrow?'

'Who's this?' she asks, and it further breaks my already broken heart.

Jack sees the state I'm in and asks no questions. I walk into the living room and Dom and New Guy vacate it without even looking at me.

I remove my jacket and throw it out of the window. I leave the window open to rid the room of the aroma of piss I've brought into the flat.

I go to kick bottles and cans away from the base of the sofa but my housemates have already tidied them away.

I drop onto the cushions and close my eyes.

I pray to any god that will have me that I won't wake up in the morning.

I imagine how much blood would come out if I opened my wrists with a razorblade.

16

Rob marches me to his office and I leave a hand resting on the bottle in my pocket.

'You've got a lot of explaining to do,' he says when we sit, and I respond with: 'Mate, just cut me some slack.'

'Why should I?'

'Because I don't want to be like this any more,' I say. I massage the neck of the bottle and tap on its glass with my index finger. I add: 'I want to work for you because I'm passionate about teaching and I very much enjoy watching students develop their English language skills.'

'You're joking, aren't you? You're here for work? You wouldn't believe the shit you caused after the inspection. Karen, the other teachers and myself – we're on our last legs now.'

'I am, too,' I say. 'Seriously.'

'Oh, that's so good to hear. I must remember to tell everyone you said that at our next meeting. I'm sure a lot of your ex-colleagues would love to hear about how much you're struggling.'

'I truly hope that's of some comfort to you all,' I say with a straight face. He leans back in his chair and wraps his hands around the back of his head.

'Can I ask you an honest question?' he says.

'Of course you can. Be my guest.'

'After all the trouble you caused, after everything it cost you, I have to know: was what you did really worth it?'

'None of them are worth it, Rob,' I tell him.

He changes position, leans forwards, and plants open palms onto the desk in front of him. He looks me in the eyes and says: 'If you ever come anywhere near this school or one of its students again, you'll get what you deserve. You'll get everything you've had coming to you for the last few months. Am I making myself absolutely clear?'

'Kind of,' I say, 'but if you really want to hurt me, then just go ahead and do it. I couldn't get much more damaged than I already am.'

'Believe me, I'd quite happily take you outside and beat the living shit out of you if it wouldn't get me fired. The girl's barely sixteen, you sick bastard.'

'Legal, though,' I say.

'Not the point. The job we do here comes with a certain amount of responsibility. You were briefed when you signed the contract. We are *professionals*. Using this job to sleep with poor, vulnerable young girls is fucking *outrageous*.'

'Yeah, yeah, that's true. I agree with you. But two points that might placate you, Rob: firstly, that girl is in no way poor or vulnerable. Secondly, I've seen the error of my ways. That's why I'm here. I'm here for a second chance. I'm here to make things right –'

He moves as if he's going to lash out at me but instead he lifts me out of the chair and forces me out of the room, back through Reception, towards the front door. On the way out I notice Sophie conversing with friends, no doubt discussing at length my length and girth and the pitiful way I behaved.

17

I leave the school and walk towards Tottenham Court Road. I drink dregs left in crumpled cans in bins by tramps and liquid mixed with ash in glasses propped on outer windowsills of clubs and bars. I pick up three apples from a box outside a corner shop. I eat one and throw the other two away for being too sweet.

'Spare change?' I ask, walking against the lunch-hour tide, getting hints of La Défense, hits of British Utilities, thoughts of Jess dressed for a day at the office in a clean white shirt, grey skirt, red lipstick.

I walk into Boots on Oxford Street. I spritz myself with a dozen different perfumes from the toiletries section and slip a box of condoms into the inside pocket of my jacket. I browse other aisles on the hunt for medication, settling on a vial of mucus cough medicine that I unscrew and tip into my mouth; not to rid my chest of mucus but to rid my head of a few hundred cells.

I slide a sandwich into my waistband and flee security when they catch me in the act.

I walk to the river and toss the box of condoms into its rippling skin.

A young Japanese girl adjusts her handbag as she walks beyond the theatres of the South Bank, bound for Waterloo.

She's wearing knee-length boots with heels, so is easy to catch up to. I angle my path to step ahead of her then turn to face her with both hands raised.

She touches her hair nervously. I point at her bag and try to explain how much I need whatever she has. She looks at me questioningly, unable to understand my intentions until I pinch its strap and pull on it firmly, pulling her towards me, causing her to almost lose her balance.

She rolls the bag from her shoulder without shifting her

attention from the lines of desperation cut into my face. I unsnap its clasps and empty it out to paw through her things; make-up, lip balm, chewing gum, tampons. I put a cigarette into my mouth and form a lighter with a trembling hand, gesturing for her to light it. She produces a box of matches from the pocket of her shorts and on the matchbook is written: *The Royal Hotel*.

I locate her purse and fill my cupped hand with coins and notes, pounds and yen.

She's whispering something in Japanese.

'Sorry about this,' I tell her with a quiver in my voice.

Her eyes dart from side to side as she searches for a method of escape.

I double over from the impact of her knee colliding with my groin. She runs to the other side of the theatre and indicates my presence here by pointing and screaming at the place where I lie.

I run as fast as I can with my stomach convulsing and my testicles throbbing, forced into hiding beneath a bridge like some sort of modern-day troll.

But at least I now have enough money for this evening's date.

18

I get to the bar already drunk, out of my head on stolen vodka, whiskey, and cough syrup.

'Hello, stranger,' she says.

'Hello, *Lollipop86*.'

'What?'

'What do you want to drink?' I ask.

'Is it too early for cocktails?'

I make an effort not to grimace and say: 'It's never too early for cocktails.'

She leads me to a booth at the far side of the bar and as she's not looking I can use the tables we walk past to stop myself from falling over. People sitting around them hold onto their drinks. I want to tell them I'm nothing but a lost cause but I don't have the energy. Besides, the music is too loud. I doubt they'd even hear me.

We settle in and she says, 'So, what have you been up to? It's been ages.'

I drape an arm across her thigh and scream into her ear, 'You know, the usual.'

'I'm glad you texted,' she says.

'You're welcome.'

'Pardon?'

'I'm quite the catch, I know that.'

'Sorry, I can't hear you.'

'Forget it,' I say. 'It doesn't really matter.'

After a few hours, the alcohol in her blood has caught up with the alcohol in mine. I turn to her hair to sniff it but my sense of smell has been deadened by all the powder I've been putting up my nose.

She starts kissing my neck and I don't want to enjoy it.

'You know something?' I shout into her ear. 'We're all skin on blood on flesh on bone. You take away my top layer and I'm nothing but gore. Do you think touching tongues together is romantic? Do you know how much bacteria we have in our mouths? The tongue is a muscle filled with veins and arteries and coated in mucus. We're suckers for sensation. The pleasure you feel, that's just nerve endings. We're full of red branches of feeling that are stimulated by contact, by friction. That's all desire is, when you think about it. But you never think about it, do you? You're too depraved. You don't know what sex is and you don't know what love is, not really, because neither actually exists. The only things that exist are blood and sweat and come and bone and brains wired up the wrong way. Take this glass, this glass of rum and coke. I'll put this into my body and it'll alter my neurological patterns, it'll spin my cogs, and I'll start getting happy, start feeling good, but if I don't keep topping up then that feeling will disappear. When time's called at the bar and no more alcohol is forthcoming, when you're cut off at the pinnacle of your high and left to fend for yourself … I'm getting at pain, I'm getting at hate, I'm getting at vomiting and headaches and shame.'

She's unresponsive.

'Romance is the tax of the stupid and sex is deranged, exploitive, twisted filth that ruins us and rots us from the inside.'

Still nothing.

'Love is pain,' I tell her.

She finishes her drink and goes to the bar and returns with two black cocktails in tall glasses, no ice.

We leave tied up in each other. Christmas decorations line the streets and I think about how funny it would be to hang myself with a piece of tinsel. She twists my arms to stop me walking and injects me with her tongue. I push her away, saying 'I can't.' She holds my cheeks to steady my head and goes for my lips, unrelenting.

'Stop that,' I say, but I'm too far gone.

She takes me into an alley and topples me against a bin.

She presses her breasts into my chest and bites my face and neck and rubs my cock.

I loop under her skirt and start pulling down her tights.

'Is this what you want?' I ask. 'Is this what you want from me?'

She wraps her legs around my middle and I almost fall backwards. She takes my penis and guides it into her and we fuck like animals, leaning against a wall for support and using each other for God-knows-what.

I make my way back to the bar for a nightcap, my jeans stained with semen and blood. I ask for a shot of tequila and a glass of wine and somehow get served.

I sit on a barstool facing a mirror and use its reflection to straighten my tie. She was wrong – it doesn't bring out my eyes. All it does is remind me of my inability to get on with things and the struggle I have to be someone worthwhile.

I finish off the drinks and ask for two more. I raise a shot to all the girls I've wronged and swallow it whole. I attempt to ask for a cocktail but by now I'm too drunk to speak.

I go to the toilet and collapse into a cubicle. I cover it in vomit and piss and phlegm.

I struggle to get back to the barstool and now even I know I've had enough. I pick up my suit jacket and take my time locating its sleeves.

I button it up and check my phone: no messages.

I walk towards the exit and stop halfway when someone catches my eye. She sits with a straw resting on her bottom lip, staring at the man opposite her as if trying to make sense of what he's saying.

I take a few moments to consider who she might be.

I adjust my tie, a gift from her, and walk out of the bar.

I close the door behind me as I don't want her getting cold.

Fin

Other titles you may enjoy

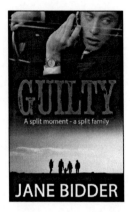

For more information about **David Rogers**

and other **Accent Press** titles

please visit

www.accentpress.co.uk

Lightning Source UK Ltd.
Milton Keynes UK
UKOW03f1143120514

231522UK00001B/3/P